Once Upon A Blade

Kailey Alessi

THE WHUMPY PRINTING PRESS

To all those who love the darkness

Contents

Introduction

Mythology, fairy tales, and folklore are in many ways the original whump. These stories are often dark and brutal and violent and gory. That's why I chose the theme of "fairy tales with a whumpy twist" for this anthology. I thought it would be cool to see how the whump community interpreted these traditional tales, and I was not disappointed. Collected in this book you will find nineteen stories by fourteen incredibly talented writers. Be warned: this anthology is not for the faint of heart. Expect lots of blood and pain (and maybe a couple tears). Each story begins with a list of content warnings. Now, we'll begin our tales as so many stories have before us.

"Once Upon a ~~Time~~ Blade"

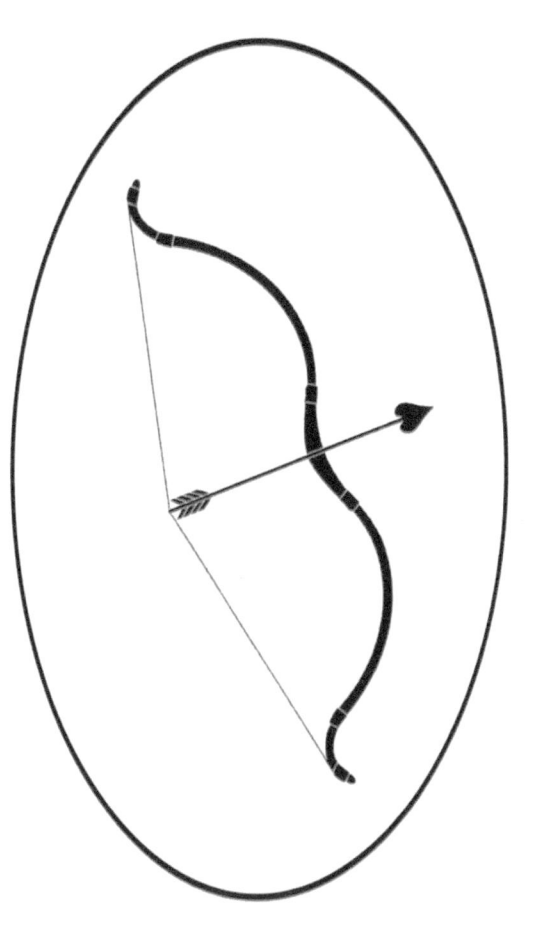

Proditum

C. M. Clarence

CW: Suicide

Whumpee: Man, women, Whumper: Man, women, Caretaker: N/A

Psyche restlessly waited for her husband to drift off. She could not turn over to check, the room was black as pitch, as it always was when he came to her, so she listened for the sounds of his breaths becoming calmer and more shallow as sleep took him in. The raging sea of confusion and pain that had swallowed her up since her sisters' departure sat to crash her against the sharp rocks of indecision. Was her husband truly a monster? That was what she had been told by the oracle of Apollo, and that was what she had accepted as she sat weeping atop a lonely mountain, dressed in mourning black and awaiting her fate. But then she had come to a treasure-castle of jeweled floors and glowing golden pillars. She had bathed in elegance and supped as though she were one of the Gods, the flavors making her realize that what she now tasted, both of the morsels in her mouth and the expansive room around her, was pure beauty in all its forms.

Despite all of this, she had felt fear at what awaited her that night. The winged serpent beast that was to be her husband. She knew he would come. And as she lay alone in bed, in the dark, in the silence, consumed by terror, suddenly a heavenly voice had whispered sweet words of comfort into her ear. She had known from that moment on that who she was now tied and drawn to was no beast, but the love she had been looking for all her life.

But then her sisters had come at her request, for though she was fulfilled with romantic love, she still yearned for the close bonds of her family.

Those words ... whispered urgently in fear and concern by those two she loved dearest of all. The scales had fallen off her eyes then, and she saw her mate for what he truly was: the winged beast she was forewarned of.

At first, Psyche did not want to see this blatant truth. But her sisters had implored her for the sake of her unborn child. They begged and pleaded with tears in their eyes that not only would he devour her, but the being growing within her.

So, they made a plan ... and now it was Psyche's duty to carry it out.

She lifted herself from the plush bed that pleaded for her to stay within its warm confines, to ignore everything her sisters had warned her of, and to instead indulge in the lie of a happy marriage and true love.

Psyche placed a hand upon her growing stomach and set her heart in stone, resigned to her task. She fished the blade she had concealed under her pillow and fetched the lantern with a cloth cover, filled to the brim with oil to cast the greatest light upon the mystery that was her husband's true form. Though she had felt him, she had never seen him, forbade as she was to do so by his own word. Nor was she to ask anything about him or his appearance. She agreed with her sisters that this could only be for nefarious reasons.

Though as she walked around the bed, feeling her way in the dark, she could not help but think, "I love him." For she did. Even now as she planned to dispatch him from this world forever. Her stone heart began to crack and she felt tears come to her eyes. Tears of sorrow at losing the sweet caresses and gentle words she had experienced every night. Tears of fear for what she would see when she finally unveiled the lantern and laid eyes upon her husband for the first time. And lastly, tears of rage for the unspeakable plans this beast had for her and her unborn child.

Standing at the edge of the bed on her husband's side, she trembled slightly as she lifted the cloth from the lantern.

What she saw brought her to her knees.

Before her lay not a slumbering serpent, but a man. With rose-colored cheeks and soft auburn hair that curled delicately behind his ears and against his forehead, he was the very form of beauty. She gazed at him, heart filling up so intensely with such love and such regret at the actions she almost took, that she wanted to take her blade and plunge it deep within her breast, if only to find some semblance of relief from the sensation that her heart might burst. But she did not, too fascinated by who lay before her, a man she had known most intimately and then again not all.

She thanked the Gods and rose to her feet to examine her lover once more. That is when she noticed the bow and arrow at his feet and the pearlescent wings draped on either side of him. Again, her breath was stolen from her lungs as she realized not only was this the most handsome man she'd ever laid eyes upon, but that he was in fact not a man, but a God. The God of love: Eros.

Mesmerized, she drew a finger along the tip of a glowing arrow, accidentally pricking herself. The effect was instant.

Suddenly overcome with passion, she draped herself over his sleeping form, placing gentle kisses along the skin of his exposed face and chest. She feared to wake him and cast away the spell of the moment, but could not control herself. Though she had loved him before, more after seeing his beauty, she was now mad with it.

In her wild ministrations, she forgot she held the lantern. Perhaps in envy, or out of a want to join in, the burning oil spilled forth, splashing with a sickening hiss onto the skin of her beloved.

Eros woke with a cry of pain, causing Psyche to jump back in shock. She dropped the lantern on the floor, causing its flame to dance about wildly. She was in agony over what she had just done, that agony echoed in her lover as he grasped at his face and writhed upon the bed, image flickering in and out in a sickly manner with the lantern's confused light.

It took several terrifying moments for him to realize someone else was in the room with him. He sat up and scrambled back against the jewel-encrusted headboard, unseeing and afraid of more torture.

"Psyche," he gasped, and Psyche recoiled at the sight of that beautiful face now marred with burns. He seemed confused for a moment, pain hindering his ability to think. But then he noticed the blade in Psyche's hand, which she tossed the moment his eyes graced it, as though his very vision had made the metal too hot to touch. However, it was too late, and he had realized the betrayal for what it was. "What have you done!" he shouted at her.

Guilt crashed into Psyche with the force of a thousand horses stampeding into her very soul. It was not just from what she had done to his face, now an angry red and hosting hot blisters, but from her betrayal of his trust. She had promised time and time again that she would not look upon him. And yet, twisted by the words of her sisters that she now recognized as poison, she had done just that.

Without another word, Eros fled, Psyche giving quick chase. She screamed after him to stop, to let her beg forgiveness. But he would not yield in his escape.

All around them echoed the wails of those invisible servants who had seen to her every whim since she first stepped foot in this place, screaming at Psyche for what she had done. The wails grew louder and louder until Psyche felt a sharp pain in her ears and then the wet trickle of blood.

They exited the palace doors out onto the front gardens, darkened by night, twisting juniper trees casting ghouls and demons in every shadow. They reached for her with clawed hands and gnashing teeth as she pushed her body to its limits to catch up with her lover. They tore at her dress and flesh, leaving deep gashes upon her flank, but she would not be stopped.

Eros took to the sky, but not before Psyche, close behind, found his thigh in an iron grip.

Either Eros did not notice in his agony of both body and mind, or he simply no longer cared. Regardless of the reason, he continued to climb high into the sky. Beautiful wings beating the air as though it had been that which betrayed him.

Though she scrambled to hold on, Psyche found herself waning quickly in strength. She clawed at his flesh in her desperation, leaving long bloody marks, and when she saw what she was doing, that she was hurting him even more by holding on, she let go.

She fell through the sky, white dress billowing in the wind like a dove that had been struck down midflight.

Her heart pounded loudly in her ears, blocking out the rushing whistle of wind as she fell. She felt it might seize her and declare her dead before she had a chance to hit the ground. But it did not, and as the ground approached, she closed her eyes.

The hard unforgiving earth came up to meet her, and it was not kind.

Landing feet first, her right ankle snapped, and she dropped to her side with a painful thud, finally feeling some of the pain she had caused her partner. It was a white-hot agony, and she felt herself scream before she had given her voice permission to do so. Psyche looked down to see her foot at an unnerving angle. She reached for it, but at the mildest of touches, it sent throngs of pain up her leg that then radiated throughout her whole body, like knives scraping across her skin.

The sound of wings approaching distracted Psyche from her torment. She looked above to see Eros flying overhead before landing a short distance away in a cypress tree.

"Psyche, are you—" But he stopped himself. His ruined face turning cold before he continued on, words just as frigid. "I went against my mother for you. She would have seen you end up with a true beast, and not just one of my fictions. I left the heavens for you. I pierced my breast with my very own arrow so I may love you." He sneered then. "I must have blinded myself. I thought you ... But no, it no longer matters. You believed me to be a monster, despite my loving words and affections. And for this crime, you aimed to cut off my head!" His voice rose sharply at the end, making Psyche flinch.

"No!" She sobbed, "My sisters—"

"I warned you not to heed their words! I told you it would spell ruin for us both!"

"I know, I know!"

"They will get what they deserve. As for your punishment ... I—" His voice broke. "I still see you through that most damned haze of love!" His breaths came heavy for a moment before he settled once more. "I cannot bring myself to do any more to you than withdraw my presence."

"No!" she shrieked, the very idea leaving her in more pain than anything that had befallen her this night. "Please!" she begged.

"Never again shall I give in to the indulgence of love, for it is a poison! That I see now."

"I love you!" It was all she could think to say.

Eros turned away with a look of disgust on his face. "Keep your venomous words. They only aim to cause me more pain."

"I would never hurt you willingly—!"

"Enough!" Eros bellowed, and the winds blew harder to carry his voice more forcefully into Psyche's breaking heart. "Just ... enough." And with this final, awful goodbye, he took to the skies once more.

Psyche screamed as her heart was torn in two. "Eros!" She called out her lover's name for the first time. But it was to no avail. He did not stop his flight.

Psyche let her pain out through voice and action, as she pounded at the earth and screamed at the skies. She hated everything then. The land, the sea, the very air, and the people who breathed it. But nothing did she hate more than herself. For she carried the burden of blame. She had let the corrupting words of her sisters enter and twist her mind.

After a time of seemingly endless suffering, she began to notice the color and light bleed out of everything. A world of monochrome greeted the broken Psyche as her gasps settled and her sobs quieted and she began to feel nothing at all, just an emptiness she had no desire to fill. Like a hunger that you no longer cared proved fatal.

She got up on her broken feet, heeding not the pain as it meant nothing. All meaning having left with the colors of the world.

She began to limp forward, dragging her more damaged foot behind her.

It did not take her long to find something to pique her interest: a violently running river, waters white with their rage.

Psyche dragged herself up to its grassy shore. She gave one last look to the skies, in hopes of seeing that beautiful winged creature once more, but when she did not, the last of hope died within her.

She flung herself into the rapids below.

Engulfed in the freezing water, breath knocked from her lungs at the shock of it, she let her body be tossed here and there, waiting to crash her head against a rock or for the need for air to overwhelm her so she would be forced to drag the frigid waters into her lungs.

Perhaps hope was not gone after all. The hope for death still lingered.

But even this was denied her, as the waters carrying her took pity and gentled themselves. She floated for a moment in their embrace, confused, before she was deposited onto the shore once again.

She lay there on the bank, drenched to the bone and shaking from the cold of the water that had delivered her. She sobbed against the grass, clutching it in her fists of rage and sorrow.

"Oh, my child," a voice whispered in the gentlest of ways, and suddenly there were hands on her, helping her to sit up.

Tears and pain blurred her eyes, so it took a moment for her to recognize the being in front of her. With horns upon his head and the furred legs of a goat, it could only be Pan.

"I saw what you did, and I know why. You bear all the markings of a heart greatly in love."

Psyche did not respond; her only movements were the shallow rise and fall of her breaths and the tears that slipped down her face.

"Please, do not try and harm yourself again. I may be rustic and rude, a simple herdsman, but know that in my great age, I have gained the wisdom of a thousand mortals. And this now I impart onto you, sweet child." He brushed a damp lock away from her face. "Take heed and pray to the God of love. Surely Eros will see your pain and come to aid you in but the time it takes to beat his wings only once."

At her husband's name, Psyche felt speared anew. Her heart caught in her throat, making her unable to respond even if she could get her voice to work, hidden away in her mind as it was. Eros *had* seen her pain and had felt it much deserved. This was her punishment for trying to slay the love of her life. And now, unable to slay herself, Psyche had nothing left.

Psyche stumbled to her feet with the aid of the hooved creature and looked around at where she had washed up. Flowers grew here along the river's edge in an explosion of color, young goats grazed upon the green further up on the shore, and the stars blinked overhead, giving the only light now that the moon had abandoned them to make way for the sun. It was beautiful, but it did not fill Psyche's heart as it might once have done. For she had now learned of true beauty, and how easily it could be lost, like water leaking from the cupped hands of a man desperate with thirst, like the blood that now poured freely from Psyche's broken heart, no shell of flesh left to contain it.

Psyche moved then, body and mind numb to the world around her. She limped off into twilight, not knowing where she was headed and not caring in the slightest. What was there for a soul without the light of love? Nothing could be illuminated. Nothing could matter. Nothing *did* matter. Psyche dragged her broken body forward, alone, and sent out one single prayer with all the will she had left, for any God that would listen. She prayed that if there was any mercy left in the world, she would not have to endure this silence alone for long.

About the Author

As an autistic, gay, trans man with chronic pain, Clarence finds an escape in literature, both in reading and writing, as well as a way to express himself, with the hopes that other people might feel heard as well.

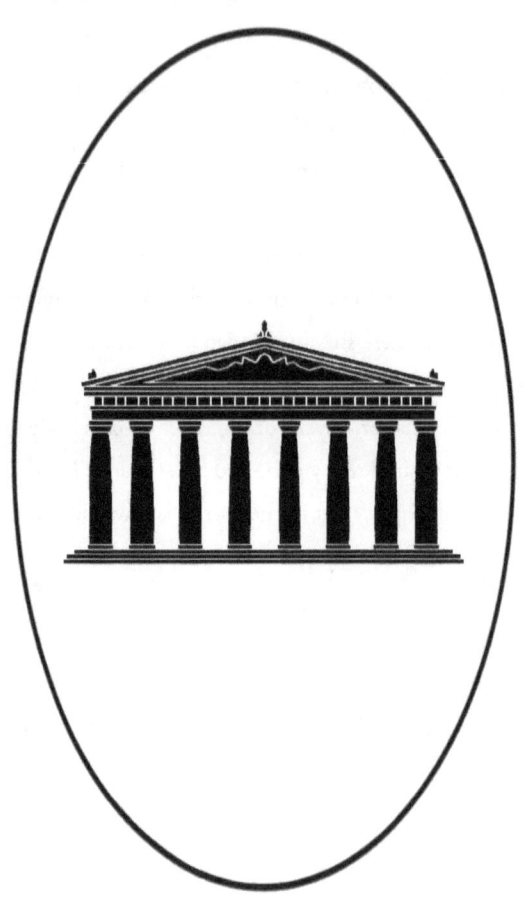

Interemptor

C. M. Clarence

CW: Character death

Whumpee: Man, Whumper: Man, Caretaker: N/A

Talos ... the very name offended Daedalus. Along with his clever inventions of saw and compass. And the young years of his nephew only stood to rub salt in the wound. Soon Talos, a youth of only nineteen, would surpass even the genius of Daedalus himself ... Rage boiled within Daedalus at thoughts like these.

Taking on pupils, he had thought to tutor the next generation of craftsmen, and when his nephew had asked to be taken on, Daedalus could not have been happier. This gleeful naivety did not last, however, for soon Talos' skills emerged. Where Daedalus thought he would find pride in his student, he found only bitterness and, dare he say, hatred. This dark feeling grew inside of him, and he would admit to feeding it with even darker thoughts on occasion. Until one day he could contain it no more. One thought chanted over and over in his mind, and that thought was "Talos must die."

"Would you like to join me on a walk?" Daedalus asked his nephew one late night.

"Certainly," was the cheerful reply. Daedalus had to do all he could to hide his disgust.

They walked at a quick pace, Daedalus both eager to accomplish his goal and also wary of anyone catching them on the road together.

"Where are we headed?" Talos asked, breathing hard to keep up with his teacher and uncle.

"The Acropolis," Daedalus replied, now quickening his steps.

They climbed up to their goal, looking out at the moon as it rose fat and orange on the horizon. Daedalus looked down over the cliff's edge upon which they stood, catching their breath, and decided this would not do. One might survive a fall from such a height, only to be maimed but still able to identify their attacker. No, if Talos were to fall from this height, Daedalus would have to traverse the rocks below and finish the job, though that did hold some appeal ...

"Come, the best view is from the top." And so, they ascended further.

Once upon the roof of the Parthenon, Daedalus found himself overcome with so much glee that it had to escape as laughter.

"What's so funny?" Talos asked, innocent smile painted on his face, waiting to be let in on the joke.

"I'll tell you, but find myself short of breath." A dark smile overtook his face. "You must come closer."

A slight apprehension crept in on Talos' features, peeking out around the edges of his mouth and eyes, the minute downturn of his brow. He could smell danger on the wind, but trusting that the blood that ran through his veins also flowed within his uncle and knowing no stronger bond could exist, at least in his artless mind, he decided to ignore the strange sensation and approached as he was bidden.

Daedalus' eyes grew wide, his smile became unhinged, as he reached out with both hands and pushed his nephew.

The look of betrayal on young Talos' face was worth more at that moment than all the riches of the world to Daedalus.

He fell without a sound, no scream, no cry for help, just a shocked silence. And then he was out of view, but Daedalus heard a satisfying thud.

Daedalus peered over the edge and was met with the gruesome sight of Talos' body, arms, and legs at odd angles, a pool of blood gleaming black in the moonlight spreading from Talos' head.

Laughter escaped Daedalus once more. He laughed so hard he nearly toppled over the edge, but righted himself just in time, falling back against the roof and continuing his maniacal fit.

Soon though, the laughter turned to tears. They weren't tears for Talos, which he still carried a bitter rage for, but for himself. What had he done? What crime had he just committed? Anyone could walk by and see now, even given the late hour. Suddenly fear swamped his mind and he rose to his feet, stumbling slightly in his hurry to reach Talos.

Murder... Murderer. That's what they would call him.

Daedalus reached his nephew and grasped him by the collar of his shirt and shook him roughly, to no avail. Talos was very much dead, no hope there of undoing his great wrong. Why did he listen to those evil words? Why?!

Panicked, Daedalus dragged the body out of view, hiding behind a bush, a smear of red leading any who would happen by to the grisly scene.

Daedalus, in a rage, began clawing at the dirt. He must bury this body. Why did he not think this through and bring a spade?

As Daedalus dug, a strange cawing echoed above him. There, a partridge flew in circles, as if it thought it were a scavenger of the dead.

"He's mine! Go, you! Go!" Daedalus shouted at the bird, out of his mind with fear, convinced this avian creature meant to tell on him in some way.

Daedalus dug until his finger bled, and then he continued on until the hazy fat moon had set and the glory of the sun was beginning to cast its rays. Daedalus felt burned by them, as if Apollo himself had seen what he had done and set out to punish him.

Soon others would be upon them. Soon they would know of his crime. "Daedalus the murderer!" He could already hear the shouts of the angry citizens.

Daedalus prayed to Athena for protection. And dug. And he kept digging ... and digging ... and digging ... The only sound to accompany him was the hollow wail of the strange partridge, its song never far off, driving him to madness.

About the Author

As an autistic, gay, trans man with chronic pain, Clarence finds an escape in literature, both in reading and writing, as well as a way to express himself, with the hopes that other people might feel heard as well.

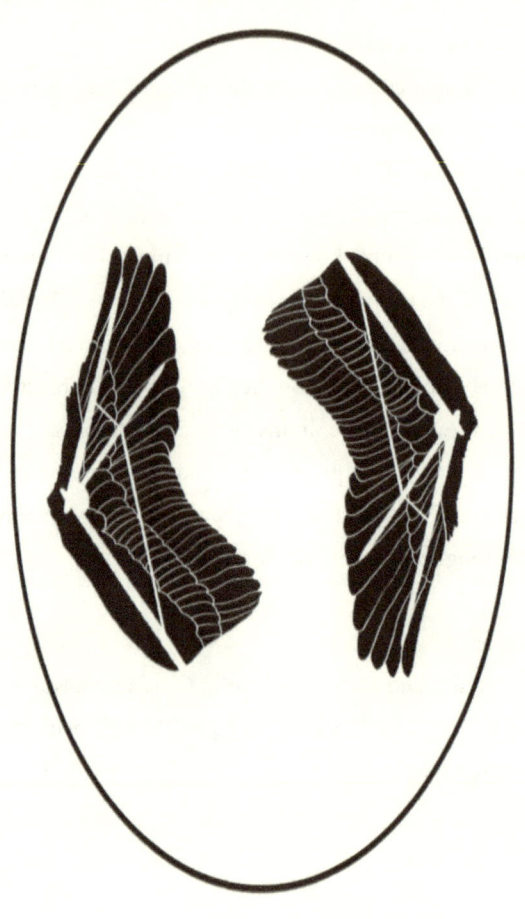

Melting Away

Leanne Albillar

CW: Chronic pain

Whumpee: Man, Whumper: N/A, Caretaker: Man

"Father!" the stranger cried, twisting in the narrow bed.

Phaidros sighed, tempted to keep mending his nets. After over a month of caring for the youth he'd dragged from the sea, he tired of plaintive wails.

"You're safe now." Phaidros rested his aching hand on the youth's arm. "Just sleep."

Usually, the stranger slipped back into a fevered, restless doze once Phaidros soothed him. But today, as the rain drummed down outside, the stranger opened his eyes and tried to sit up. "Where am I? Where's my father?"

Phaidros straightened quickly—too quickly for his old bones—and steadied the stranger before he could fall. "You're on Icaria, boy. I only found you, not your father, and you cost me an entire haul of fish. I couldn't have saved your father if I tried."

"No, he was ... flying. I was flying too." The stranger held up a trembling hand and studied the rough, still-healing scars that stretched from fingertip to shoulder. "But my wings melted."

Oh, the gods were cruel in their answer to prayers. They'd not only sent Phaidros an invalid instead of a helper, but a mad one. "Wings?"

"Yes. My father, he told me not to fly too high, but I didn't listen ..." Tears glistened in the stranger's eyes. "I have to find him, to tell him I'm sorry. You must have heard of him. He's famous."

Sweat beaded on the stranger's brow, chest heaving as the words drained his limited strength. Phaidros patted his arm again. "Easy, now. Who's your father?"

"Daedalus." The youth's voice weakened, but his eyes burned with conviction. "I'm Icarus."

Silence stretched between them, and Phaidros cleared his throat to break the quiet. A mad one indeed. "Daedalus is known to me, aye. But they say Icarus is dead."

***

Icarus gazed across the coast of Icaria, swollen fingers clumsily working at a torn net. What a fate, to be trapped on an island named in memory of him, and yet to still be forgotten. He'd melted away, just like his wings.

No one believed him. Not Phaidros, not the inhabitants of the nearby village, not even the sailors who came ashore.

Some days, Icarus didn't even believe himself.

His father had found a body, after all, and said it was Icarus. But the seas near this island raged, and many people drowned. Any waterlogged body might be mistaken for another.

"We'll catch no dinner if you work that slowly." Phaidros groaned as he sat on the beach beside Icarus. "Let me help, boy."

Icarus passed the partially repaired net to him, then flexed his stiff, quivering hands. The wax wings had scorched him with the heat of the sun as they melted. Droplets of burning wax spattered across the rest of his body as he plummeted towards the sea, but the worst of the burns wreathed his arms and hands.

Shuddering, Icarus glanced at the sun. Tears came to his eyes, not caused by the glare. Sunlight inflicted the memory of melting wax, yes. But a slow realization had crept up on him over these past weeks, as painful as the burns.

"I have no hope of finding my father, do I?" He rubbed his hands together, trying to massage the ache from his stiff fingers. "I can't even find work as a sailor, not with these hands."

He thumped one hand against his thigh, which only worsened the throbbing. Phaidros cleared his throat, his own stiff hands slowly mending the net. "You can stay here with me. I can use the help, bad hands and all."

Something other than pain burned through Icarus, a lightness, a distant echo of the bliss he'd felt as he soared close to the sun. The offer of a new home melted the grief, just a little bit, and ignited a flicker of hope.

Bad hands and all, Icarus picked up the next net and pulled it into his lap. If he and the old man worked together, even at their slow pace, perhaps they could finish in time to catch something for dinner.

About the Author

Leanne Albillar is a disabled writer and artist with a passion for exploring pain through art. Writing is her preferred method of coping with chronic illness. Other loves include Scott (the family cat), painting, drawing, and single malt scotch.

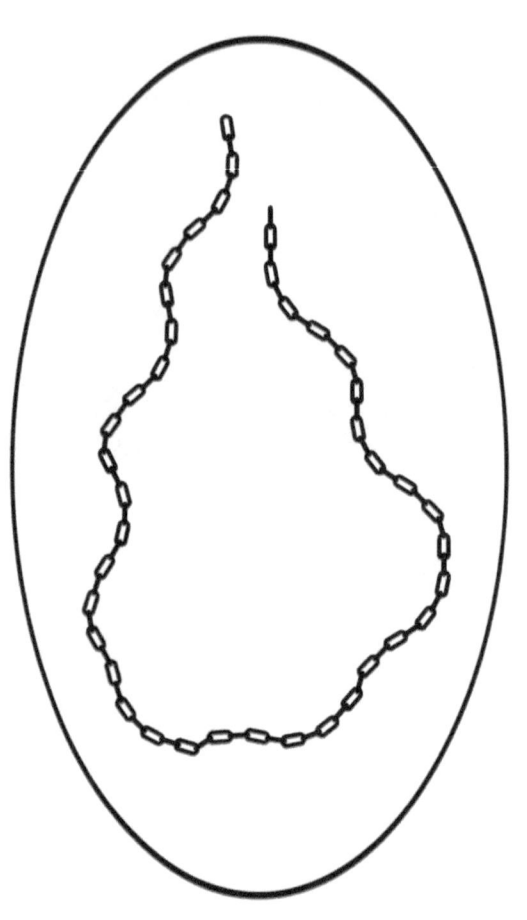

Words Cause Trouble

Archer L

CW: Body horror, mouth whump

Whumpee: Man, Whumper: Man, Caretaker: Woman

"Thor, is this really quite necessary?" Loki asked, trying to sound more annoyed than afraid. His hands were manacled together with iron chains, and Thor had a hold on his elbow to drag him forward.

Thor smiled at him in an almost cruel way. "You mean losing your head?"

"I lost a wager to some dwarves," Loki responded with an eye roll. "Let me go and let them forget about it."

"I think not," Thor said. "You need to see how your words cause trouble."

"But—"

"Quiet your silver tongue!"

Loki did just that, clamping his mouth shut. Fine, if Thor didn't want to talk, maybe the dwarves would.

The dwarves he'd wagered against, Brokk and Eitri, were waiting for Thor and Loki at the entrance to their forge. They were in Nidavellir, a realm deep underground, dark and dank and mysterious. Loki didn't like it here. He *especially* didn't like the two dwarves he was being faced with.

"Ah, Loki," Eitri said, stepping forward, his long red beard swaying. "Come to give us your head?"

"Actually, no," Loki said as he and Thor came to a stop. Thor would still not let go of him. He shot him a look, though.

"No, that's what we're here for."

"Well, I realized there was a bit of a misunderstanding in my wording," Loki began. He knew exactly how to get out of this. Dwarves were very particular about rules, especially the rules of a bet. "I said I would give you my head if I lost. However, as you can see, my head is attached to my neck. I never said you could take any of that."

It sounded terribly silly, but Loki thought maybe it was the thing that would save him here. He was afraid, for sure, as he was with three people who arguably *wanted* his head and his life, and the only defense he had was his words. Luckily, he was good with those. *Very* good.

Brokk and Eitri exchanged looks, then looked at Thor, who was scratching his head.

"That doesn't make sense, Loki," Thor said.

"Of course it does." Loki stepped *closer* to the dwarves, trying to make his point. "You see, I said that I would give you my head but no harm was to come to the rest of me. In cutting off my head, harm would come to my neck."

Brokk shot forward, reaching up an arm to put a hand around Loki's throat. He was shorter than him, but strong, and Loki doubled over and choked in his grasp.

"How about we cut off your head just beneath your chin? Can't get your neck then, can we?" He nodded to Eitri. "Get the axe."

Loki struggled in his hold. No! They weren't listening!

He managed to pull away, and he brought up his manacled hands to rub at his throat, gasping. Eitri was heading back into the hall to retrieve the axe, but stopped when Loki once again began to speak.

"That would still bring harm to my neck," he gasped out hoarsely. "A thing which you agreed *not* to harm."

Brokk looked at Eitri, clearly confused. "Is that what we agreed to?"

Eitri sighed, turning back to face Loki and Thor. "Yes, I believe it is."

Thor grabbed Loki roughly under the arm. "Forget his head! Do something to show this snake that his words have consequences! Or to at least shut him up!"

Loki said nothing, keeping his tongue firmly behind his teeth. He certainly didn't want to lose that. One could argue that, his tongue being in his mouth, it was attached to his head, and therefore they could cut it out.

Brokk smiled in a very unnerving fashion. "I think I know just what to do with you." He nodded to Thor. "Bring him into the hall."

Loki struggled and shouted out a "no!" as Thor dragged him into the dwarves' hall by the grip on his arm. He tried his best to get away, managed to slip out of his grasp. But, before he could run for it, Thor had a fist in his red-gold hair and was pulling on it so hard his head snapped back and he released a pained yell.

"You're not getting out of this," Thor growled. He used his other hand to grab the iron around Loki's wrists, spun him around, and dragged him forward with that. Loki's scalp *ached*, and tears had come unbidden to his eyes.

Once in the hall, Eitri and Thor wrestled Loki down onto his back on one of the tables. Loki kicked and yelled, but it was worthless. There was nothing he could do.

Brokk had gone off into the shadows, and Loki couldn't see what he was doing. He watched him, panicked. What were they going to do to him?

Brokk came back with a needle and thread, and Loki glanced at Thor and Eitri, perplexed. Eitri was just smiling. He knew what his brother was going to do without him speaking it into existence.

"Maybe this will teach you a lesson," Brokk snarled as he threaded the needle. "Thor, keep holding him down. Eitri, hold his head still for me."

Big, filthy hands grabbed Loki by the jaw as Thor just put more pressure on his chest and arms. He understood now.

They were going to sew his lips shut.

"Thor, you can't let them do this!" Loki pleaded as Brokk approached. "Think of all the good times we've had together!"

Thor sneered at him. "Think of all the lies you've told."

Loki didn't give up struggling despite being outmatched and outnumbered. Eitri, however, overpowered him and tilted his head so that he was facing Brokk. Loki squeezed his eyes shut as the needle neared his lips.

It hurt.

Loki had never had a wound stitched before, had never felt needle and thread through flesh, so he hadn't been ready for the immense pain of it, hadn't known what to expect.

He screamed through his teeth as the needle went in one lip and out the other. Dammit, this was going to scar for sure.

He forgot how to breathe as the process continued. All he had to do was inhale through his nose, but he felt like he couldn't, even as he grunted and moaned and yelled. It all happened through clenched teeth, as he could no longer open his mouth. His chest felt like it was going to burst open, his heart pounding and pounding. He wanted to beg and plead for it to stop, but he couldn't speak.

It hurt the most when Brokk got to the middle of his lips. He renewed his struggles, which Thor responded to by pushing his hand into his chest so hard that Loki felt ribs crack. He inhaled sharply, the only reaction he could give.

His face was wet. He didn't mean to be crying. By Yggdrasil, this was humiliating!

He was learning now that his words did indeed cause trouble, and could come back with consequences. Maybe once he was released, he should just leave the thread there, so that he would never speak again.

Thor and Eitri let go of him once Brokk tied off the thread and drew a knife to cut off the extra length. Blood was running into Loki's mouth, down his chin and under it. He wished he could spit it out, but now his mouth was firmly sewn shut.

Loki nearly vomited once they let him sit up. The pain was too much, as was the horror of what they'd done to him. He felt at his lips, closed his eyes and shuddered at the horrible feeling of the thread there. Valhalla above, he couldn't believe this had happened to him!

"Go, Loki," Brokk said angrily. "Before we *do* agree to take your head."

Loki simply nodded, feeling utterly defeated.

He wasn't given any time to rest. Thor grabbed him by his chains and pulled him off the table and to his feet. Loki's stomach was roiling, his lips burning. He wanted to say something, was *desperate* to speak, as was the norm for him, but not a word could leave his mouth.

Thor *smiled* and *thanked* the dwarves as he led him out of their hall. Loki wished he could insult him for such a thing, or use magic, smite him down with words.

He was silent as he was led out of Nidavellir and back to Asgard.

***

Sigyn heard the door to her chambers open and close. Forgetting to leave her paint brush, she took it with her as she left her work on the balcony.

"Who is it?" she asked. Usually her husband announced himself when he came home. Now, the entrance had been quiet, and there had been no knock. She was a bit perturbed.

She came into the main room, and her mouth dropped open in horror at the sight of her husband, her paint brush falling to the floor, smearing blue onto the polished bronze tiles.

"Loki, my goodness!" Sigyn nearly shrieked it. "What happened to you?!"

Loki, his mouth sewn shut, came over to her silently, because he could do nothing else. He dropped his head against Sigyn's shoulder, wetting her hair with tears. Sigyn's arms looped around him, holding him tight. She didn't care about the blood getting on her dress. What was a little more color when it already had tiny smears of paint on it?

"Do you want me to cut the thread?" Sigyn asked.

Loki hesitated, and she didn't know why. But eventually, she felt him nod against her. Sigyn directed him towards the sofa before going to get a small knife, not sure that he'd be able to stay standing on his own.

She retrieved the knife, then returned to where Loki sat, despondent. She sat beside him, and he turned his head towards her. By the Valkyrie, this was gruesome! There were lines of blood from his lips going down his chin.

Sigyn very gently took him by the jaw, but he flinched at her touch.

"Did that hurt?" she asked, quickly drawing her hand away.

Loki nodded.

"I'm sorry. I just have to keep you steady." She reached for his jaw again. "May I ...?"

Loki nodded again.

Sigyn carefully held him by the jaw and raised the knife to his lips. Her hand shook slightly, so she tightened her hold on the knife. She didn't want to mess this up and end up hurting Loki *more*.

Loki inhaled sharply through his nose as the first part of the thread was cut. Sigyn didn't know if she'd hurt him or not, but she had to keep going. There was no way she was allowing this. She was certainly going to ask what happened once she was done.

Pulling the thread out was worse than cutting it. Loki was gasping, mouth now open, as Sigyn gently pulled them from his flesh. She winced each time he made a sound, unable to help herself. She hated seeing *anyone* in pain, never mind the man she loved.

Once it was done and the thread cast aside, the knife put down, Sigyn ran a hand carefully through Loki's hair. It was mussed, as if someone had pulled on it. His eyes were red with tears.

"What happened, love?" she asked.

Loki, now able to speak, did not do so. He just shook his head and once again embraced her. Sigyn did the only thing she could do and held him.

Hopefully her husband would one day speak again, but she feared that the ghost of the thread and the scars it would leave would keep him silent forever.

About the Author

Archer has been writing whump for about 10 years. His favorite genre to write for is fantasy. Read his work at evilwriter-originals.tumblr.com.

Venom

Puck

CW: Torture

Whumpee: Man, Whumper: Snake, Caretaker: Woman

The twin drops of gold-tinted poison quiver on the snake's fangs.

And, in perfect unison, they fall.

An echoing splash, thudding like distant war drums, reverberates through the cave. Loki closes his eyes on instinct and opens them again, staring up at the copper bottom of Sigyn's bowl.

He has no sense of how long he has been here. He has no sense of anything at all. There is only the rock, and the chains, and the serpent.

But there is also Sigyn.

He can barely see her anymore. She is little more than a patch of color in his ruined eyes. His vision is blurred, near-blinded by the acidic venom that falls on his face whenever Sigyn turns to empty the bowl. But she is there, and that is enough for him.

Loki would rather Odin had sentenced him to death. A quick death, a final death, rather than this drawn-out hell. Then again, he could hardly have expected anything less. He runs his tongue over his lips, feeling the long-healed scars from when they sewed his mouth shut, a long time ago now, but still a memory that fills him with anger. *They've always been a new kind of creative when it comes to tormenting me.*

A gentle hand brushes his shoulder, and Loki flinches before berating himself for doing so. *See what they have reduced you to. A cringing coward, afraid of a mere touch.* He will repay them all, someday. That is something else he can cling to, despite all they have taken from him. He has Sigyn—and he has vengeance.

"My love," Sigyn whispers. "The bowl is nearly full."

Gods are not supposed to be afraid, but a chill runs through Loki at his wife's quiet words.

"I'll be as quick as I can," she promises, her voice heavy with sorrow. She hates to see him this way, bound and helpless and tormented. Loki summons his voice, viciously glad that they did not take it from him again. Words have always been his best weapons.

"Hurry back," he tells her. "I need you."

It is not a lie. It may be the truest thing he's ever said. He would have gone mad with pain and hatred by now, if not for Sigyn. Sometimes he thinks he's gone mad anyway, but she's always there to bring him back from it.

The splash comes again, and Sigyn turns, hurrying away. Loki stares up at the snake, locking eyes with its slitted golden gaze. It flicks its tongue out, taunting him. He felt sorry for the creature at first, as much a prisoner as he is, its mouth held open by some magick, forced to venom down onto the helpless man chained to the stone below. Now he just hates it, and the snake hates him back. Whatever sort of serpent it is, it is malicious. It seems to enjoy his suffering, and being the cause of it.

The beads of golden venom start to form at the tip of the snake's fangs.

"Sigyn, hurry," Loki breathes.

He has felt the acid before. He knows his face is burned from it. It hurts more than anything he can imagine, far more than even the awl hurt when it punctured his lips. He hasn't seen his own face since he was made a prisoner here, and he is chained so he cannot touch it—he wonders sometimes if it is still there or if the acid venom has melted it away. Whatever the case, he is terrified of the agonizing splash of liquid. It seeps into him, sets him afire from the inside out, and the pain does not abate for hours. And, of course, there is always another drop waiting.

The droplets are larger now, like liquid gold in a forge. *Sigyn, where are you?* Loki tries to turn his head, but he cannot move it far enough to look over to where she must be. The spell is meant to keep his face positioned directly beneath the serpent's open jaws. "Sigyn," he calls, desperate. "Sigyn, please!"

There is no answer, no gentle reassurance that she has nearly finished, no splash of liquid on stone as she pours the poison out. There is nothing at all but the sound of his own words ricocheting from the cave walls.

"Sigyn!" Loki cries one last time, but he already knows that it is in vain. Whether she has left, or been taken, or whether she was ever there at all, he does not know. But she is gone.

The twin drops of gold-tinted poison quiver on the snake's fangs.

And, in perfect unison, they fall.

About the Author

True to her name, Puck has a flair for the dramatic and enjoys a little chaos. She's currently pursuing her theatre major- hence her Shakespearean psuedonym- and is also training as a dancer. Puck has been writing whump on Tumblr since 2021, and this anthology is right up her alley!

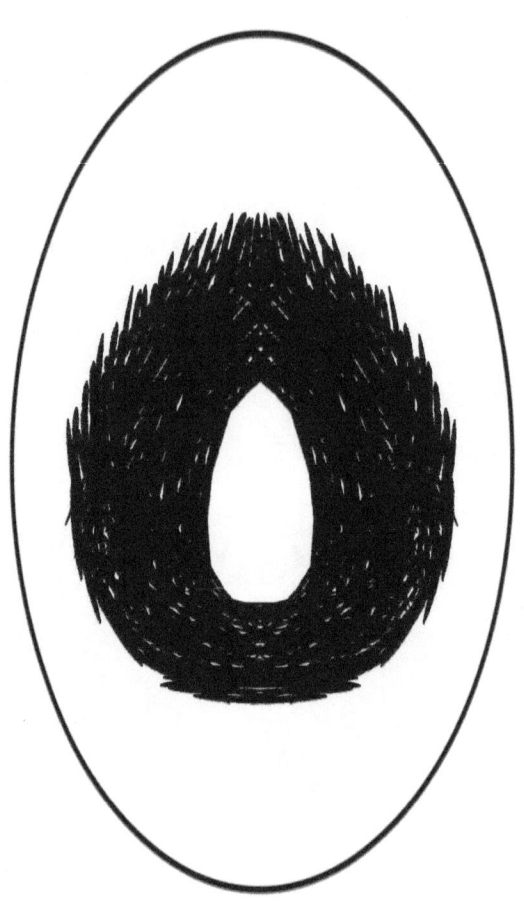

Blue Dress in a Bower Bird Nest

Breanna Bright

CW: Kidnapping, animal death

Whumpee: Woman, Whumper: Woman, Caretaker: Woman

Mora's mother made her a dress of blue, the sort not found in nature. It was deep as the sea and rich as a miser. Mora ran through the fields, sharp even against the clear sky. A gem in her sapphire dress. She played carefully, running through the soft grass in bare feet, ever closer to the woods that bordered her home.

While playing, a bower bird—who loved anything blue—spotted her. From high up she looked small enough to grab and store in his nest. It dived down and snatched her up, flying her far away, clutching her arms with its talons. Mora watched the world pass under her feet in a blur.

The bower bird dropped her in its nest, which was full of pretty blue things. There were bits of porcelain, berries, ink pens, stained glass, and jewelry made of glittering blue stones, but none as fine as the bower bird's latest prize.

Mora fainted in the nest, frightened and dizzy from their journey. The gown blossomed around her like a flower that had been picked. The bower bird admired its treasures for a while, then flew away in search of food.

When Mora woke, she found herself high up in a tree, tucked safely in the twigs and brambles of the nest. Was she small? Had the world grown? If she had shrunk, then where had the rest of her gone? She had been too much of a person to fit inside something small enough to be carried off by a bird.

Yet here she was. The ground was very far away, and the leaves were large enough to wrap around her whole body. She forced her way through the cave-like nest and made her way out onto a branch so as to find a way down.

Great shadows fell over her as a gust of wind shook the tree. Leaves were loosed from their branches and began their lazy descent. Mora decided to fall as well. She jumped atop a golden maple leaf as it passed; it lifted her up and down, riding on the breeze like a magic carpet.

She held it close—it felt the same as holding another person. It even had veins. She and the leaf spun and floated. A breeze teased them higher, then lower, before finally letting them settle on top of a still pond. The leaf floated like a boat, but it was in no hurry to get to shore. With no way to paddle it, Mora sat, hugging her knees close. She watched the reflection of the sky in the water as clouds gathered, tall and dark.

A six-legged bird wandered through the pond towards her. Its long legs kept it above water. It had huge feet that seemed too big for its body. Mora realized that its other four legs were actually those of babies, tucked up under its wings.

"Hello," he said to Mora, stepping up onto a lily pad.

"Hello, father jacana. Would you help me get to shore?"

"I teach my children how to navigate the pond themselves. If you hop upon the lilies, you can find your way."

"Will they hold me?" Mora worried.

"They hold me, and I am a fair size larger than you."

Steeling herself, Mora left her boat, leaping forward onto a lily pad next to the jacana. The plant wobbled under her weight, but held her. She made her way to the next one, jumping across the water.

The next pad was a little farther, and when she jumped, Mora fell short and slipped into the water. Gasping, she surfaced and frantically scrambled for the lily pad. The jacana took pity on her and lowered himself down, closing his wing around her and lifting her up so that her legs dangled. Mora huddled down into his warm feathers gratefully.

The jacana carried her to shore and set her down on solid ground. "We're not all built for water walking, but you did well. Hide yourself now, a storm comes. I must take my children home."

The jacana jogged away, and his prophecy came true. Rain fell, great drops of water muddying the ground, knocking Mora over with the force of their fall. Mora quickly found shelter under the giant leaf of a young foxglove tree.

She stood wet and trembling while raindrops burst like bombs around her, mud seeping between her toes. She remained stagnant, watching the giant world glisten with dampness. When the rain finally stopped, she left the foxglove tree, beginning to ponder where she was and how to get back home. The shadow of a bird flitted by, and Mora quickly ducked out of sight, fearing the return of the bower bird.

She looked down at her perfect blue dress, then at the mud at her feet, thinking of disguising herself. She hated the idea of ruining the lovely blue, given to her by someone she loved ... It was her own fault for drawing attention to herself, she decided.

As she gathered mud to camouflage herself, there was a rustle from the tall grass. Mora looked up and saw a stoat slip through the flora. It paused its journey to stare at her.

"I thought you were a flower at first," said the stoat, "but I see you walk on two legs."

Mora nodded. "I was taken far from home. A bower bird snatched me up because of my blue dress."

"It is very beautiful."

"It has put me in this predicament."

The stoat shook her head. "You cannot cast blame on a garment. The bower bird knows better. Don't tarnish yourself. I will help you."

The stoat stepped forward and lowered herself so that Mora could slip onto her soft back, covered in smooth fur. The stoat moved like water through the brush, twirling and twisting through the bramble smoothly, barely disturbing the vegetation. They soon came to a berry bush, and the stoat stopped for a snack. She stood on her hind legs, and Mora stood on her head to reach the fruit. She was small enough to slip through the thorns and pick the blackberries within. Being so small, the thorns were the size of swords and posed a real danger. Mora snapped one of the thorns from the branch and slipped it under the ribbon around her waist. A substitute for claws and sharp teeth.

The stoat accepted the blackberries that Mora passed down, and they shared the meal until they were full. The berry juice turned Mora's arms and chin deep purple.

"You are a good berry-picker. You can live with me if you want."

"I'd rather go home."

"The only ones who would be able to find it are the birds. We are deep in the woods, far from two-legged homes."

Mora worried at this, unsure if there was a bird she could trust. She asked the stoat if she knew any, and after a brief thought she said, "Let's ask a bat instead."

The stoat carried Mora through the forest and took her to a rocky place full of dark nooks and crannies. They seemed like great caves to little Mora. She slipped off the stoat's back and stared into the darkness.

"What's in there?"

"Hard to know without going in."

So, Mora went in. She saw nothing in the dark, and could only hold her hands out in front of her as she walked. The ground beneath her feet started hard and cold, then began to turn soft. She heard something in the darkness, a squeak, a flutter. Then she felt a spiny hand grab her arm and lift her off her feet. A slippery tongue lapped over her arms. Mora squealed.

"You taste of berries," a voice said, "but you're the wrong shape."

"Certainly," Mora said, "since I am a girl who was only eating berries."

"Why are you here?"

As Mora's eyes adjusted to the darkness, she could make out a pair of large, friendly eyes looking at her, with equally large ears flitting back and forth.

"I was looking for help. I need a flying creature to take me home."

"So, you ventured into the darkness to find one?"

"I cannot ask the birds, it is because of a bird that I am so far from home in the first place."

"Poor child." The bat turned her so that Mora hung upside down just like her new acquaintance. The bat wrapped her up in its fleshy wings, hugging her tight as they hung from the ceiling.

"It was my blue dress that caught its eye," Mora said sadly.

"Still no fault of yours," the bat said, "you taste of blackberry, but I do not eat you. I will make you a deal: if you help me retrieve this fruit—whose thorns keep them guarded—I will help you get home."

"I would be happy to."

"We leave at nightfall."

"I'll return then."

"You're welcome to stay in our cave. You will be safe here."

As comfortable as Mora was wrapped in the bat's embrace, the blood was rushing to her head, and the draftiness of the cave was making her throat sore. She thanked the bat, but insisted she return to her stoat friend. The bat took her hands and lowered her back to the ground, bidding her farewell. Mora followed the wink of light of the cave entrance back outside, happy to breathe in the fresh air and sunlight.

But she found that she was enjoying these things alone. The stoat was nowhere to be seen. She stared about, trying to see through the tangle of weeds and shadows, but it was impossible to discern if there were any creatures hidden within.

Mora walked away from the cave, calling for the stoat. Bugs scattered at her shouts, skittering past her—ants and beetles the size of dogs. Mora shuddered at the sight of them and ran away. Blades of grass made papercuts on her soft skin, devastatingly painful on her tiny body. Rocks that she would have crushed under her foot now left nicks and bruises on her legs. She had to climb over sticks that she would have snapped in her bare hands, and swim through puddles she would have taken pleasure splashing in.

The sound of wings made her look up in alarm, and she saw a hawk circling like a storm cloud. No doubt the reason behind her friend's absence. Mora could only hope the stoat had found cover and not been taken away by the winged death-bringer.

Mora decided she needed to find a safe place as well, and began searching for a warm, hollow place not already taken up by the horrible, giant bugs. She found a bramble of thorns and crawled inside, avoiding the thorns, which would have only left a dot of blood before. Now they grabbed at her dress and threatened to stab her with fatal repercussions.

She found a gap of safety and wrapped herself in a still-soft leaf. Feeling safe at last, sleep came rushing in, demanding its due, and she let it take her away.

She woke, luckily, before the night, but the shadows were growing long with the sun's descent. Eager to reach the caves before nightfall, Mora risked another venture through the thorns, and carefully extracted herself from the brush. She reached the open air without harm, but a new risk awaited her. Mora heard the flutter of wings, and looked up in time to see the bower bird rushing down at her. It spread its wings and aimed its talons down for her. Mora ducked to the left, avoiding the bird's sharp claws. She kept her eye on it as it rose back into the air and circled around.

Mora thought quickly as the bird reset its sights on her. She could remove her dress and let it take the garment, but a hardness in her heart resisted this idea. She disguised it as sentimentality for the craftsmanship that her mother had put into the beautiful dress, but underneath she simply didn't want to give the bower bird what it wanted.

Instead, she removed the thorn tied around her waist and held it aloft as the bird began a second dive. Its reach was longer than hers, so Mora let it snatch her up, and as they began to ascend, Mora raised the thorn and drove it into the bower bird's breast.

The bird screamed and crashed back to the ground, dropping its prize. It flapped its wings erratically, talons and beak searching for Mora. She countered its attack with another strike of her thorn, this time pushing it deep into the bower bird. Its blood coated them both, feathers were cast away, it kept twitching and fluttering in defiance of death, but finally, at long last, its feet curled up like a dry leaf, and its body became stiff. It was dead.

Its feathers were caught in her hair and dress. Mora left them there and turned away from her opponent. Something else would find him and live another day because of it. Mora walked back to the cave; this time she did not flinch from the bugs, the grass did not cut her, and her feet moved surely over the ground.

When she reached the cave, she heard the bats leaving with their familiar squeaks and flutters. She waited outside the entrance until one landed in front of her, walking about on its hands and feet.

"You smell of blood," her friend noted.

"Life is much harder when you're very small."

"Let's get you home then. Will you share some fruit with me?"

Mora could not show the way, but the bat already knew the location of all the fruit bushes and trees in the forest. Mora climbed onto its soft back and kept her arms around its neck as they took to the sky. Its large, funnel-like ears twitched and wiggled as the bat sang its way through the forest, seeing in the dark what Mora could not.

When they reached the blackberry bush, Mora maneuvered through the thorns and picked the dark fruit, passing it to her nocturnal friend, who hung upside-down from a nearby branch. The bat ate happily, its little tongue lapping up all the juices. Mora fed it patiently until the bat was full.

They resumed their flight. The bat chatted about what a splendid feast it was as they flew over the treetops. From her perch, Mora took in the sight of the stars, losing track of the bat's conversation. She saw lights on the horizon and hugged her friend more tightly until they were close enough for her to see that it was indeed her home. There was the tree she liked to climb, there was the field where she played.

The bat took refuge in the tree and helped lower Mora down to the ground, which suddenly didn't seem so far. She thanked the bat, but it was already returning to the strange world behind her.

Mora walked home, climbing the stairs and opening the door. Her mother was inside, face red from crying. She screamed at the sight of Mora—limbs covered in a mixture of blood and blackberry juice, feet coated in excrement, feathers in her hair. Mora offered no explanation, only left to clean herself.

She saved the feathers, keeping them on a bracelet around her wrist. She hung soft fruit on the porch (it was always eaten away by morning), she kept a knife on her person, and she commissioned a rainbow of gowns from her mother that glowed with color, making her look like a drop of sunlight, a shining emerald, or a midnight clear. The blue dress remained forever her favorite.

About the Author

Breanna Bright is the author of 'The Shepherd and the Horned Girl'. When she's not writing she's on adventures to find her next story.

Earthly Knight

Lady Wallace

CW: Noncon, kidnapping, slavery

Whumpee: Man, Whumper: Woman, Caretaker: Woman

I was ten years old when I first met the Faery Queen.

I think that I knew something was coming. It was not unusual to feel the presence of the Fair Folk in the days before Samhain, but that year was different. I felt that I was being watched, targeted. I feared going outside to walk in the woods like I usually did, and yet, the young, daring boy in me forced me to overcome my fear. It was foolish, and I would learn to regret my decision heartily in years to come.

It was the day before the feast of Samhain, when the veils between the Worlds were thin. The Fair Folk weren't supposed to be able to cross over until that night; that is always what we were told, but of course, many things about the Fair Folk are not known, and the Queen has powers of her own that no man can understand or account for.

I was in the woods gathering firewood for the bonfire that night, and she came out of nowhere, appearing right behind me as I turned around. She was the most beautiful woman I had ever seen. Her skin was pale, her eyes an icy blue, almost silver, like her gown that shimmered with unnatural light, made from a fabric that had not been woven on any mortal loom. Her hair was long and dark, reaching down to her knees. I knew instantly that she was not human, even before I marked the pointed ends of her ears. There was an aura around her that felt like the presence before the veils ripped, but it was ten times that and so overwhelming I could almost smell it. I wanted to run, but my feet were held fast to the ground, whether in fear or awe, or some spell of her own, I didn't know.

"Tam Lin," she said, speaking in a voice that sounded like all the wind through the trees, and yet was as soft as a butterfly's wing. "Come with me."

I had heard stories all my life about the faery dances, and been warned against going into the woods after dark at any time of the year, for some of the Folk never hide behind the veil.

Still I did not say anything. She took a step forward. Then another, and another, until she was standing only a foot in front of me. She reached out and put a hand under my chin, raising my face so that I would look her in the eye. I gasped, or tried to, but I had no breath. Her eyes were deep, bottomless, and one could so easily be lost in them. Lost and never return. There was so much to see in those eyes. On the surface, they seemed kind enough, but underneath there was deadly deceit, power, and a wickedness that I had never before seen in my young life. I suddenly felt an icy hand grab my heart and I froze.

"So fair," she said, her fingers brushing my cheek gently, making me shiver. "I would have you in my court. Will you come?"

I finally found my voice, though it broke haltingly as I spoke. "I must stay with my family." I clutched tighter at the rowan twigs that I had in a pouch around my neck. Everyone wore them this time of the year. It was too unsafe to go around without. I wished I had a piece of iron, though some said even that did little good when it came to some of the faeries.

She smiled, seeming to mock me and my rowan twigs. I should have known better than that they would affect the Faery Queen. "Perhaps not now. But someday, you will come with me." And then she was gone, so suddenly that I blinked several times trying to make sense of how she had managed it. I was finally able to move again, running all the way back home to cower in my bed. I did not come out until the next morning when I was sure that the Wild Hunt had passed back behind the veil and we would be safe until the next Thinning Time.

***

I was fifteen when I was taken.

I was squiring by then, and hoping to become a knight by the time I was eighteen. I was riding through the woods one day, when without warning, my mare spooked and I was thrown from my saddle, hitting my head. When I came to, I thought I was dreaming, for I was in a land so fair that I could not believe it to be real. It was a forest like the one I rode through, on the lands of the family I stayed with, but so much more vibrant. Every color was rich and saturated and there was a particular floral sweetness in the air that I did not find cloying at the time. Along with the visual aspect came a heightened sense of all things—birds, small animals, the water running in the brook not far away.

And then I noticed I was in a cage, and I knew within my heart what had happened to me.

In my lifetime, I had known several people who had gone missing for several years, only to appear again, mad, or worse, having been caught in a Faery Dance and thought to be gone only a night. They were never the same afterwards, but they were not like me. I had not stumbled upon a dance or a mushroom ring unawares, had not been called by the music that was too lovely for human ears to resist. I had been captured on purpose, with wicked intent by the Faery Queen.

I knew the stories—everyone knew the stories. The Queen liked to keep fair human men around her all the time as her courtiers, her favorites—her lovers. I had feared she coveted me when I met her all those years ago in the woods for the first time. I had tried to forget that meeting, but sometimes her wicked eyes would find their way into my dreams and plague me. *I* had not forgotten, and I should have known better than to think she would as well.

It was not long before I saw her again. She came walking with two courtiers—one Fae, the other, a mortal man; fair, like me, fine-boned with thick locks of golden red hair framing his thin face. His gaze was what caught my attention first, even before that of the Queen, for he gave me such a look of pity and heartache and pain, that one would expect tears to fall down his cheeks at any moment. That was the first time I met Owain Johnstone, another fated meeting that I would never forget.

The Queen knelt by the cage and I instinctively pulled back to the other side as far from her as possible. She smiled.

"Don't be afraid, Tam Lin. Whether weal or woe, you are mine now, and you shall never walk a free man in the mortal world again." That smile that flicked across her lips as she said this made my stomach turn, and I knew she meant it. And at that time, I feared she was right. The Fae guard unlocked the cage and dragged me out, keeping a hand on my shoulder as we marched through the woods.

Eventually, we ended up at a castle, the Faery Gard. It was the most beautiful place I had ever seen in my life, looking like something more from a dream than any reality of either the mortal world or that of faery, but I was too scared to appreciate it then. I was taken to the royal hall where the Queen took her place on her delicate crystal throne, surrounded by her men and maidservants, her warriors and her courtiers, the lesser ones, some younger than I, crouching at her feet while the man I would come to know as Owain stood at her right side, his head bowed in submission and his hands clenched behind him. Even in that current state of mind, I saw how his body shook in unbridled anger, and I was only able to tear my gaze from him as the Queen spoke to me.

"You will now be one of my courtiers," she told me. "You will serve me with your life, and swear fealty only to me, and if you fail whatever order I ask of you, you will pay with your life. Is that understood?"

I nodded, unable to say anything else. The guard, who still stood at my back, put a hand on my shoulder and shoved me to my knees on the dark stone floor. The Queen reached out a hand and I took it carefully, with all reluctance, and kissed the delicate, marble white fingers she offered.

A jolt went through me as my lips touched her skin and before I could recover, the guard behind me had grabbed me by the back of the neck and ripped my tunic from off my left shoulder. He drew a sharp dagger and I screamed as he carved out a symbol in my flesh. Another guard took a goblet the Queen handed him to catch the blood that fell from the wound. Once he was done, I curled over with the pain, but looked up as the Queen settled the goblet on a pedestal beside her throne. I later learned she kept the blood of all her subjects in there to bind them to her so she was in full possession of their lives.

"Now you are mine, body and soul, Tam Lin," she told me, all false pretenses of kindness gone; only the dark Queen remained. "And if you ever betray me, I shall tear out your heart."

I gasped for breath, still in pain from the cuts on my chest, but I managed to look up at the man who stood at her side and this time there were tears flowing freely down his face. I did not fully understand then, the full cause of his grief, but oh, how I would understand all too soon the suffering and everything that came with it. And then I would find myself reduced to tears on more than one occasion myself.

***

I was brought to some sort of dormitory where the mortal courtiers of the Faery Queen stayed. There was a wing for maids as well, for the Queen would also take fair maidens for the fae nobles, and also sometimes took girls who were half fae into her house to act as ladies' maids and tell her of the outside world. All of this I learned later, of course, for that first night, I was too scared to think or care about the happenings of this magnificent palace of the Otherworld. It would have fascinated and enchanted me if it had not been ruled by the evil that was the Faery Queen.

My bed at least was soft and I sunk into it and immediately curled into a ball, finally letting the tears flow. I feared then never to see my kin or my comrades again, and I mourned my position as a captive of the Faery Queen, no better than a slave, and possibly worse off, for a slave could always escape if brave enough, but the Queen had bound me to her loyalty by blood ritual and I would not even have the luxury of hoping that I could escape one day.

I didn't know when I fell asleep, or even how I could be still of mind enough to do so, but when I woke to my unfamiliar surroundings, I turned from the wall and saw the man I had seen at the Queen's side, watching me with sadness on his face. I sat up slowly and turned to him, wanting to know the cause of his great sadness, yet, at the same time, fearing the answer.

"Sir," I began hesitatingly. "What ails you?"

"Oh, what ails us all?" he replied grimly. "You will find out soon enough. My dear lad, you should have run when you had the chance. Should have fought and died before she marked you, for now your soul is hers as well as your body and you cannot even escape this life with death unless she wishes it."

I was shocked then, but I would understand perfectly in time. "Why do you say such things?" I asked. "Surely, with life there is always hope?"

"Not here," he whispered bitterly, his voice choking as if his throat were constricted by sorrow. "Not here, lad. It's best you know that now. I have been here for ten years, and have been her favorite for four. In three more years, she shall have to pay the tithe and that shall be me, and all my suffering will be over."

"What suffering?" I asked, for I was really only a boy then, and knew little of true suffering of any kind.

He shuddered. "Whatever pain pleases her, whether it be degradation, torment either physical or mental, it matters not. We are only here to serve whatever cruel whim she wishes and nothing more. Once I am gone, you will be her next favorite. So it is only fair I tell you, lad. You see me now, and I am a broken man. I wish only to die. It pains me to see one so young and full of life come here because I know that you too will be like me one day."

Fear clutched at my heart to hear his words. I did not want to be broken like him; I never wanted to be in so much pain that I wished for death above freedom. I suppose death was a kind of freedom, but was it better? I didn't think it would be. I knew that I would at least have to try to escape before I could let myself hope for death.

"What is your name, lad?" he asked softly, breaking me from my dark thoughts.

"Tam Lin," I told him.

"I am Owain Johnstone," he replied.

***

Owain looked after me there when he could. Helped me navigate the ways of the Faery Court so that I would not garner any extra attention.

Luckily, my time spent with the Faery Queen was limited in those days to dinners and attending her in court, which mostly consisted of standing near her throne and bringing food and drink when she requested it. She rarely addressed me at all, for I was not her intended target at that point. I was hers, body and soul. She was confident in that fact, thus she needed to pay me no mind. And because of that, none of the other members of her court dared touch me, even in drunken revelry during the copious parties and dances.

For the most part I was able to blend in with the other humans living there. Most of them did not interact with me. It was like they knew that one day I would be held above them as the Queen's favorite, which ultimately only led to one thing and why bother wasting time on someone who could not be saved?

Owain, however, was different. His fate was already sealed, and he gifted me with a small portion of the quiet care and love that he must have once had in abundance, treating me as something of a younger brother to him. I came to love him likewise in return, which was, perhaps, my first mistake.

***

The beginning of the end began about a year after I had arrived, when I was walking back to the dormitories and happened to spy Owain in a corridor. He was holding close one of the maidens and burying his face in her hair. I began to realize this must have caused the change in him of late, how his whole demeanor seemed more quiet, speaking less of his dark cynicism and instead of simply taking things as they came. It was as if there was ... not peace in his heart—never peace in this place—but at least something to ease the pain a little bit. I felt happiness for him, and horror at the same time because I knew that if the Queen found out, he would be killed. But I would not say a word or think on it a moment longer, for I knew that Owain needed the small consolation he could find in lovely Annabelle's arms more than anything else.

But it was only a matter of time before the Queen found out, and when she did, it marked a new passion in me.

The court was called randomly one day. I had not seen Owain all day and I worried, feeling in my heart that something was wrong, but I knew for certain as I saw him dragged into the hall and cast down before the throne. On his knees at the feet of the Faery Queen he was stone quiet, braced, and stronger looking than I had ever seen him before. I knew with sickening certainty that he was at peace with his fate, but I was not. I did not want to see my only friend killed.

"You have betrayed me, Owain," the Queen said coldly, standing up to stare down at him. He turned his face up to meet her gaze in a defiance I had never seen in him before.

Fury crossed the Queen's face and she snapped her fingers.

My heart sank further as I saw two of the faery guards dragging Annabelle into the court. Her face was streaked with tears and she looked like she had been beaten, blood and bruises covering her exposed skin.

"Anna." Owain turned to her desperately, looking to get up before the guards forced him back down.

The Queen grabbed his chin and wrenched Owain's head back around to face her. "You dare look at this lowly serving girl in my presence?" she demanded.

Her fury felt palpable, as if a miasma of darkness had permeated the room. I could barely breathe, terrified of what was to come.

Owain simply stared at her and the Queen's lip curled in fury before she turned sharply toward the guards that held Annabelle.

"Do it," she commanded.

"No," Owain tried before his voice simply died away as if he knew how futile any protest would be.

I watched in horror as one of the guard's drew a dagger and dragged it across Annabelle's throat; a garish crimson ribbon painted the front of her dress the same color before her eyes dimmed and they simply let her fall to the floor.

The Queen watched with cruel satisfaction before she turned back to Owain, drinking in the pain in his eyes.

"Will you repent and come back to me?" she asked.

"Nay," he said quietly.

"Very well then, you shall meet your fate, Owain, I have no more need of you." And she pulled a small, thin blade from her sleeve and grabbed Owain by the back of his neck, jerking him forward. A quick slash of the knife sprayed droplets of red, before she plunged her hand into his chest. He gasped, but his mouth soon twisted into a smile. He looked up at her as she pulled his heart, still beating, out of his chest, and then dropped his lifeless body back on the ground.

I choked back a sob and rushed forward, unable to help myself. I fell to my knees beside the body of my dear friend, the only man who had been kind to me at all in this strange place. I gathered him into my arms and held him tightly, rocking back and forth, but I could not ignore the look of peace that was on his face, an expression I had never seen there before, and I think it hurt me all the more to know that he was happier in death than he had ever been in life. I feared that it would be like that for me one day, sooner than I thought.

The Queen spoke, jolting me out of my grief. "You should not mourn him, Tam Lin," she said.

I forced myself to look up at her, for ignoring the Queen was never a good idea.

She was gazing down at me with a hard expression on her face, calculating. She then turned to her guards, flicking her fingers in dismissal. "I'll need another for the tithe. Have the other courtiers brought before me. We only have a few months to decide now."

I was too distraught to even think about what that meant but could only shudder in grief, trying to hold back my tears as the Faery Queen turned her attention to me once again.

She crouched, her hand still bloody from ripping Owain's heart out. She reached that hand out and cupped my face with it, forcing me to keep her gaze. "He betrayed me, Tam Lin. Now you see what happens to those who break their bond of fealty to me. Do you see now? Do you see why you should not do the same?"

I nodded, but deep inside, I knew I didn't mean it. I would never stop trying to find a way to escape, and I was determined to do so; to have freedom again, even if it was just for a moment before I met my doom. I was not going to die like Owain, wishing for the calm blackness of death, until finally dying in captivity in Faery. I would be free again one day. I swore it.

***

I don't think I ever fully understood what the Samhain tithe was truly about until I witnessed it myself that year. Owain had never elaborated on it, and though back in the mortal world we had plenty of stories that told of the Wild Hunt and why you stayed safely locked away on that night, clutching your iron and rowan, no one knew what really went on.

But it seemed that even the Queen was held to a darker power, one she had to pay a tithe to as all of us did to her.

I watched, guarded and tense, as the preparations were made. The courtier who had been chosen as the tithe was bound and taken to the stables. I was surprised when the Queen herself addressed me.

"You will ride with us tonight, Tam Lin," she said.

So I rode with them in the Hunt that night for the first time and, oh, what a ride. The horses galloped with an otherworldly speed I had never known. It would have been exhilarating if I had not been so terrified of what was to come. I concentrated on simply staying in the saddle, worried that if I were to tumble off the horse now I would fall somewhere between Faery and the mortal world, stuck there forever in some horrible limbo.

Perhaps that would be a better fate when all was said and done.

The feeling of urgency only intensified when we finally crashed through the veil. I breathed in the air of my own realm, shock and familiarity swallowing me as the moon shone down, cold and uncaring as it lit the way for the Faery hunt. The white fae hounds bayed, dashing around the horses.

Finally, we made it to a crossroads and the party slowed as the Queen pulled her horse to a stop.

"Bring the tithe," she called.

The unfortunate man was brought forward, taken from his horse and pulled toward a large stone that was illuminated under the moonlight.

I could only watch in a sort of fascinated horror as the man was pushed down on the stone before the Faery Queen stepped forward with a knife and slit the man's throat.

As blood spurted and dripped down on the stone, filling carven runes and symbols that I had not seen before, the atmosphere became dense and charged, like the feeling before a storm. It was then a veil was ripped open in the night, swallowing the dying man before dissipating, leaving nothing behind but the blood trickling down the stone.

"It is done, for another seven years," the Queen said and then, oh, and then, she turned to look at me and I had never felt such abject terror, even in all my time spent in her court. I might have been newly eighteen, a man in the eyes of the world, but in that moment, I experienced more fear than I ever had as a timid child left alone in the dark of night.

I knew then that the prophetic words Owain had spoken to me the day I was first taken to the Queen's Court were to come true. In seven years, I would be the next tithe.

My true hell began that night.

The Hunt continued and we returned to Faery as the sun began to rise in the east. It brought no joy or comfort to me. I was shaken by what I had witnessed that night, and what I knew was coming.

As I was putting my horse away, two guards approached me.

"The Queen has requested your presence."

I walked as a man doomed toward the Queen's chamber. Yet a man heading to his execution would at least be left at peace when it was over. I, on the other hand, knew that my torment was just beginning as I entered the Queen's private chambers, and saw her standing there.

She was undeniably beautiful, especially now bathed in the glint of tinted sunlight from a high stained-glass window. Her long black hair was down, reaching past her waist, and she wore a gown of sheer midnight blue silk that clung to her pale skin in the most alluring fashion.

Having grown to manhood, I could easily recognize her sensuality, but instead of feeling any arousal at her presence, I could only feel terror. No more than a small animal caught by a dangerous predator. A bird standing in front of a wildcat. A bird that had already had its wings clipped with no hope of escape.

"Tam Lin, you shall be my new consort now that Owain is dead for his betrayal," she told me firmly, walking toward me. "You are to attend me in all my needs, you will not hesitate to be by my side whenever I call you." Her hand fell to my chest and delicately pushed aside the collar of my tunic, revealing the scar that rested above my heart, the mark she had put there when I had first been captured. "You are mine, body and soul, and you shall serve me as such." Her fingers were as smooth and cold as marble, causing me to shiver as they traced across the raised mark before she slid her hand up to my neck, slipping across the point of my pulse that fluttered under her touch. "Betray me, and you'll end up like dear Owain. Swear to me you will serve me, and only me, body and soul, Tam Lin."

I swallowed hard, but knew hesitation would only make it worse. Her eyes were so cold, I felt like they were freezing me to my core. "I swear," I barely whispered. "I will serve you. Body and soul."

She said nothing, only smiled, and pulled me forward, pressing her lips to mine.

The first kiss I had ever shared, given away to my captor. If I hadn't already had a cruel mistress, I would have said that life was the cruelest there could be. She tasted sharp, of metal and fresh snow.

She was not gentle with me that night, nor was she any other. The Faery Queen was a being used to taking what she wanted with little care for anyone else. Her teeth were sharp, her nails sharper. She berated me when I did not do exactly as she expected. She took me apart with venom and claws. I felt weak, helpless; me, a man, once almost a knight, no match for her strength as she forced me beneath her and took what she wanted from me. She had claimed my soul, my blood collected in her fell cup, and now she had claimed my body as well.

Later, as I lay upon those sullied silk sheets, that creature sleeping at my back, I felt the true disgust toward myself, toward my captor, and toward my situation as a whole. I stared up at the uncaring sun that shone through the window above. Was it truly the same sun that lit the Faery world and the mortal together? If it was, then I resented its light all the more.

I curled in my shame, and wept silently to myself.

***

It went on like that. And on and on. My life soon became nothing but serving the Queen in her every whim. She broke me like a horse until she was certain I would do as she asked, and truly, my defiance had worn thin years ago. Once I had seen there would be no point in it.

It was then she set me to other tasks. As a human I could travel through the veil, if she allowed, at any time of the year. Because of this, I was sent out to collect a new batch of young maidens to serve in the court.

"You are fair of face and sweet of tongue," the Queen told me before she sent me out. "They will flock to you. Bring back only the choicest among the maidens."

I went, and did as I was told.

It was painfully easy. I would go into town, and though whispers would follow me, the young women would always fail to heed the warnings of those more wise in the ways of the world. Those who perhaps might even know why a young man who dressed in noble clothing, who rode a rich white steed, might come around with seemingly no intention of business.

I would charm the maidens and lead them into the woods where they would then meet the same fate as I had. I truly despised this job, but I was to find out soon enough what would happen if I disobeyed.

There was one maiden, far too young, barely older than I had been when first captured. I told her to go home, but stubborn as girls are at that age, she followed me into the woods against my warning. It was then, with the Queen's guards waiting, that I forcibly turned her around and sent her home with fury enough to terrify her.

When the Queen found out what I had done, she struck me across the face, her nails cutting into my skin.

"How dare you keep a willing girl away from me!" she snarled.

I would have replied, tried to make some excuse for myself, but her hand suddenly clenched and agony tore through my chest, stealing my breath.

I fell to my knees, the scar above my heart burning like a brand pressed into my flesh. I felt as if I were being torn apart from the inside out. I wished for death in that moment perhaps more than I ever had before. This red agony was like nothing I have ever experienced. Truly, I understood in that moment that she was torturing my soul as much as my body.

When the pain finally subsided, I could only lay, limp, on the ground, sweat and tears streaking down my face as I shook in my skin.

The terrible visage of the Faery Queen loomed above me, looking down with the slightest upward curl of her mouth as if my torment amused her—I knew it did.

"Defy me once more, Tam Lin, and you will never see the light of day again. Pity one of those maidens and I shall rip your heart out and replace it with stone. And it would be such a shame to have to ruin such a warm bed companion."

I rolled over until I was kneeling with my forehead on the ground at her feet. Partly in some form of penitence, and partly because I could barely stand to move farther in my current state. "Forgive me, my lady," I gasped. "I shall not fail your orders again."

"Kiss my feet to show your humility."

A black silken slipper was presented before my eyes, and I felt the slightest flare of disgust and humiliation. But I still leaned forward and pressed my trembling lips to the cold skin above the slipper.

"My loyal Tam Lin," she cooed as if I truly were some pet. She crouched and cupped my face, finally forcing me to look up at her again. Her silver eyes were always so unnerving, sickly to look into, yet impossible to look away from.

"You will attend to my pleasure now and perhaps then I will fully forgive you."

I rested my cheek against her knee in acceptance of my position, affecting gratitude for this chance to prove myself to her, trying not to let my disgust show.

I never let it show; I kept myself passive, perhaps even smiled at her when she was in one of her better moods. I knew how to play my part. Had learned what she wanted out of me when. I hated myself, and yet, even if I had chosen death, I believed she would never let me die. And the certainty of being gifted with death at the time of the tithe was better than an eternity of what I had now. Of worse than I had now.

I was nothing but her plaything. An object to break, to abuse and throw away when she was bored of it.

I began to count down the days, the weeks, the months, to the time when I would be given as the tithe and my torment would be over.

***

Traveling back to the mortal realm was always strange to me. It had been so long since I had mingled among humanity as a whole. I had almost forgotten that I was still mortal myself. Nothing but an earthly knight in the realm of the Fae.

It was the only time I was allowed to be truly alone. The Queen trusted I would come back, because I, of course, had little choice in the matter.

I usually stuck to the towns, wooing my way into the hearts of the maidens—not too many and not too frequent. Otherwise people would talk more than they already did.

But I also snuck away from my duties on occasion and rode my horse through the hills outside of the cities.

It was one day that I happened upon familiar land and, recognizing where I was, I slowed to a trot and stopped to dismount, continuing by foot.

Carter Hall looked sad and ill compared to when I had last seen it. Quite like my parents the last time I had seen them before the fever took them both within days of each other. I had been away, squiring at that time. It seemed no one resided there at the hall now. Why would they? After all, I was the only heir and had no siblings, without me being around there would have been no one to take it under their care.

I left my horse to graze and walked up to the aging hall.

Ivy had grown over its stone walls. Several windows were cracked or broken with time. The door was rotted so that I was certain animals had made up their residence inside.

A deep sadness tugged at my heart as I slowly trod my given land like a ghost who refused to leave. A monument to a life long gone. A life that I had trouble recalling if it had even truly happened, or if it had simply been the product of a dream.

I recalled then the garden bower behind the hall where I had played many days as a child and continued on my way, hoping, perhaps, to find some sort of peace there. If only for a few moments.

It turned out I was to find something entirely different.

Indeed, I was so astonished at the sight of another human amidst this crumbling ruin that I simply stood in shock for a moment before I was able to fully take in the scene.

A young woman stood in the garden with a basket over her arm, reaching boldly into the tangled, overgrown briars to cut roses until a bundle of crimson velvet settled in the basket.

I did not know what befell me in that moment, but I experienced a brief sharp anger. How dare this woman trespass on my family land and be so bold as to cut my roses? The ones my mother herself had planted.

"Lady," I called sharply. "What mean you by cutting my roses?"

She startled, an obvious reaction considering I must have seemed to come out of nowhere. A small gasp escaped her as she caught herself on the briars while quickly pulling away.

But instead of cowering in fear, she faced me boldly. "What mean you by *your* roses, sir? This land belongs to my father, therefore I have the right to pick all the roses I wish."

This stopped me for a second. "Your father?"

She raised her chin, green eyes meeting my own as auburn hair tumbled over her shoulders with a defiant toss. "My father received this vacant land from the king himself with the death of the last heir. If you truly claim it as yours you'll need the proof."

It was then I saw the drop of crimson blood, brighter than the roses, trembling from her fingers. I swiftly pulled a handkerchief out of my pocket and stepped forward to press it against her hand, feeling her freeze.

"Then I suppose you have the right to it, my lady. I have no proof that I can show you, for I am no better than a dead man."

She stared at me as if trying to read my expression. I busied myself tying the kerchief around her hand tight enough to stop the bleeding.

"I have never seen you around these parts. What is your name?" she finally asked.

I sighed and released her hand. "I have been called Tam Lin."

She took a step back, fear now flashing in her eyes. "I have heard of you," she said, voice barely above a whisper. Her hand reached for the knife she had been using to cut the roses but iron wouldn't do anything to me aside from the natural sting of the blade. "They tell tales. They say that when you come to town, maidens disappear."

"And what do you believe?" I asked.

I expected her to simply run, and truly, she should have, but she did not. Instead, she stared at me even longer, until I felt like she was peering inside me, seeing places I didn't want anyone to see, and yet ...

"Truly, I do not know," she admitted, adjusting the basket of roses. "I feel I see a man with a very heavy heart."

I offered a sad smile. "You see through me, my lady. And because of that, I promise you that I will not steal you away."

She seemed to settle then, but I had already spent as much time here as I could allow.

"You may pick the roses if you wish," I told her. "My mother would have wanted to see them enjoyed as she enjoyed them."

The lady's face changed to one of shared sadness and understanding, and I turned away briefly before glancing over my shoulder.

"My lady, tell me this one thing—What is your name?"

She straightened and clutched the basket tighter. "Janet is what I am known by."

"Good day then, Lady Janet," I told her and returned to my horse.

Unbeknownst to me at the time, I left part of myself at Carter Hall that day. Part of me that was not owned by the Faery Queen, and that was indeed a dangerous game to play.

***

It became more of a habit than I had intended to stop by my old family land whenever I crossed to the mortal realm. While it may no longer have been mine, I still felt some duty to check in on it.

I also, admittedly, hoped to meet with the Lady Janet again, as shameful and foolish as that was to admit at the time. I would keep my promise to her and would not steal her away. Because of that, there was something freeing about being around her. I should not have been so comfortable, and yet I could not deny that she had brought a strange sort of peace to me that day picking roses in the garden.

The next time I saw her, she was walking up to the garden with a cloth-covered basket over her arm. She offered a small, tentative smile as she saw me.

"I heard that you were in town," she said. "I thought you might visit again. Would you like something to eat?"

I could hardly form the words to speak, but I watched as she settled the basket on the low garden wall where I sat and began pulling out food. Rich dark bread and cheese, the kind of which I hadn't tasted in years.

I could hardly resist and ate with her, the two of us sharing a companionable enough silence.

"What burdens you, Tam Lin?" Janet finally asked.

I swallowed the bread and cheese slowly, savoring every mouthful. "You should not ask me that, my lady. Nor any questions you do not want the answer to."

But she persisted, seeming unbothered. "The people talk; they say you were taken by the Fair Folk. Is that true?"

"Perhaps."

Green eyes settled on me, not with pity, but rather contemplation. I somehow knew Janet would pry the information out of me one way or another, and, in truth, I didn't mind that. Though, I knew how dangerous a game that was to play. For both of us.

"My lady," I said finally, turning to her. "You should not ask me such things. I am not a good man. In fact, you should not even be around me."

I made to stand, to leave, but before I could make it more than a step, her hand descended on the one I had braced against the stone bench. Her skin was warm and supple, soft, the press comforting.

"You seem so alone," she said and actually sounded sad as if she had the gall to care for someone of my ilk. "Would it not help you to unburden yourself to someone else? I promise it will not go beyond me—I have no one to tell."

I should not have. I should have sealed my lips and left, but I had never felt so at peace with anyone as I did with Janet in that moment, far enough away from the reaches of the Faery Court that I was able to experience some sort of dangerous false security.

So I told her all. The story from the beginning when I had first had that fated meeting with the Faery Queen in the woods, that day so long ago now.

"She holds me," I explained, pushing aside my collar to show her the mark on my chest. "I can never be free of her until the day she grants me my death."

"And when is that?"

"About three years from now," I told her, unable to keep the weariness from my voice.

Janet leaned toward me. "Then until that time, come see me. You'll be safe here."

And before I knew it, she had pressed her lips to mine. The kiss was soft and giving; kind, not at all possessive. Janet tasted warm, of cinnamon and honey, memories of sunshine despite the overcast sky.

A little piece of me cracked, the chains the Faery Queen held me with seeming to weaken just slightly. I emerged from this state only when Janet pulled away, to find myself lost in her emerald eyes.

"Look for me the next time you come here, Tam Lin," she said as she cast her eyes downward modestly and gathered her basket. She stood, leaving me sitting there, both elated and terrified of the feelings surging through me.

What had I done?

I could not be truly penitent, though. And I did return. I met with Janet every time I went back to the mortal realm. Somehow, she always knew when I would be there and would greet me with the utmost kindness, and sometimes with a honey-tinted kiss.

While the Faery Queen was spiteful and cruel, all cold edges and sharp claws, Janet was warmth and soft touches, supple fingers soothing the scars that had been left on me, body and soul.

Janet was the only thing that could quell my nightmares. The only thing I would truly consider living for, no matter how foolish a thought that was.

I, in my weakness and my stupidity, grew to love her, though I knew there was no way we could share the life together we both secretly wished to. How I longed to stay in Carter Hall, to return the place to its former glory, to take Janet as my own and raise a family with her like I might have now, had I never gone to the woods. But those dreams were so far from my reality that they were laughable to even think about. The chain around my heart would not allow it, and, selfishly, I realized I could stand to leave Janet, but I could not stand to see her taken from me should the Queen ever find out.

Janet was an insanely brave woman to love me at all. Many times I could not believe she was more than a figment of my imagination, but her soft words, kind eyes, the feeling of her body, warm against mine, were too real to be a trick of the mind.

Even now as we lounged in the grass of the garden, my head in her lap, she was more than real, her fingers soothing through my hair.

"I wish you could stay here with me," she whispered.

I took her free hand and kissed the palm, remembering how she had caught herself on the thorns that day we had first met. "I do too."

She was silent for a long moment, tangling her fingers with mine before she said, "I hear there might be a way to win someone back from the Fae."

I flinched. I was not interested in false hope. I too had heard the rumors of ages past, but I could not allow myself to put all my hope into old tales.

"They are just legends."

"Maybe, but what if they are not?"

I couldn't reply. How I wished it was that easy, but I had lived enough life in this world, and the Otherworld, to know that there was nothing without a price.

I raised myself on an elbow to look up at her. "Janet, do you have no better prospects than me?"

She smiled sadly. "I had a man who I was to wed, but he died. Now, I am nothing but an almost-widow who should have gone to a nunnery a long time ago. Aside from my father, you're the only thing I have left in this world."

"But I am not of this world," I protested.

She bent to kiss me and my eyes fluttered shut briefly in a moment of longing bliss. "You are still my earthly knight, Tam Lin, and I will save you if it is the last thing I do."

***

I knew the effort would be foolish, but still, the thought was now in my head, and I did my research quietly, knowing full well how it would go if anyone caught on.

There was not much on this side of things. Faeries liked to keep their secrets and weren't in the habit of writing anything down that might cause them trouble. Still, I hoped to find something among the histories that would hint at a way to escape a bond like mine.

One day I even stared at the cup full of blood that sat behind the Queen's throne, wondering what would happen should I simply tip it over. Would that free me and the others under her curse? However, unless we were to all be instantly sent back to the mortal realm by some magical power, I feared such an action would result in only more death, mine included.

And recently, I had begun to realize that I didn't truly want to die anymore.

What I wanted was to spend the rest of my life with Janet at my side. I fully understood now why Owain had risked everything for Annabelle and yet, maybe, I had even a little more hope than he had. Maybe I had not yet lost my will to survive.

"What do you do here, Tam Lin?"

The Queen's voice was like an icicle in my chest, but I quickly schooled myself, turning around and leaning back against her throne with a coy smile, the kind I used to bring the maidens to me.

"I was looking for you, my lady," I told her.

"Were you?" One slim eyebrow raised as she moved forward. "And why suddenly so eager?"

"Am I not your loyal servant?" I inquired, hoping I could entice her away from any suspicions she might harbor.

"Loyal only in a dutiful sense. You only ever come when I call. What do you want?"

I tried to keep my heart from pounding as I shrugged, reaching toward her. "I am simply in a good mood today, my lady. I thought it would please you to know that. And that, perhaps, you may like to share in my good mood."

It was a mistake.

She had me against the wall in a second, her strength far surpassing what it should be in a woman her size—but then, she was not a woman.

Cold fingers tightened around my throat, restricting my breathing.

"Tell me, Tam Lin, why are you in such a good mood when you have failed me so?" she demanded. "Where are the maidens you are supposed to bring to me? Three times you have gone to the mortal realm this year and you have nothing to show for it."

"My lady," I croaked. "They have started to become suspicious of my appearance. It will take me a little longer to gain trust. The women of the town have been warned that I might steal them away and they—"

Something clenched around my heart and I gasped in agony before the Queen's fingers tightened around my windpipe and I could no longer draw breath. My eyes fluttered as I choked, hands weakly clutching her wrists.

She sneered and threw me to the ground where I curled, catching my breath.

Something pressed under my chin and raised my head up. I looked up the length of a switch to see the Queen staring down at me with her cold silver eyes.

"Did you think to distract me from your failures, is that it?" she asked darkly, as the switch traced up my throat. "Did you think to entice me, and put me in a fair mood before you begged more time?"

"My lady, I—"

The switch lashed out like an adder, and I barely closed my eyes in time, feeling a cut sting high across my left cheekbone.

"Do not speak," she said, pressing the switch up under my chin again, raising my face. "Now get on your feet, Tam Lin, and strip. If you wish to please me, then I shall have my amusement by humiliating you in front of my court, and next time, perhaps you will think twice about failing in the tasks I appoint you."

I rose slowly to my feet, a new defiance, a new loathing, seeping through me. My hands shook as I removed my clothes until I stood naked in her throne room. But part of me was glad for her assumption. It was better she think me trying to buy back her good graces than trying to escape her altogether.

Whatever I had to endure, I would do it knowing that I would eventually be back in Janet's arms.

Such a dangerous thought to have so close to this powerful creature.

With my clothing discarded, she found cord and bound me by my wrists to her throne.

The switch cut across my bare body with the sting of a thousand wasps until the Queen finally exhausted herself, or at least tired of that particular form of torment. She grabbed me by the hair and wrenched my head back so that I was forced to meet her eyes.

"Next time, simply admit to your failures, Tam Lin. I will not be so lenient should you think you can woo me again like one of those silly maidens you are supposed to catch."

"I will remember, my lady," I whispered hoarsely.

She leaned in and licked away the blood beading on a mark across my neck. I shuddered in disgust and terror as she finally pulled back, her lips tinged crimson as her tongue flicked across them.

"You shall stay here until I think you have paid your dues," she said in no uncertain terms.

I slumped on my knees, leaning against the throne, my hands already numb from the tight bonds and my body stinging with pain from the thrashing. I shivered in my skin and closed my eyes, imagining that I was back in Carter Hall, lying in the grass with Janet.

It was thoughts of her that kept me sane those three—perhaps four—days that I stayed there tied to the throne, enduring the abuse from the Queen as well as her courtiers. I was given no food or drink and no one dared try to sneak any to me. All I received were sneers and kicks, base cruelties meted out by those who wanted the Queen to look favorably on them.

When she finally saw fit to release me, she cut my bonds and shoved a glass of wine against my lips.

It barely touched my tongue before she pulled it away and I whimpered shamefully.

"Have you learned your lesson, Tam Lin?" the Queen asked, holding the glass just out of reach.

I gathered the little bit of wetness on my tongue and managed, "Your servant has learned his lesson, my lady."

She didn't reply, but offered the glass again and I gulped down the wine this time before she could think to take it away again.

Her hand landed on the top of my head, petting me mockingly like a favored hunting hound.

"Attend to me in my chambers and then I will allow you to eat and return to the mortal realm where you can resume your duties."

I stood dutifully, body aching, and followed her silently to those hated bedchambers.

Once she had finished having her way with me, she lay curled against my side in a strange affection. I, of course, was not so foolish as to think she cared for me at all like that, but I had come to realize that she enjoyed my warmth at least. A cold-blooded creature who liked to sun itself, like the adders who waited under rocks for unsuspecting travelers.

I longed for Janet's warmth, her soft, gentle hands, plush lips. There were no sharp edges to Janet. Round-faced and well-endowed. Pink cheeks and smiling eyes. Not skin and sinew and sharp teeth. I wanted to go back—and I would soon.

Pain flared briefly in my side as the Faery Queen dug her nails into my belly, pulling me back from more pleasant dreams.

"You are even more distant than usual," she said, continuing her digging into my flesh until she drew blood.

I refused to squirm away, instead swallowing carefully before speaking. "I am merely ill for want of food, my lady. I am not at my best."

It was not necessarily a lie. I was starving.

She made an annoyed sound and finally pulled away from me, reaching over to ring a bell. I gave a barely audible sigh of relief. I wondered briefly how many times I would be able to get away with these excuses.

Soon, I was brought food to eat. And once I had finished she watched me dress, a certain possessive look in her eyes as she seemed to count the marks she had made in my skin as I covered them up. It made my flesh crawl, and I was glad to be rid of her for a while.

"Do not fail me this time, Tam Lin," she said in parting.

I bowed to her and left for the stables, saddling my horse and galloping away as fast as I could.

***

To my shame, I did do as she asked. I wooed maidens and sent them to the forest—rather, to their doom, for I knew they would never escape.

Perhaps I never would either, though the thought was still a pleasant one, dream or not.

I finally allowed myself to visit Carter Hall and, as always, Janet was there to meet me with food and a soft kiss.

This time I simply fell into her arms, holding her tight as I leaned over to rest my head in the crook of her neck, releasing a sigh of relief and longing.

"Oh, Tam," she whispered, and that was enough for me to feel at home, burying my face in her hair and simply breathing her in for a long time.

Later we lay in the grass of the garden, my head pillowed upon her breast as she gently stroked my hair, tracing a finger across the cut on my cheekbone.

"I found a way," she said finally after a long silence. "To free you."

My breath stopped, and I turned to look at her. "You jest."

"I could never," she replied, turning on her side so that we were facing each other. Her hand went to the open collar of my tunic, tracing the fresh scars across my chest, a furrow in her brows. "She hurt you."

I caught her hand to still her touch, meeting her eyes. "It matters not. Janet, this plan, the risk involved ... I could never stand it if I lost you."

"It's a risk I'm willing to take," Janet said firmly, raising herself on an elbow and cupping my cheek with a warm palm.

"And if she catches you ..."

"Once I have you she will not be able to do anything as long as I hold on," Janet told me. "The Fair Folk might be powerful, but they follow their own rules. If I can pass their trials and not give you up, you will be mine by right. Not hers."

The thought was dizzying and I sat up, taking hold of Janet's shoulders as I looked her in the eye. "You're truly willing to do this? For someone like me?"

"I am."

My eyes stung angrily and I clenched my jaw. "Why would you risk so much? I am nothing but a lowly hound for the Queen to enjoy tormenting. You truly want me after I have been hers for so long?"

"You will not be hers for much longer, Tam Lin," Janet told me firmly. "You will be mine soon." She reached up to take my face between her hands, wiping a stray tear away. "She will be nothing but a terrible memory."

"And what if you're to find there's nothing left of me?" I whispered, my own truest fears finally reaching the surface.

"I will cherish even the smallest bit of my earthly knight," Janet replied as she took my hands, tracing her fingers across my palms. "Do not think of her. She cannot reach you here. It's me who's with you now. Your Janet." She guided my hands around her waist and I pulled her closer, leaning in to press my lips against hers, soft at first, then hungry, needing her taste of warm cinnamon to flood my senses.

I eased us back on the grass and reveled in this brief moment of stolen bliss. Janet's touches soothed across my scars, erasing the Queen's sordid pleasures. Nothing could erase the truth, though, as sure as the binding scar she had marked me with.

"She owns me," I tried to protest against Janet's lips. "Body and soul."

"Not here. She has no sway here in the mortal realm this day," Janet replied, kissing her way down my neck until her lips found the scar on my chest and grazed across it as if it were nothing more than another hurt to soothe.

"She has ruined me, broken me," I bit out, my own disgust so much that I could hardly bear to touch Janet with the same hands I'd been forced to touch *her* with.

"Then allow me to put you back together, my love," Janet breathed as she moved so that she hovered over me, eyes gentle and asking.

I finally allowed myself to give in, leaning upward with a ravenous kiss, Janet's touch bringing a solace I had not thought possible anymore. I felt no disgust, only elation and shared joy as Janet and I moved together, warm and needy, lost in the world that only true lovers can find until nothing else matters and everything is one soul coupled together in true bliss.

If I never experienced a happy moment again, I knew that I would remember this until my dying day.

***

My dying day.

A phrase that would have made me laugh had I known what was to come as consequence of my lapse of weakness.

Samhain was approaching and I knew it was closing in on my time to act as the tithe. Once, I would have been relieved; now all I could feel was terror. Janet and I had made our plans, but there was no guarantee the trick would work and, even if it did, whether or not we would even both survive. As long as the tales proved correct, I would be leaving this wretched realm for good within weeks; but if they did not then I shuddered to think what might be in store for me. Would the Faery Queen even have the mercy to use me for the tithe then? Or would she contrive some worse fate for me?

I was able to slip away one last time as part of a patrol of Fae who went out looking for other mortals to steal away. I hurried to Carter Hall as rain began to fall and I huddled with Janet under the shelter of the rose bower, both of us pressed together for warmth.

"You'll have to take me at a crossroads," I told her. "You'll be able to see the hunting party clearly there."

"And you'll be on your white horse?" she asked.

"Behind the blacks and browns." I nodded, looking down at her hands twined in mine. "Janet, are you sure this is what you want?"

She looked up with a soft expression, stroking my cheek. "I told you I want nothing in the world but you, Tam."

"When you take me, they'll try to fool you, but whatever you see, you must remember that I will do you no harm."

"I will not let go," Janet said sincerely.

The rain had slowed, and I held her tightly, in case this was the last time. She kissed me fervently before I left, and it was like a promise that we would see each other again.

I rode back toward the woods and found the hunting party readying their return.

The Fae captain glanced at me, eyes narrow. "Where were you?"

I shrugged. "Patrolling to the north. But no one would be so foolish as to come this close to the woods this time of year. I see that you had little more luck than I did."

He did not look happy, but the Fae guard had little to worry about. I was the whipping boy who would always take the brunt of the Queen's frustrations.

I rejoined the party and we returned to the Otherworld. It was now a week before Samhain and there was a peculiar charge to the world. The feeling of the veils thinning. A certain charged energy that sent goosepimples down my back.

The Queen was indeed not pleased with the results of the hunting party. I thought, fool that I was, that she had overlooked me as the culprit this time, but everything was only to devolve from there.

I meant to go bathe the rain and mud off, but the Queen caught me before I could get to the bathing chambers.

"Tam Lin, my men say you went off alone today," she said, a frostiness in her voice like the coming winter. "Where did you go?"

"I knew I would have better luck alone so I went to the north," I replied as casually as possible.

"And yet you have nothing for your troubles."

"I'm afraid, my lady, that people are cautious this time of year. They are careful not to be caught out alone near the woods."

She was not happy with this explanation. "You're hiding something," she hissed and stepped forward, taking my cloak in her hand. "What are you hiding from me, Tam Lin?!"

As she tugged on my cloak to pull me closer, something fluttered to the ground and I watched as two rose petals fell onto the floor like drops of blood. I froze in horror. They must have clung to my clothing while I sat in the bower with Janet.

"Roses," the Queen muttered darkly, hand clenching even tighter in my cloak. "That's what you always smell like when you come back." She was in my face within the blink of an eye. "Where do you go when in the mortal realm, Tam Lin?"

"My lady, I was only holding roses to give to any maidens I might spy. It acts as a disarming gesture."

"No," she practically growled and leaned close, nose pressed against my throat, sniffing like a dog. "You smell of another woman."

Her eyes were ice as she pulled away and I could almost feel the electric charge of power pouring off of her as she slammed me back against the nearest wall.

"Who is it, Tam Lin?" she demanded. "Who is this little harlot who thinks she can take you from me?"

"No one," I gasped.

She slapped me across the face, her claws raking furrows into my cheek as I staggered.

"How long, Tam Lin?" she demanded. "How long have you been going behind my back to sully yourself with some mortal wench?"

I refused to answer. Instead I put my hands on her shoulders and pushed her away.

It was a bold move that did not make her any kinder toward me. I was on the ground in the blink of an eye and she kicked me hard enough to crack ribs, leaving me gasping for breath.

Her hand was in my hair, wrenching my head up so I was forced to look her in the eye. "Tell me, Tam Lin, and I might have mercy on you."

"I will never tell you," I said firmly.

"You wretch!" she screeched and started attacking me. Biting, clawing, breaking bones, until I collapsed on the floor, my world nothing but agony and blood.

She was on me, straddling my hips as she loomed above. I blinked and suddenly her clawed fingers plunged down toward my heart, breaking the skin.

I screamed, sure that she would take my heart there and then, but she pulled back, lips curled in disgust.

"I should have taken your heart out a long time ago, Tam Lin," she said in a dark voice. "If I had known that another would steal you away, I would have given you a heart of stone. I would have torn your eyes out and put in ones of wood!"

I got my arm up in time to block her from scratching my eyes out. She snarled in frustration, but rose and grabbed me by the collar, dragging me along with her.

"The time for the tithe approaches too quickly," she growled. "I cannot afford to give another proxy. But if you think that I will have mercy on you while you await your fate, then think again, Tam Lin. Everyone will know you for the traitorous wretch you are."

She dragged me to the throne room where the courtiers loitered as usual and threw me to the floor.

"Tam Lin has betrayed me," she wailed. "Bring the cage and chain him up!"

I had seen the cage in use before. It was like some macabre bird cage that hung from the vaulted ceiling. Barely the span of a man's shoulders.

I watched with wavering hope as it was lowered to the ground. When they came to take me, I fought for the first time since I had been here. It did little good for their strength far outweighed mine and I was lifted up to be put inside the cage. My wrists were bound and chained above my head, before the chains were firmly wrapped around the rest of my body, finally securing my feet fast.

I could not move to alleviate any pain. I was simply stuck fast, completely at her mercy.

And yet, I still lived. I might be foolish to still hold onto such hope, but I could not help but consider the fact that I was still alive. I would still be taken from this cage on Samhain to be given as a tithe.

Janet would still be waiting at the crossroads.

The Queen might know there was a woman, but surely, she would never guess that she would be brave enough to try and win me.

If I had learned nothing else during my time at the Faery Court, it was that the Queen in her pride tended to underestimate humans. And I was determined to make sure that would be the cause of her downfall.

***

The bindings were too tight, ever tightening the harder I struggled until they forced the breath from my lungs, and I could barely draw another.

The Queen seemed to enjoy me all the more in a cage like this, as if I were an exotic bird. If I was, I was one who refused to sing—a lovebird trapped away from its mate. I'll admit that the lack of food and the elation of finally allowing myself defiance toward my tormentor was playing with my head, but there was a certain joy in counting down the days to the tithe for a different reason than I once had.

I only had to endure for a small while longer and then, hopefully, I would be free.

"It is the night of the Wild Hunt tomorrow," the Queen informed me one day as she circled the cage, having it drawn downward so she could look me in the eye.

She reached through the bars and put her hand under my chin but I pulled away. Her eyes flashed and I screamed as she sent a sudden stab of pain through my heart. It stole the last of the breath I had.

I hung in the chains, my only support, as I felt her look on, watching with a satisfied smile.

"It would not be ideal to find another sacrifice at the eleventh hour, but I have done it before." She stroked my face now with a mocking affection that caused my skin to crawl. "There is still time to recant your love for the mortal girl," she added, voice syrupy, coercing. "I'll give you one more chance to prove your loyalty to me. You will never leave these halls again, but I will allow you to live."

"Being trapped here with you is not living," I told her firmly.

"You hate me so much that you would rather die?" the Queen demanded.

I looked her in the eye and spat, "I have always despised you."

The room was suddenly full of the sensation of an impending lightning strike. I realized then that I should be more careful as the Queen was at her full power now.

"Then you are truly no more use to me. You shall die as the tithe this year," she said darkly. "Such a fair sacrifice shall please the gods. I'll regret your loss, but you disgust me, Tam Lin. How angry you made me, breaking your vow that you would serve only me. You forget that I still own you, body and soul, and that will not change until the day you die—and only if you die at my own will. Even that is not your own, Tam Lin. The time of your death belongs to me as well, did you know?"

Her fist clenched around the air and I screamed again as she raked me with pain once more, digging deep until the invisible claws radiated from my chest to the tips of my fingers and toes. I sobbed for breath once it subsided and she was right next to the cage, her face beside mine. Her hand tangled in my hair as she dragged my head up, forcing me to look her in the eyes.

"You could have been powerful, Tam Lin," she whispered, caressing my cheek with her pale fingers. "You could have been mine forever, but you chose to run back to your mortal realm and find a mortal girl after everything I gave you. You're no better than any others of your ilk."

I found myself letting out a breathless laugh, head light and high on adrenaline. "Your one mistake was only binding me body and soul," I told her. "You left me my mind, and you are delusional if you ever thought that you were more than a cruel captor and tormenter to me."

She looked, if possible, even more furious at this statement. "If that is what I am to you, then I shall be happy to play the role well," the Queen hissed, clenching her hand again.

My body snapped taut and I threw my head back as she stabbed with me such pain that I couldn't even scream for want of breath. Nothing but silent tears slid down my cheeks. My eyes rolled up in my head, on the verge of blackness, unable to withstand it anymore. She finally stopped and I sagged, choking for the breath that the chain refused to give me, only barely conscious of my surroundings.

"I will see you later, Tam Lin," she said finally, in dismissal. "When you shall pay with your life."

***

Mercifully, the Queen ignored me until it was time to ready me for the Hunt. The guards took me from the cage and sat me upon my horse, still chained tightly. My hands were bound to the saddle and I would have no control over the horse. It wouldn't matter, though. Once in the Queen's party, I could do nothing but follow her lead. It would take an outside force to interfere.

My stomach was in knots, fearing for Janet in the woods alone, but I trusted her to take the proper precautions. As long as she withstood the trials, the Queen would not be able to touch either of us.

She came to me as I sat waiting, dressed all in black with glints of silver. Her hand landed on my thigh, possessive still, as she glowered up at me.

"If not for your betrayal, I would have kept you by my side forever, Tam Lin," she said. "But you did teach me a valuable lesson. I will not be so careless with the next one."

I shuddered at that and tried not to think of the next poor soul who would fall into her clutches. There was nothing I could do once gone. I knew for certain that I would never step foot in those woods again.

"You have nothing to say to me?" the Queen asked then.

I stared down at her, meeting her eyes. "Only that I am glad that, whatever comes this night, I will finally be rid of you."

Her face darkened and for a moment I thought she would strike me down right there, but the hunting horns sounded their readying call and the dogs started baying.

The Queen left my side and mounted her horse, taking her place at the head of the Hunt.

As soon as the horns called the start of the Hunt, everything was a blur of motion. I held on for dear life, my restraints making my position awkward and precarious. I knew I would not fall, though, and my horse would not stray from the path of the Hunt.

I could barely tell where we were, but then I saw it. The crossroads up ahead, a patch of moonlight shining down on the spot.

I held my breath as my horse barreled forward. With a strength I didn't know I possessed, I ripped my hands free of the ropes that tied me to the saddle and just as I crossed over the moonlit road—

A figure loomed out of the darkness, a flash of green as I sped by, but hands latched onto the chains wrapped around me and tugged me down.

My momentum sent me flying off the horse, tumbling into the shadows with the dark figure until we both came to a stop and I saw Janet hovering under me, the hood of her green cloak having fallen loose.

"Tam," she breathed.

An inhuman shriek split the night, sending all the hairs on the back of my neck standing up.

"He's away!" I could clearly hear the Faery Queen scream. "Tam Lin is away!"

The Hunt came to a halt and the Queen rode back down the line. I could feel the moment her eyes landed on me.

"Tam Lin!" she snarled. "You will not get away from me!"

I could feel my body shifting, contorting. I clutched Janet's shoulders. "Hold me. Hold me and do not let go," I told her breathlessly.

Janet didn't hesitate a second before she threw her arms around me.

I screamed as I could feel the Queen's power assaulting me, tearing at my body as she covered me in Faery glamour so that to Janet my form would appear as that of a giant snake. She did not recoil, only held me tighter.

Next, my form changed into that of a lion, my screams turning into roars. But Janet still held me fast, keeping her promise.

The Queen finally turned my form into burning iron and though Janet cried out from the heat, she didn't waver, not fooled by the illusion.

The chains around me finally broke, falling into dust, and I was released from the Queen's glamour, returning to nothing but a naked man in Janet's arms.

Janet sobbed and swiftly tore her cloak from her shoulders, wrapping it around me as she continued to hold me tightly.

"Tam Lin!" the Queen screamed at us, coming forward with all the fury of a thousand storms. "You think you can run from me so easily? Your mortal wench cannot keep you from me forever. I will kill you both! I will have your heart!"

Janet and I held each other, primordial terror keeping us in place.

But as the Queen took another step forward, just past the stone where the tithe was to be sacrificed, a tear opened in the air, revealing an eldritch darkness. I could only watch in horrified fascination as hands reached out and took hold of the Queen.

"No," she gasped. "No, you cannot! Take *him*! Tam Lin is the sacrifice!"

There seemed to be no reasoning to be made. The hands pulled the Faery Queen back into the rift. Her bloodcurdling screams cut short as it fused back together with a gust of freezing air.

The horses and dogs bayed in terror and the rest of the Hunt sped away from the crossroads as if hell itself was on their heels—perhaps it was.

Soon, there was only silence, Janet and I still holding each other tightly, before she finally found the courage to speak again.

"I know not what that was," she whispered.

I swallowed hard. "A tithe needed to be paid."

I finally took the chance to look down, pulling the cloak aside to see that there was no longer a sigil carved into my chest. It was like there had never been a scar there at all.

I could not say the same for the rest of me. My body ached in the cold night air, the copious injuries pulling me down to a comforting darkness.

"We should leave here," Janet finally said. "Can you stand?"

I did my best. At least long enough for her to retrieve her horse. I mounted with difficulty and wrapped my arms gratefully around her waist as we rode through the trees.

But before we even left those cursed woods, my strength failed me. Perhaps it was pure exhaustion, perhaps relief, but whatever it was, I found myself slipping away into a dark embrace, no longer caring, for I knew Janet would catch me.

***

I woke to warmth and the friendly crackle of a fire, the sound of someone humming softly. For a brief moment, I was taken back to my childhood, thinking it was my mother. When I finally opened my eyes, however, I saw that it was instead Janet who was sinking down next to me.

"You're awake." She smiled as she presented a cup. "Here. Drink."

I raised myself onto one elbow with difficulty as she held the cup for me to drink. It was then I realized we were in Carter Hall. The area of the main hall had been cleaned and a fire burned merrily in the hearth. I lay on a pallet beside it, warm blankets wrapped around me. The soft light of early morning was filtering in from above, another comfort to mark the end of the night.

"How do you feel?" Janet asked, green eyes showing concern as she took the cup away.

I focused on my body then, realizing all my hurts had been tended and bandaged with clean linen. I lifted a shaking hand, looking down at the spot on my chest that was now bare. I traced my fingers over the spot where the scar had been and suddenly felt a lot lighter.

"I truly am free of her," I whispered, unable to believe it.

Janet leaned over with a smile and took my face between her hands. "You are. I told you I would win you for myself, didn't I?" She leaned in and brushed her lips gently against mine.

I pulled her close, one hand cradling the back of her head as I deepened the kiss, drinking her in. I was too overwhelmed to say anything else at the moment. What could I even say, after all?

When we finally parted for breath, I smiled more broadly than I had in a very, very long time. "It is truly so much sweeter to kiss you as a free man," I told her.

Janet kissed me again before she pulled away. "There will be plenty of time for more." She ran a hand through my hair. "For now, you should rest. I'm sure it has been a long time since you have slept."

It had and I was indeed weary. But I could tell Janet also was.

"Rest with me," I told her, holding out my hand. "It has been a long night for both of us."

Janet's face was soft, and she nodded. She slipped out of her mud-covered dress and joined me on the pallet, tucking us both up under the blankets. I held her close, resting my chin against her head. This felt like heaven. I wanted to stay here forever, even though I knew there was better even than this to be had—a whole life for me lay ahead. A life that, before I'd met Janet, I never dreamed would be possible.

I started sobbing without knowing the reason. I think at most it was because I was now free and I didn't think I was truly ready to accept that yet.

"Oh Tam," Janet said softly and simply held me while I cried, until I had nothing left in me.

"I am well," I assured her with a smile to prove it, kissing her forehead. "I am simply overwhelmed. Ten years of my life I lived in the Otherworld. I'm honestly not sure what to do with myself now."

"I can't imagine," Janet said quietly, stroking my hair. "But you are safe here now. And she will never hurt you again."

I'll admit that knowing the Queen was no longer in this world or the Otherworld was a huge comfort to me. I would not have trusted that she wouldn't try to cause me or Janet more misery. I'm sure she could have found a way.

"I will be fine as long as I have you—if you'll still have me, anyway," I told Janet.

"Of course I'll have you," Janet said with a soft smile. "I won you fair, my earthly knight."

I kissed her again. "You did. You won me heart and soul."

***

Over the next few days as I recovered, Janet brought me stories from the town that spoke of people stumbling out of the woods who had been missing for months or years. They brought strange tales of the Otherworld and a goblet of blood that had seemingly tipped over at random, releasing the binding that was keeping them there.

I was relieved to know that all of my fellow captives had been freed as well. I hoped that the Faery Court was in turmoil over what had happened. Perhaps they would even move their court elsewhere.

As for me, I met Janet's father and asked for her hand in marriage. I did not know what he knew, but he did not ask questions, simply gave me his blessing, and promised to return Carter Hall to my name. I made plans to repair it so that Janet and I could live there together.

My story ended well, but take this as a cautionary tale to never go into the woods near Samhain Eve or you may meet a fate worse than mine.

About the Author

LadyWallace is a long-time artist and writer—and nocturnal creature. When she's not drinking coffee, crafting, and running her online shop, she's usually dreaming up some sort of whump scenario for her favorite characters and OCs.

For the Queen's Honor

Aiden E. Messer

CW: Torture, broken bone

Whumpee: Man, Whumper: Man, Caretaker: Man, Woman

It had been a few weeks now since Lancelot had fled with Guinevere from Camelot. He knew he had taken a great risk leaving with the Queen, wife of the great King Arthur, but he loved her, and she loved him, so it was worth it.

Love conquers all. At least that's what he thought until he came face to face with Leodagan, Guinevere's father, during his morning patrol around his camp.

Before he had time to react, Leodagan was on him. Lancelot tried to protect himself, but the King of Carmelide was too strong. The knight fell to the ground as Leodagan punched him in the face. When the blows finally stopped, Lancelot laid on the ground, helpless, too weak to move. All he hoped was that his beloved Guinevere had fled far away, and that no one would find her and punish her for her adultery. He closed his eyes, ready for his execution.

Lancelot did not remember losing consciousness, but he woke up tied to a table in some sort of dungeon.

His head hurt. He tried to move, but the ropes were too tight, and struggling only made them bite deeper into his flesh. A cold draught made him shiver, and he realized that was naked. He tried to speak, to scream, but a gag prevented the words from forming.

Panic started to fill his lungs. This couldn't be happening. King Arthur was strongly opposed to any form of torture. It was even one of his most controversial stances. The knight felt the nausea rising in him. King Arthur was opposed to torture but Leodagan, on the other hand, was a great supporter of it. If the Queen's father was acting on his own behalf and not on behalf of the King of Britain as Lancelot had first thought, anything could happen.

Leodagan looked at him with a cruel grin.

"So, the great Knight of the Cart is finally awake. Did you have a nice nap? Did you really think you could harm my daughter without any consequences?"

Lancelot looked at him with imploring eyes. He tried to speak, to make him understand that the love he had for Guinevere was pure, but all that came through the gag were desperate moans. Leodagan's smile widened as he ran his hand lightly against Lancelot's cheeks.

"Did you want to say something? Maybe you were hoping for a quick death? Well, that's too bad. I'm the one in charge here, and no one will come to save you."

Leodagan took a knife out of his pocket and ran the blade against Lancelot's cheeks, retracing the path that his fingers had taken just a moment ago.

The cold metal bit into Lancelot's skin, leaving a trail of blood and fire behind it. Lancelot clenched his jaw, trying his best not to scream. He didn't want to give Leodagan that pleasure. The knife continued its course, slashing his arms, his legs, his torso.

Lancelot was squirming and whimpering, but he was still resolutely fighting the urge to scream. Then Leodagan lifted the blade in the air, buried it deep inside Lancelot's shoulder, and it was suddenly too much. A shriek escaped his chest. Leodagan burst into wild, sadistic laughter as he twisted the blade into Lancelot's wound. He then slowly pulled it out, only to slide two fingers in its place.

Lancelot's eyes widened as a burning flash of pain shook his whole body. He screamed once more, to Leodagan's delight. There was no point in trying to resist it anymore. The pain was just too much to bear.

"Was that enough to break you?" Leodagan laughed. "That was only the beginning."

He took some kind of iron shoe from a table and showed it to the knight. "This is the perfect opportunity to test these beauties. King Arthur didn't like it, but I knew I wouldn't regret buying them."

Leodagan placed the iron shoe on Lancelot's foot and turned a crank on the side of the device. The shoe tightened, its cold contact becoming an unpleasant pressure, then a painful one. Lancelot screamed again as the first bone snapped with a sinister *crack*. Far from stopping, Leodagan laughed and continued to turn the crank. A second *crack* sounded, then a third. The door of the dungeon suddenly opened, and King Arthur walked in. His voice was firm and filled with barely contained anger as he asked:

"Leodagan, what is the meaning of this?"

About the Author

Aiden E. Messer doesn't exist. According to one of the children they work with, if they were a teacher, they would be as tall as a human. They are not a teacher. They have studied psychology, and have always had a penchant for horror and the macabre.

In Bloom

Vanessa Roades

CW: Character death, body horror

Whumpee: Man, Whumper: Woman, Caretaker: N/A

Once upon a time, in a kingdom with a lost name, a princess fell asleep and didn't wake up.

Curiously, no one seemed to know the princess. Not the gentry. Not the peasants. So the news trickled down into the towns, sour and cold like snowmelt, and there was no ritual or funeral. (Though the temples whispered that after she was inspected for plagues and parasites, she was sent away, not to the cemetery at the top of the hill or the crypts within it, but to the clock tower in the center of town.)

Her death was a merry excuse for a mourning holiday. First a day, then a week, where the peasants told stories about how the princess loved cupcakes and fiddle music and no work, so they must honor her accordingly. The King and Queen didn't seem to care for this ruse.

They cared so little that they ignored it. They ignored the princess entirely. As if they forgot her.

And then they forgot everything else.

The people watched the castle, day by day, month by month, year by year, be swallowed up by its own gardens. Arrow-head ivy, silky flowers in white and pink and orange, wisteria reaching and willows weeping. As the garden grew up the castle, a civil war raged over which flower would consume the most. Once it enclosed all the windows and barred all the doors, the winner was clear: the blood-red rose.

The roses took the town, and then, last of all, they took the clock tower.

***

He said he was a prince.

He *was* charming, well-dressed, well-armed, and (most importantly) catastrophically handsome, so who were the pixies on the border woods to say that he wasn't a prince? They didn't quite believe him, but they didn't care. They didn't care about the kingdom-eaten-by-roses, either, besides what a curious and silly tale it was. If the prince tried to take on the garden, the tale could only get sillier.

The pixies tittered because he was catastrophically handsome, after all, and they had heard about Narcissus enchanted by his own reflection, Tam Lin bound in a queen's shackles, Beast cursed on his own doorstep.

They drew him a map of the town-that-once-was, and off he went to the clock tower to do what princes did in those days.

***

This town should be full of bees, the prince thinks.

A century's layers of flowers bend, then crunch, then squish beneath his calfskin boots. Proudly preening, they've swallowed every other sign of life. And yet there are no insects to pollinate them.

Maybe the bees are smarter than me and saw the thorns before the roses.

Maybe they saw the slashes in his trousers before they saw that alluring tower. The cuts on his hands before the sleeping princess. The empty, echoing, heartless kingdom before the starry chance for heroism.

Surely some poor townsperson fell to the curse in the street, or near enough to a window that the prince could spy them within the nets of thorns. Surely someone will wake up and see what he's done.

If the clock tower has doors, they're hidden under the thick overgrowth. Scraps of clothing, so shredded by the wind that they're thin as strands of hair, twist around the thorns. The prince steps over bones and hollow armor to scale the tower with a sword at his hip and riding gloves.

He's climbed a tower before, but that tower didn't have a predatory mind. This one pricks his fingers and catches his wrists, stripes his calves, reaches for his face, so once he's squeezed through a narrow opening into the belfry, his lips sting with the hot tang of blood.

The belfry is as dense with thorny stalks as the village. They crawl up the walls and hold the enormous gold bell captive, constraining the clock's gears even as they still, after a century, strain to turn. The greenery piles in the corners of the room like snowdrifts but nothing stirs.

No evil witch weaves, waiting, here.

But there, lifted upon a bed of bruised roses with a funeral shroud and mourning silks spilled open like bed dressings, is the princess of the tower. Hands folded on her heart, hair splayed around her like she floats underwater.

The prince approaches the princess. Her tiara still glitters. Her skin is dustless and soft. Silver rings on her fine fingers, amethysts at her throat. It's as if she arranged herself for this eternal sleep. Pricked her finger on the spinning wheel and put on her best dress.

As he looks over the sleeping princess, behind him, above him, past his decorated shoulder, is a reflection of her.

Not in glass, but in a nest of thorns tucked inside the dark of the golden bell–and not in rest, but in wait.

The reflection unfurls her vines. They strike him, plunging into his back between the embroidery and the bone, like monstrous teeth locking into prey. He falls without a sound into the bed.

The princess dreams.

***

The prince is calf-deep in snow.

It's not dissimilar to his journey through the dunes of dead flowers to the clock tower (whenever that's meant to happen, or if it's happened already). His steps are heavy and undignified and again, he's had to leave his horse behind, but this time it was to let it die after the cold froze in its eyelashes and the snowdrifts broke its ankle.

A group of men gesture him on. They're dense and severe like cannons, weighed down by their bear-skin cloaks and the steel lanterns in their fists, but still faster than him in this gloomy pine forest.

And there—a princess, just as the rumors said! Her hair's as black as charcoal in a hearth, skin white as the frost he scrapes off her glass casket.

His fingers skim over the smooth surface, hunting for seams left by the welder or cracks by the harsh winter, but the casket is perfectly fused.

So he strikes it with his sword at her feet, over and over, until it makes a hole. He wraps his hands in the thin straps of his horse's reins to break the glass apart like a predatory bird breaking open the eggshell of a rival's young.

And with a kiss on lips as red as the blood on his fingers, the princess wakes up.

He carries her through the snow. In his arms, like a bride already. She accepts this, because back then, all little princesses were told what to do if a magical this-or-that got cross with them and gave them a curse.

(Do not fuss. Do not challenge. Do not seek fairies to make it right, because they don't like right. Above all, do not dream of avoiding it or fighting it. It's up to your family to see that you're comfortable.)

At the end of the snowscape is a road where the little men bundle everyone into their oxen-towed cart and bring them to town. The prince sits with the princess in the snowdrifts of blankets and furs and pretends he doesn't hear the fatherly weeping of the dwarves as the castle draws near.

The princess's family thanks him with tears, titles, and gold. The prince wipes away the tears. He turns away the titles. He meticulously wraps the gold in the bed linens (just as expensive, he warrants). He collects baubles off his princess's throat and ears when he flirts. He makes the court adore him. He watches. Everyone. He kicks away lines of salt that the cowardly staff draw outside his private chambers. He has no privacy any longer and he's all cramped in his own skin. He buys a new horse. He boards it and watches the schedules of the grooms.

On their wedding night, he's as polite as he can manage when he asks for separate rooms to sleep.

And in the morning, he imagines that she wakes up, drifts to his room in her lonely waifish way, finds the ruby-red apple and a splash of brighter blood on his empty bed, and perhaps she supposes that curses don't end with kisses.

***

The prince snaps awake.

He's pinned against the princess's bed of thorns, but there's no princess, not anymore. Only the creature in the golden bell, crawling down to drink him in.

She could have been the princess once, despite it all, or maybe only something wearing the princess's skin (he's seen some pretty horrific princesses, once the curses get feisty and the veils (and inhibitions) between realms get thin). Flaxen hair hangs in long curtains, rows of black eyes ladder up her gaunt face, slit nostrils are carved into the waxy skin, and lips like lines of confident calligraphy frame a sharp-toothed maw. Petals white as bone grow down her lithe form like a gown, vanishing into the bell where she bends into its darkness. Perhaps it's her more than the room who smells so overpoweringly sweet.

The thorny stalks on his wrists crawl down his pulse. They trace little cuts everywhere they touch, so light they feel like a gentle scrape of nail or teeth until the stinging sets in. In his periphery, he can see his clothing torn apart and his heart beating hard enough to jolt the hollow under his ribs, juddering the few vines that have wrapped all the way around him—that movement flows into their razor-edged leaves, off the bed of greenery, until every vein in the room is throbbing with his own heartbeat.

And the princess hangs above him, focused face turning like the hands of her clock would, had she not wrangled it into stasis.

"Who are you?" he hisses. It's worked before. It could work now, even if his sword is pinioned in a thatch of thorns. Evil witch? Wicked stepmother? Fairy curse? *What* are you? Wicked humans like to wrap their intentions up in pretty cloth and coy smiles, but most wicked creatures like to be beheld.

So he says, "Let me behold all of you."

The monster crawls out of the dark bell. She's one set of arms away from being shaped like a spider, but she makes an impressive impression of one in her movements. Each distended limb curls around the edge of the metal, pulling herself with the ease and long, elegant reach of a weaver pulling thread from the skein.

She replies, "I was a princess, once."

It's the voice of a girl, naive, high and wondering.

This is more than he's ever seen a curse do. He's bartered bones and briars with witches, bowed to fairy queens, begged to fairy kings, bent the laughter and logic of hags. They all love beauty so much that they're loath to ruin it despite all their other evil wishes. Or perhaps it's the one thing they can't touch.

Perhaps it's something they want. She's lying.

"Where have you taken the princess, *now*?"

She tilts her head. It swivels on her neck like an old, creaky wheel spins on a boat.

"The princess." His voice doesn't sound like his own. The plants around his ribs are still shuddering. "The princess of this land who slept for a century. I saw her, moments ago."

"There's only you."

"Astute, my dear. You see, I scaled the tower," he says, trying to steady where his voice slipped, "so I get to make my stand, start my fight. I get to look upon her at the very least. You know, for bravery."

"Everyone here stopped dreaming," she breathes, "but you still remember."

The stalks wrap tighter around him, sliding up his inner arms, cutting channels in his shirt to nestle tight against the skin. The pain is so acute that it seems like strident music or metal scraping against metal. It shivers in his teeth.

One rises like a snake and strikes into the source of the room's pulse, the echo of his heart in his stomach, and the force of it arcs his back off the silks. Its thorns catch in his shirt and then in his skin. It writhes and swells with his rhythm like a lover, catching his breath in his lungs.

A bright red rose blooms from that stalk, growing so suddenly and heavily that it bows against his ribs. The creature picks it. Puts it to her face, and for a flash she looks like any other princess, eyes fluttering shut as she breathes in the aroma.

"You remember," she repeats like a prayer, and drops the flower. It leaves a stain of red, strange wet red, all over her mouth.

The thorns twist tighter. He falls again.

**

This time, the prince is leaning over the edge of a boat while the crew haul up a straining fishing net.

The crew. Not his crew. Not on paper, anyhow. But they transform into *his* crew whenever they dock. The prince has that effect (even if he's never called himself a prince to these folks).

Something about his fine clothing, his soft leather boots that, each night, he uses his rationed fresh water to clean while he never gets thirsty. Something about his *air*.

What a curious thing to have, he'd thought when the real captain sneered at the poor mistaken dock worker, snatching the ledger away from the prince. *An air! Not something you can buy. Maybe a thing you can conjure.*

Now, because that air has him standing aside rather than hauling the heavy, scratchy ropes, the prince sees what they've caught: the flash of long, bony limb, the curve of snake-like back, the slimy sheaf of dark hair.

A corpse? But when they drop the net on the deck, a webbed hand clutches at its confines, and that grip is strong, sinewy, alive.

The prince unsheathes his dagger (sapphire in the hilt, unmarred engravings in the blade) and hacks at the net. The captain heaves him away but not before a wave of panicked fish wash onto the deck, a tide of wet scale bringing the mermaid with it.

He's read his fairy stories. He's sung his child ballads. He's a good prince, learning with the best of them (curses aren't just for princesses, after all). He skips over being alarmed, unlike the rest of the crew.

She sees him. So deeply that he shudders.

He doesn't trust her.

Against the crew's wishes, he lets her go free, but she follows.

They dock in another kingdom. The prince makes his goodbyes to the crew (some goodbyes are with words, and some cost the price of a purse, or chain, or ring, or dagger, or engraved spyglass, but who's counting?).

Here he finds the princess he originally sought (he's always seeking), but his mind lingers on the mermaid and hers on him: he hears her foreign, watery croon outside the palace that hosts him. He sees her in the sallow eyes and death-pale skin of the strange, silent woman who fumbles her way through the little palace. He recognises the clawed grip of her hand around his wrist.

The princess and the mermaid both know *of* him, one from stories at bedtime and one from the thrum of the earth itself. But the mermaid knows *him*.

She returns to the rocks beneath his window every night and regains her voice with her fins, only to sing, on and on and on, trying to lure him down into the dark.

Despite it all, he has an *air* that lets him charm the princess regardless of his locked windows and fragile sleep. And the night before the wedding, he wakes to the shadow of those webbed hands wrapped around the sapphire knife that freed her.

"The crew saw you as a bad omen. They would have strung you up, had I not gotten to you first," he says, very much soberly awake. Seeing a knife poised above your heart will do that.

She doesn't speak.

"Do you intend to protect her with that? I won't hurt her, I promise."

She *can't* speak. The knife wavers. She should wonder if plunging it will do anything at all.

"I'm much less safe when I'm freed," he advises gently. "As are you. Drop that knife and this form. You embarrass us both."

What does she know about him? Enough to persuade her, apparently. She glides to the window, naked and swift as a snake, and plunges between the curtains. He leans over the sill to watch her hit the water, her legs vanishing under the waves. She took the knife. Damn her.

The wedding is the following morning. The prince is rumored to have fallen on the same rocks as the mermaid.

***

The prince tumbles into the room. His body jolts on the silks—the vines are inching out behind him from where they were wrapped around his spine. He flutters back to consciousness. He forces himself into the sweet-smelling cage, fast enough to see that she, too, has to *come back*, by the way her six beetle-black eyes clear before taking him in again.

She lowers entirely to the floor. She approaches the nest she's caught him in, walking like she's unpracticed, teetering for those two, three steps on a deer's thin legs. The thorns waver around her, floating, ready to catch her.

She's observing him so closely that she must have picked up on the little scars of that memory. She's looking for the truth that the mermaid had no voice to say, the truth that is so normal to him that his memory needn't have defined the hard lines.

Is it worse if she knows or doesn't? His head is foggy. Blood pools in the silks beneath. Wet and cold on the small of his back, shirt clinging to him. The room is suffused with the reek of flowers, fresh and rotten in sickening concert. They took a century of growth and waiting and feasting (on what, on minds? On dreams?) to make a gag that now seems specially tailored for him.

The mermaid didn't stop him. She *couldn't*.

The princess's weight pulls the old, musty sheets into the sharp net. One knee, then the other, framing his thighs. He holds his breath. Instinct pulls at his wrists, but somehow, that tiny pinch of the thorns digging too deeply is enough to make him stop.

But his shifting pushes a blade into his back. One very sharp dagger, clipped in a sheath on the back of his belt.

If he can get a hand free …

Every nerve is alight. He can feel her breath, the way his wet clothing releases from his skin with every swell of the greenery beneath him, like a wave, like he's lying on a boat.

The princess lowers her face to his. He denies the jerk of fear in his stomach. He gives his wrists another wrench but nothing gives.

The mermaid didn't stop him, but he wasn't in her trap.

"I have never," she breathes, "smelled the sea before."

"The sea?"

"The acrid paint you coat the ship's wood with. The sway when you try to sleep. The wind full of rain when it isn't raining. The cold slime of the fish kicking around your knees as you pulled her from their pile."

He runs his tongue over his teeth. Flexes his hands in their cuffs, accidentally dipping his fingers into the sticky smear of sweat or worse in his palms. But she's given him a spark of hope. "Where were you before this tower, my dear?"

"The shine of water on rocks. The foamy crash of it. The blade balancing on its sharp little point against my chest."

"Oh, I could show you that again if you let me go."

"The rush of fear, first cold, then hot." She bares her teeth, two full sets of them, sharp and lined up neatly. White enough that he's suddenly sure she doesn't eat her victims.

And he's *also* suddenly sure that doesn't matter. The stalks squeeze violently tight around his chest and then his throat, leaving threads of red shallow enough to bead but not drip. He lifts into the pain, every nerve and muscle pulling taut in panic.

He sees the flutter of a muscle in his jaw, the tendons rising white on his wrists, the tight arch of his ribs against his open shirt and bloody skin, the vine still sunk into the crest of them like a worm buried in the dirt.

He's seeing himself through her eyes, like she saw through his.

He needs to buy time before she gets bored with him like everyone else in this town. One hand free, and he can cut himself loose …

The prince gasps through grit teeth, "Has this sustained you, princess?" Why can't he get control over his spine? She's winding him like a screw. "Eating the bland memories of maids and grocers?"

She's perfectly still as her vines unwind and unwind and unwind: snaking over him, slotting into the shallows between his ribs, biting up his spine and jaw and slicing needle-thin cuts on his lips and cheeks. They're blurry and green in the corner of his eye; they're everywhere around her. But she's focused on him, he knows it. His palm is slick and slippery, gaining centimeters of freedom–

He speaks fast, losing air. "You ate nobles once. I know the story! You went for them first, greedy thing. The best sorts of memories are in them, right? Great food, fancy clothes, all the sex, all the adoration. Looking at the world from up on high. I bet you saw so *far* with them. But you wasted all that and now—"

His voice is strangled out of him. The snaking vines rip through his skin, wrapping around the ladders of ribs like ivy into trellises.

He says with his last gasp, "I've seen *so much more* than kings."

***

This is not the prince's first tower.

He knows which lands have recently harvested a fresh batch of cantankerous fae, so he follows their footprints to see what they've left behind. Sleeping princesses in glass caskets in the snow. Peasant girls fleeing in rags at midnight. One sister doomed to vomit up snakes and toads, uprooting any chance for her to cool her poisoned tongue of adolescence, and a sister charmed to smile diamonds, learning only how to be so sharp that the cuts wouldn't leave a scar.

Eventually the prince finds the tower. No doors, no stairs, no ladders. Only a song, swirling from the single window like a ribbon.

He calls out to the girl inside. She's resistant at first, but he can wield his charm better than a wizard wields a wand. She throws down her golden braid for him to climb.

She's awake, which makes her more complex than most other princesses he saves. She's a bit batty, having grown up locked in the tower, but that also makes her fascinating: her mind takes unexpected spirals into unexpected tunnels. She understands so little.

But she does know who she is.

She tells him like a secret. He figures sharing that with him is like lovemaking for a girl who thinks such a thing begins and ends with her own hand under her covers.

The witch is not my mother.

I've read enough stories with stolen princesses.

Like all stolen things, there's a bit of magic to her, inherited in the stealing (or is it in the losing?). She learned it from the birds, she says.

In actuality, her parents are peasants.

She's not a princess at all.

What can her parents give him? A bundle of cabbage? A terrible poem? Gratitude? A warm bed?

Her *hand,* obviously. That's how things work these days. They'll be so grateful to have her back–and so stupid in the face of royalty. They won't know what to do except give this girl away again. They know all they have to barter with is beauty.

Still ... there's a witch in the mix, too, and witches never stop at peasant girls. The rulers of the land must know that. If they don't, he'll just have to show them.

However, the next time he climbs up the golden hair and claws into the window (armed, this time), she greets him with the brutal binds of a spell. She's holding a grimoire in one frail arm, balancing a candle in the other.

"The witch has been teaching you," he says. Interest blooms in him like a flower. The spell's a minor annoyance; he lets her have it so she feels safe enough to keep talking.

"I know what you are."

"Do you now?" He laughs. "We're rare in number, but in variety we're beaten only by insects."

"You're a fairy."

"And what does that mean to you? I'm your thumb-tall prince? Your beastly king? Your keeper of realms? Clearly it doesn't mean enough! You gave me two secrets already. Some of us can use those like collars."

"I know you don't really look like that," she says, chin lifted. "I know if I cut you, you'll heal. I know you'll never die. And ..."

"And?"

She glances at her grimoire, at the spell she's caught him in. Fear crawls over her features. "And I know you'll never forget."

Then the room fills with smoke as the witch conjures herself a doorway.

The prince knows what he came here for, so he's the only one unsurprised. He slides out of the peasant girl's binds like a rabbit from a snare and brings out his knife. Witches are not fae; they have to cast spells with grimoires and chanting and time, so the kill is easy once he gets her claws and screeching out of the way.

When she dies, her shape transforms. The face elongates, the ears stretch to such long points that they droop like a bat's, the eyes go milky, the skin crusts over with birch bark.

The prince cuts off her head, preserving as much of the earthy skin and greasy moss hair as he can. He stands to find the not-princess staring at him, grimoire clutched in her shaking hands.

"Every ruler wants a dead witch," he says, "but no one wants a living witchling. We'll both need a way out, because I doubt you can conjure a door. You can cut your hair, if you can spare it."

A wildness flashes in her eyes. The kind of wildness that comes from being raised in a closed cage by a hag.

She shoves him, head and all, out the window, into a patch of rose bushes.

***

The prince landed in roses back then, and now he resurfaces in them.

He's lived a long, long time. He's lived on the road with nothing to spare, in palaces with everything he could dream of. He's traveled through smoky pine forests, caustic sand dunes, cracking snow and blistering winds, over the high hills on the crown of the world and deep, dark tunnels on its soles. He's kissed princesses and maids, dukes and farmer's boys. He's slayed majestic dragons. Slept cozy in their hoards, long enough to awaken some of their habits that were hibernating in him. He's charmed sirens right back.

He has no shortage of memories. But he can run out of blood.

Nothing is really immortal. Nothing is, except *her*, he thinks, staring up into her fathomless eyes.

She could feed off of him forever. At least that gives him forever to think of a way out.

"Do you want to hear more?" he asks, out of breath.

The thorns that punched through him are squirming; his skin scratches from the inside, stretching around the thorns as they wrap his bones, his organs. The pain's spread a wobbly fog from the tips of his toes to the cold top of his head. He tries his wrists again, but he's getting weaker.

"I've run into real princes, you know. They're all looking for a story. Something to stab, something to save."

A stalk seeks his mouth; he jerks his head away and keeps talking, so it diverts to the soft underside of his jaw, tracing thorns like a lover's sharp fingernails as it goes.

"I've found those princes. Them, I hurt. The princesses I don't, I just forget them; they've been through enough. But the princes? Them, I have to stop. If you were ever a princess at all, you've figured out what they do."

Deeper, deeper, deeper. Tremors run through his body. His thumb joint grinds in protest as he tries to squeeze it through the cuff of thorns.

"I kill them with blades, swift through the ribs, once they've led me as far as I need to the next curse. Or slowly, if they refuse to tell me what I need to know."

She's bowing over him, eyes wide and unblinking, black as the infinite, musty inside of that golden bell.

"I know what they want. I can read them. I break them."

The vine plunges through his jaw, out between his teeth, crawls over his cheek, seeks his eye.

Panicked, muffled, he snarls through teeth grit around the thorns, "Don't you want to see how something with hands like me, blood like me, *freedom* like me can break something?"

The princess crawls closer, bracketing him in. The plants carpeting the tower pulse and pull, a gigantic, thorny throat swallowing more than it's due.

Flowers begin to sprout and bloom. First in the room. Then pressing against his skin from the inside. Their points, like fine chisels, rip out of him, and they bloom heavy and brilliant red, dripping blood off their petals.

His hand shoots free of the thorns and flashes to the blade beneath him.

And she says, "I do."

***

Our prince leaves the tower, skin covered in needle-point cuts.

He crosses the town's sea of vines without a stumble. When he finds his horse at the edge of town, she turns tail with a high whinny, but he doesn't mind. Not once in that long walk from the tower did he tire, and the lands from here on out, he remembers, are much easier to cross.

From all corners of the land, he hears rumors of princesses being cursed. Sometimes even princes. He follows them, sword at his hip, gloves tight over his hands. He takes meticulous care of himself, touching up the thin incisions with salves that scour then soothe. He sews shut the hole under his jaw. He carefully binds that dislocated thumb. He's immortal, but not to everything, and regardless, it's important to treat the body with care. Beauty has uncountable value these days.

He finds the princesses and princes. They're always so full of dreams: dreams of shaking free of their curse, dreams of everlasting love, dreams of fairies, dreams of being saved, dreams of revenge, dreams of living forever and ever and ever.

Invariably, they fall for that catastrophically handsome face and his heroic deeds (or else they feel like they have to pretend to do so, if only until their parents praise him and they can run back to their dragons). If they notice a strange stillness in his countenance, a glint of fathomless black in his stare, they don't say anything. If they notice the way he leaves roses in his wake, they know not to touch them–each cursed princess is born wary of thorns.

When he takes them to bed, those roses break through the stone streets and crawl up their castle walls, spill through the windows, wrap around them like a caress.

Their thorns bury deep and the princess who outlives them all begins to dream.

About the Author

Vanessa Roades is a Canadian writer who is making up stories about fantasy pantheons and their meddling gods, wicked women, LGBT+ characters, and all types of elves.

Dance To Death

Puck

CW: Implied character death

Whumpee: Man, Whumper: Women, Caretaker: N/A

He falls to his knees, gasping, soaked in sweat. His legs are shaking, his muscles spasming so hard it feels as though they're tearing in two. His heart is nearly pounding out of his chest with exhaustion and terror.

Trembling, he looks up at the girls. They stand in a circle around him, staring with unblinking eyes. Dressed in white, all of them, like brides. Like his beloved, whom he came here to mourn. At least she is not among the circle of murderers. He couldn't bear to see her face set in the cold, dead expression of his tormentors.

The queen slips forth again, her crown of white roses marking her out. The roses are dead, he notices now, dead like the girls—the ghosts—that surround him. And behind them is the black, cold river.

"Please," he gasps as two of them take his arms and pull him to his feet. "Please, no more. I can't—"

Myrtha, Queen of the Wilis, presses a finger to his lips. She steps around him, her dainty slippers silently floating over the forest floor.

She strokes his face gently, her hands chilled. Her long, bony fingers creep across the back of his neck like a spider, combing through his sweat-drenched hair in a cruel mockery of comfort. He shudders at her touch, knowing what is coming, helpless to resist it.

Myrtha's cold, dead lips brush against his ear. "Dance," she whispers in her death-rattle voice.

Hilarion dances.

About the Author

True to her name, Puck has a flair for the dramatic and enjoys a little chaos. She's currently pursuing her theatre major- hence her Shakespearean pseudonym- and is also training as a dancer. Puck has been writing whump on Tumblr since 2021, and this anthology is right up her alley!

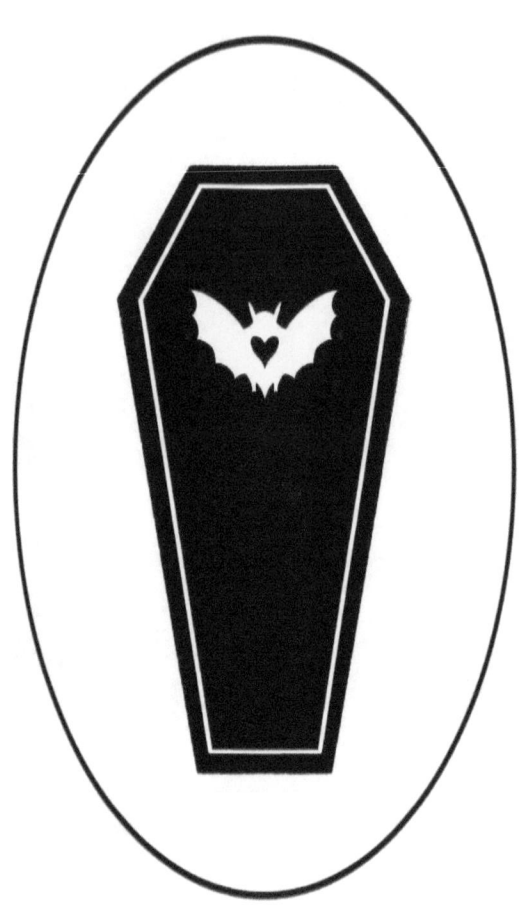

Have Mercy

Archer L.

CW: Sickness, desecration of corpses

Whumpee: Man, Whumper: N/A, Caretaker: N/A

Edwin's sister Mercy died the winter of 1892, right after the New Year. He wanted to mourn her properly, but, wracked with consumption, he couldn't cry without hurting himself.

And that wasn't all.

The town of Exeter, Rhode Island, had decided that his family wasn't just afflicted by consumption, but something else entirely.

They were vampires.

Edwin thought this the cruelest thing that had ever been done to him. His family was sick and dying, and they thought they were *vampires?* That they *deserved* to die?

Edwin slept fitfully most nights now. If he wasn't awake coughing up blood, he was worrying about the townspeople. He only had his father left, and he was worried about him too. Would he become sick? Would the townspeople come after him as well?

For now, George Brown was protecting his last living child, locking the doors tight at night with a padlock and keeping a weapon close by. He'd told Edwin that he would not let the townspeople take him.

The sound of shuffling footsteps and orange light coming through a slit in the thick curtains woke Edwin that March morning of 1892. He had only been half-asleep, the taste of blood in his mouth, a cough rising in his chest, lungs pierced with needles. He was quick to roll out of the comfort of his bed and creep over to the window, floor cold on his bare feet.

Very carefully, heart pounding, he peeked out.

There was a mob outside his house. They made it to the door, torches burning. He didn't see too many weapons among them, but a mob—armed or not—was dangerous.

Edwin pulled back from the window as if burned by the early morning sun. He didn't want to be caught.

He was about to rouse his father when he heard him downstairs, yelling through the door.

"What do you want with us?!"

"Bring out your son!" the mob yelled.

"And leave him to you wolves?! Never!"

There was silence for a long time, chattering of voices.

Then, someone spoke, a woman:

"We want to cure him."

Edwin's face went as white as snow. He knew what they meant by a cure. They'd have to ... No, he couldn't ... He ...

Feeling like he was going to be sick, Edwin sank down onto the bed. Would his father fulfill the mob's wishes?

Apparently so, because it wasn't long after that George Brown was barging into his room and demanding he dress. They were going to the graveyard where his sisters and mother had been buried.

"I can't." Edwin was surprised at his lack of a stutter.

"You must. It's the only way to appease them."

"Father—"

"And what if it works?"

I don't care. Edwin didn't *want* a cure from his supposed vampirism, or even from his consumption. He just wanted to be with his family again, not desecrating their graves to live longer than they.

Edwin knew he couldn't argue with his father, though. He dressed slowly, feeling mechanical as he did so, like there was no life left in him.

Once the two men had their coats and boots on, they left the house, and the mob escorted them to the graveyard, pushing and shoving, jostling Edwin. He coughed. Blood came up on his lips. He didn't even make a face; he was used to the taste of it by now.

Edwin could hardly see by the time they reached the graveyard. It wasn't the mist that surrounded everything in a cold blanket of vapor. No, it was the tears in his eyes.

The digging started.

Edwin had to stand the whole time, even as fatigue made him shake. His father wrapped an arm around him to keep him up. He, at least, was not afraid of consumption or vampirism or whatever the Hell it was that Edwin was afflicted with.

The bodies of his mother and sister were decomposing. The smell was awful, and the sight was ghastly. The mob agreed that, no, they hadn't been vampires, and thus the cure would not come from them.

But Mercy. Dear Mercy. She was not decomposing, and it looked like her fingernails had even grown.

They cut her open with a giant, serrated blade used for butchering pigs. They took her liver, her heart. The heart still had blood in it, as if she had fed.

But Edwin knew she hadn't. She wasn't a vampire! She wasn't! He didn't want this cure!

They had to hold him down for it.

Once they'd taken her organs, they'd burned them and mixed the ashes with water.

And told him to drink.

Edwin refused. How could he not?

So, they held him down, pinched his nose to make him open his mouth. There were too many of them! He tried fighting, but was weak from his illness, no strength left in him. Sobs wanted to break free. He couldn't breathe, he couldn't breathe!

He was made to drink the horrid mixture. He choked, spluttered, but down it went nonetheless.

They let him up once every drop was gone, and Edwin ran to the edge of the graveyard as well as he could on wobbly legs. He tried to vomit, to get rid of the wretched thing they'd made him drink, but nothing came up but blood.

He heard faintly, over his heaving, his father's voice:

"Lord, have mercy on us."

About the Author

Archer has been writing whump for about 10 years. His favorite genre to write for is fantasy. Read his work at evilwriter-originals.tumblr.com.

The Nutcracker Prelude

Puck

Whumpee: Man, Whumper: Woman, Caretaker: N/A

The shop window read 'C.E. Drosselmeyer, Fine Watches and Clocks, Machines of All Sorts,' and it was the only shop on the street still lit. The lettering, painted in gold, curved across the top of the display window in which lay several of the fine watches and clocks promised. And they were fine indeed, wood and bronze and gold and silver decorated with fanciful designs that must have come in a dream, so strange and fantastic did they look.

Snow fell on the steps outside, but inside the shop was warm. The shop owner, a short, thin man with an eyeglass strapped over his right eye, sat at his workbench, humming a snatch of folk song. His deft fingers set a new hour hand into a man's gold pocket watch, working with precise movements and careful deliberation. Christian Elias Drosselmeyer was a master of his trade, and he saw no need to hurry through his work. He liked to say that if you rushed the making of a clock, it would always run fast, and if you were lazy with the piece, it would always run slow.

A clock shop was never silent, but this one came close. The clocks ticked the minutes away, and the clockmaker's tools clicked against the casing of the watch, but that was all. Though the shop was open, no customers were expected—the hour was nearly midnight, as proclaimed by the tall wooden grandfather clock in the far corner. This was the only clock not for sale, and all the other pieces took their time from its cold face. Customers often remarked upon the curious nature of the clock—it was plain from base to trunk, but the top had been exquisitely carved. The smooth wood transformed into the figure of a fierce owl with wings spread, the clock face itself serving as the bird's heart. Its feathered head bore a striking resemblance to the wild, graying hair of the clockmaker, and its hooked nose and hooded eyes seemed almost to be a reflection of his face.

The clockmaker lifted his eyeglass as he glanced at the owl clock. "Quarter to midnight," he announced, pulling the eyeglass off. "We had best be getting to bed."

His apprentice, a golden-haired young man who had been quietly polishing the pieces on the display shelves, nodded. He left his work and came to stand just behind his master, looking over the clockmaker's shoulder at the timepiece on the bench. "Is that the judge's watch?" he asked.

Drosselmeyer frowned at it. "Yes, and what a troublesome little thing it was. The hands were installed badly when it was made—set too close. The minute hand had gotten lodged against the hour hand, which only bent it worse. See?" He held up the old part, which was indeed misshapen. "I also replaced a few of the springs. Rusted. Not badly, but I can't bear to let a watch go with rusty springs." He laid the pocket watch on a piece of white cloth and wrapped it carefully. "Here, Hans, put this in the back. The judge will be by to collect it sometime tomorrow."

The apprentice took the piece and disappeared into the back room. Drosselmeyer sighed. He interlaced his fingers and stretched his arms over his head with a groan. Running his hands through his hair, he stood up and pushed back the stool he had been sitting on. He opened a little drawer and swept the bits of metal left on the table inside, bending down with a groan to make sure none of the tiny pieces had fallen to the floor.

The bell above the shop door jingled.

Drosselmeyer apologized from underneath the bench. "Oh, I'm sorry, I was just closing the shop. We'll be open tomorrow, if you—"

"But this is an *emergency!*"

At the sound of the shrill voice, Drosselmeyer straightened up so fast he nearly hit his head. His jaw set in a strange resignation as he turned to face the new customer.

It was a woman, a wealthy one, dressed in expensive red silk and accompanied by two footmen in neat gray and black livery. All of them, however, looked strangely similar to each other. They all three shared their round faces, their oddly long noses, their beady black eyes that flashed brightly at the clockmaker from underneath hats that did not seem to fit quite right. The footmen also wore sharp swords at their sides, the type of sword that was clearly not only for show.

"If it's an emergency," Drosselmeyer said slowly, "I suppose I can take a look. What sort of machine is it?"

The woman flounced over, setting down a cloth-wrapped bundle on the workbench. "A clock, sir," she announced. Her voice was high, almost squeaking, and she spoke far too loudly for the little shop. "It has stopped working entirely. I cannot think what must be wrong with it!"

Drosselmeyer unwrapped the cloth, and if his hands faltered a little his face never changed. The clock in question was a fantastic bronze creation, shaped like a grand castle. As the clockmaker opened the back panel, several small, brightly painted figures presented themselves, all lined up to parade across the castle's balcony at the stroke of every hour.

"It's a wonderful clock," Drosselmeyer said, unrolling the bit of leather that held his tools. "And it doesn't work at all?"

"Not a tick nor a chime. It is a lovely creation, though. The artist who made it must be a master of his work."

"Indeed."

The door to the back room opened just then, and the young apprentice looked out into the shop. "Are you coming to bed, Uncle?"

The clockmaker looked briefly over his shoulder, then back to the castle clock. "You go along, Hans. I'll be there shortly."

Perhaps it was something in Drosselmeyer's voice. Perhaps it was the clock on the workbench. Perhaps it was the odd faces of the wealthy woman and her footmen. But the apprentice saw something that he did not like, and he shook his head. "I'll wait for you."

"Hans-Peter." This time the clockmaker spoke sharply. "I won't tell you again. Go upstairs."

The apprentice hesitated a moment. Then, in silent defiance, he moved into the shop and shut the door firmly behind him, standing sentinel before it with his eyes never leaving the new customer.

Drosselmeyer sighed and turned his gaze back to the woman. "About how long ago did it stop working, meine Dame?"

"A few days," she said carelessly. "I only noticed it this afternoon." She reached out a hand, gloved in black, to caress the casing. "I would be delighted if you could repair it,

Herr Drosselmeyer. I should have gone to the man who made it, but he seems to have ... slipped away."

"Yes," Drosselmeyer replied, inserting the first of his tools into the mechanism. "Craftsmen often disappear, for one reason or another. I'm sure the fellow who made this clock has merely vanished down some mouse hole."

He spoke nonchalantly, but the woman's black eyes narrowed all the same. "So you know me, Mechanist."

"You have an unmistakable presence, Lady Mouserinks," Drosselmeyer answered, laying down his tools and making a little bow that somehow had a disrespectful air to it. "And your tail is peeping out below your hem."

Angrily, the woman reached up and tore off her hat, which had been concealing a pair of large gray mouse ears. A golden crown sat glittering between them. The apprentice's eyes widened at the sight, but he kept silent. "Thou will address me properly, as Königin, Mechanist!" the mouse-woman snapped, gesturing to her crown. She had dropped her false German accent along with her hat, and spoke now in a strange, old-fashioned manner. "I am no mere lady, but Queen of Mousalia!"

"And where is that fine kingdom?" Drosselmeyer asked bitingly. "A hole in the wall of some grand house? Or perhaps you have found the sewers of Nuremberg more fitting?"

The Mouse Queen threw back her head and laughed, a squeaking, ear-splitting cackle. "Mock, clockmaker! Mock all thee will! But for all thy traps and tricks, Mousalia lives, thrives, *rises*. And I intend to see it rise even further."

She lunged, seizing the clockmaker by the shirt collar and dragging him half over the workbench with a strength she shouldn't have possessed. The castle-shaped clock tumbled to the floor and smashed into a thousand pieces. The apprentice started forward, but one of her soldiers stopped him in his tracks with a sword at his throat.

"Look at thee now, old owl-eyes." The Mouse Queen grinned savagely, showing large, yellowed front teeth. "Fallen so far. Surely a little shop in Nuremberg cannot compare to the royal court of the Land of Sweets?"

Drosselmeyer glanced over his shoulder at his apprentice before he replied as best he could with his voice half-choked. "Those days are behind me, *Lady* Mouserinks. I am an old man now. I prefer to spend the years I have left at peace in Nuremberg, rather than in the chaos of the court."

The Mouse Queen let go of his collar. Drosselmeyer slumped on his stool with a hand at his throat, coughing. Hans-Peter pushed past the soldier's sword and rushed to his uncle's side, throwing a sharp look at the Mouse Queen before turning his attention to Drosselmeyer.

The Mouse Queen smiled a distinctly unpleasant smile. "Such a charming little dream, Mechanist. And thou may have it still, if thou will help me."

Drosselmeyer rubbed his bruised throat as he spoke. "Not for anything you could give."

The Mouse Queen's black eyes glittered cruelly. "What I give thee is a choice, Drosselmeyer," she said. "Come to Mousalia, as my honored guest, and build machines for me. And once thou have finished, thou can return to thy little shop and die there, for all I care. Or, thou may refuse, be taken to Mousalia as a prisoner rather than a guest, and die in my dungeons. But either way, I will have what I want."

"You want weapons. Not machines." Drosselmeyer stood, leaning on Hans-Peter's shoulder. "I will not give you either."

The Mouse Queen showed her nasty yellow grin again. "We shall see how long that lasts." She raised her squeaking voice. "Kaspar, Otto, bind him. We return to Mousalia with a prisoner instead of a guest. But if that is what he chooses, well—who am I to refuse him?"

The soldiers drew their swords and advanced on the clockmaker, who made no effort to resist them as they seized his arms.

The Mouse Queen waved a careless hand. "Oh, and take the boy, too."

"No!" cried Drosselmeyer, tearing loose from the soldiers' grasp. One of them slammed a balled fist into his chest, knocking him to the ground.

Hans-Peter fell to his knees at his uncle's side, helping him sit up. He looked furiously at the Mouse Queen. "He's an old man. He's just an old clockmaker. How dare you treat him like that?"

Her smile widened. "Just an old clockmaker? Have thee told him nothing, Drosselmeyer? Then again, thou always did love thy secrets."

Drosselmeyer said nothing, one hand clutching his ribs where he had been struck.

The Mouse Queen stepped forward and bent down to take the apprentice's chin in her hand, forcing him to look her in the face. "Thou has no idea who thy uncle truly is," she said softly. "But thou will find out soon enough."

Hans-Peter jerked his chin out of her hand, his eyes ablaze with anger.

Standing up, the Mouse Queen adjusted her crown and beckoned to one of the soldiers. "Otto, take us home. I am tired of this dull, magicless world."

"If you truly looked, Lady Mouserinks, you would see that there is magic here, too." Drosselmeyer spoke in a quiet tone, and he stood only with difficulty. Yet his voice reverberated around the little shop like the clanging of a great bell.

"I do not care for this world, magic or no," the Mouse Queen replied briskly. "Say thy farewells to thy precious Nuremberg, Mechanist. For unless thou build me what I wish, thou shall never see this shop, this city, or this world again."

As one soldier bound Drosselmeyer and the apprentice's hands behind their backs, the other soldier threw down a handful of shimmering powder. The powder turned into a swirling column of golden smoke as soon as it hit the floor. The Mouse Queen made a taunting curtsy. "After thee, Herr Drosselmeyer. Mousalia awaits."

The two soldiers forced Drosselmeyer and his nephew into the sparkling smoke and followed with their swords drawn. With another squeaking laugh, this one of triumph, the Mouse Queen stepped in after them. The tornado of gold flickered and died like a candle in the wind, leaving nothing but a pile of glittering dust on the floor.

The owl clock struck midnight to an empty shop.

***

Mousalia was a buried realm. The entire country lay in an enormous pit in the earth, a cavern cradling a kingdom. The dim white light that kept it from being wholly pitch-dark came not from the sun, but from a jagged hole in the stone ceiling far above. Its residents didn't mind the lack of light—they were all mice and rats, accustomed to scuttling about in the dark.

Almost everything in Mousalia had been taken from things discarded, stolen, left unguarded. The citizens were thieves and robbers all—they made almost nothing of their own. A rickety wooden ladder stretched up, up, up to the hole in the ceiling, and a few mice at a time risked the perilous climb every night to bring back whatever food and supplies they could carry.

"This is one of two problems thee will fix for us, Mechanist," the Mouse Queen had said. She had taken the clockmaker—under heavy guard—to the parapet of her castle, showing him the hole in the stone sky. "Thou will build a machine to carry my people safely up to the opening. Not only one or two, but dozens of them at a time."

Drosselmeyer reached out and set a hand on the stone wall—the castle had been built of broken shards of limestone, fallen from the ceiling above or picked up from the cavern floor. "And the second problem?"

The Mouse Queen smiled, her whiskers twitching. She had abandoned her mostly human guise—she was fully mouse now, though she walked on her hind paws and stood taller than Drosselmeyer himself. She had also kept her red silk gown. "The Snow Wood," she said. "The boundary between my kingdom and the Land of Sweets. We have tried, again and again, to get through it. The Snow King and Queen send their storms and snowflakes to stop us. Not a single one of my mice has ever made it through the Wood."

"Well," said Drosselmeyer, "seeing as you and your mice seek to gnaw the Land of Sweets and all its citizens to pieces, I can hardly blame the Snow King and Queen for preventing it. Queen Sugar Plum is the Snow Queen's own sister, after all. It is only natural that they would protect each other."

The Mouse Queen shrugged philosophically. "And if sweet things are left too long, it is only natural for mice to devour them."

Drosselmeyer shook his head, gazing up at the hole far above them.

"I want another machine to solve the problem of the Snow Wood," the Mouse Queen told him. "A machine that can carry my troops safely through the Wood, one that even the Snow Queen's strongest winds could never blow over. Build me that machine, and the machine to carry my mice to the surface, and I will let thee go back unharmed to thy dull little shop in thy dull little otherworld."

Drosselmeyer stood silent.

"Well?" the Mouse Queen demanded. "Can thou do it?"

At that, Drosselmeyer had turned to her. "I can," he said evenly. "And I will not."

The Mouse Queen gnashed her teeth and lashed her tail in fury. "That shall change soon, Mechanist," she promised darkly. "For thine own sake, thou should reconsider." She beckoned to the guards. "Take the clockmaker to the cells!"

Those cells had been where Drosselmeyer and his nephew had spent, at their best guess, the last week. Time was difficult to tell down in the Mouse Queen's dungeons—even for a clockmaker. And they had not been left in peace. Hans-Peter was relatively unharmed, aside from a few bruises. But the elder Drosselmeyer had suffered the full attention of the Mouse Queen's jailers—torturers, rather. The latest injury had been the most severe. Hans-Peter knelt by his uncle's side, doing his best to clean the wound with the little water they had been given.

Footsteps sounded in the stone corridor outside their cell—the footsteps of the Mouse Queen. Hans-Peter looked up, his fist clenching, but Drosselmeyer laid a hand on his arm. "Do not acknowledge her," he said softly. "She loves to see what effect she has. Give her none."

The apprentice nodded reluctantly and took up his cloth again, dabbing at the clockmaker's bloodied cheek.

"Still stubborn, old owl-eyes?" The prison door slammed open with a *clang,* and the Mouse Queen appeared on the steps, flanked by a pair of burly guards. She smiled wickedly as she stood in front of the two prisoners, her long pink tail twitching behind her. "Well, I suppose that name no longer fits."

Hans-Peter tensed, an angry reply on his lips, but Drosselmeyer seized his arm. He gave the young man a warning look with the eye the Mouse Queen's jailers had left him—the right side of his face was still bloody despite Hans-Peter's attempt at bandaging the wound.

"Still insistent, Lady Mouserinks?" Drosselmeyer replied, his voice calm and cold.

Her smirk vanished. "Watch thyself, Mechanist. I can take more than thine eye."

Drosselmeyer struggled to sit upright, shaking his head. "It doesn't matter. I won't help you destroy the kingdom that was once my home. Not for anything you can give, not for anything you can take, not for anything you can do to me."

The Mouse Queen pressed a slender paw to her chest dramatically. "Not for anything I can do to thee? What a perilous situation to be in. Thou has made it awfully hard for me, clockmaker. I suppose I must try a new tactic." She beckoned with her other paw. The guards advanced on the prisoners, swords drawn. "Perhaps if thou will not do it for thy own sake, thou will do it for another's."

She raised her paw again. The guards rushed forward, seized Hans-Peter, and tore him away from Drosselmeyer. One of them wrenched Hans-Peter's hands behind his back and wrapped an arm around the young man's throat in a chokehold. The other held his sword at the ready, waiting for the Mouse Queen's next order.

Drosselmeyer leapt to his feet, his face twisted in panic. "No, Lady Mouserinks! He has no part in this—he knows nothing!"

"But thou do," she answered sweetly. "Thee knows how to build the machines I need. That is all I want, Mechanist. Just a little knowledge, and I will not hurt thy precious nephew. If not ..." She let the sentence trail off, her eyes snapping wickedly.

Drosselmeyer drew himself up to his full height, his jaw set like stone. He glanced at Hans-Peter, still held in the iron grip of the guard, and then turned back to the Mouse Queen. Suddenly he did not look so much like an old, frail shopkeeper. "Lady Mouserinks," he said in a voice of thunder, "you forget my full title. I was Court Mechanist, yes. But I was Court Magician, too."

Drosselmeyer raised a hand and flung something invisible in the direction of the Mouse Queen, shouting out a single word in a foreign tongue. The Mouse Queen stumbled backward with a piercing shriek of agony, clutching her stomach. "Aieee! Guards! Karl, Johann, help me!"

The guards rushed to her side, and Drosselmeyer rushed to Hans-Peter, helping him up from where the guard had shoved him to the floor. Hans-Peter looked at his uncle as if looking at a stranger. "What did you just *do?*"

"I put a curse on her, years ago," Drosselmeyer replied. "I've just set it in motion." He raised a hand again, looking threateningly at the two guards. They dropped their swords and scampered for the open door, squeaking in terror.

Hans-Peter looked at him incredulously. "When we get back to Nuremberg, you're going to have to explain all this."

"I will. It was time you knew, anyway. But first we—

"Uncle, look out!"

The shouted warning came with a hard shove to Drosselmeyer's back. He fell, landing painfully on one arm. But there wasn't time to think about the lightning bolt of pain that shot into his shoulder. Drosselmeyer pushed himself up as fast as he could manage, turning to see what had happened.

The Mouse Queen leaned weakly against the prison wall. In her paw, she clutched the hilt of one of the guard's abandoned swords.

The end of the blade had pierced Hans-Peter's chest, where it had been intended to strike Drosselmeyer.

All the fight and fearsomeness left the clockmaker in an instant. He caught the young man just as he fell, lowering him gently to the floor. "Oh, Hans, Hans, my boy. Why? Why would you be so foolish? That sword was meant for me!"

He didn't have to look at the wound to know that it was mortal. The dark red stain blossoming on Hans-Peter's chest told him all he needed. Tears tracked through the dried blood on Drosselmeyer's face, and he bowed his head in anguish. "I'm sorry, Hans. I'm so sorry."

Hans-Peter coughed and seemed to be trying to speak, but it was beyond him. Of all the things Drosselmeyer had ever expected he would do in his life, cradling his dying nephew in his arms had never been one of them. "You were supposed to live, Hans," he breathed. "I promised your father. You were supposed to *live*. And I—I was going to show you magic."

The clockmaker raised his head suddenly, staring at the wall, the clockwork gears of his sharp mind turning. "Magic," he said under his breath. "Magic, magic ... yes. Yes! A curse! But yet not a curse. This time it must be a blessing."

He bent his head again, speaking so low that only Hans-Peter could hear. "Forgive me, Hans. There is no other way."

Hans-Peter was far too weak to answer, but his hand grasped Drosselmeyer's, gripping it tightly with the last of his strength.

As his nephew's hand fell slack, Drosselmeyer pressed his lips to Hans-Peter's forehead, chanting under his breath.

"Crack, crack, break,

New form take,

Remake.

Clink, clink,

Shrivel, shrink,

New form take,

Crack, crack, break."

Anxiously, the clockmaker peered into his nephew's face. Hans-Peter's body grew stiff and hard—to anyone else, it would have been taken as a sign that death had come. Drosselmeyer knew better. He waited breathlessly as the spell took hold. The change would save Hans-Peter from the fatal wound, but at a terrible price. The clockmaker's remaining eye blurred with tears as Hans-Peter transformed, even his golden hair turning white as the curse affected it.

At last it was over. The musty dungeon air hung thick with the remnants of magic. Drosselmeyer knelt on the cold stone floor, holding in his arms a little wooden nutcracker. A lifeless toy—or so it seemed.

Only a little distance away, the Mouse Queen slumped against the wall. Drosselmeyer's ancient curse had her in its clutches. Still, she laughed, a wheezing, squeaking laugh. "Hee ... hee ... Drosselmeyer. I will ... have vengeance ... I will ... stamp out ... thy name ... I have ... magic ... of my own."

She raised a paw and pointed at the clockmaker, her shrill voice squeaking out a curse. Or was it a prophecy?

"Son with seven crowns will bite,

Nutcracker,

At night,

And revenge his mother's death,

Short breath,

Must I,

Die, die,

So young,

Oh, agony!"

Trembling all over, the Mouse Queen fell on her side. Amid gasps of pain, she dragged herself to the prison door and over the threshold, leaving Drosselmeyer alone.

He shook his head gravely. "So you have had a son, then, Lady Mouserinks? No matter. I can take care of that." He began to chant again, murmuring over the nutcracker in his arms.

"Strike, clock, strike,

Strike midnight.

A girl must love,

A clock must strike.

Strike midnight,

Owl in swift flight,

Then the fight,

Mouse-King must be slain,

Ere returns thy form again.

Strike, clock, strike!"

***

The owl clock struck midnight once again. And several things happened, in several different places, as it did.

In the Land of Sweets, Queen Sugar Plum opened a letter from the man who had once been mechanist and magician of her court, tears in her eyes as she read the words he had written.

In Mousalia, a monstrous mouse with seven heads found the cold corpse of his mother, the queen, and bellowed out his rage against the clockmaker and all his kin.

And in Nuremberg, Drosselmeyer, with a new black patch fixed over his right eye, stepped into his little shop, taking off his greatcoat. Smiling sadly, he went to the owl clock and stroked its casing. "So, old friend. It seems you must leave your home after all. But I've found a lovely new one for you." He sighed. "You must guard it well. For lives depend on it."

Drosselmeyer patted the owl clock one more time, running his fingers over its carved head. He turned and went to the shelf above his workbench. He removed everything that had been on it, sighing deeply as he did so. A tear or two fell from his eye while he worked.

And then, he reached up and set the wooden nutcracker on the shelf. "Wait a little, nephew," he said in a voice thick with tears. "The spell will break. I promise."

Drosselmeyer sat down at his workbench, glancing once at the nutcracker as he pulled paper, pen and ink from the drawer under the table. He dipped the pen into the inkwell, set it to the page, and began to write.

My dear Clara ...

About the Author

True to her name, Puck has a flair for the dramatic and enjoys a little chaos. She's currently pursuing her theatre major- hence her Shakespearean pseudonym- and is also training as a dancer. Puck has been writing whump on Tumblr since 2021, and this anthology is right up her alley!

Weep for my past

Aiden E. Messer

CW: Tongue whump

Whumpee: Man, Whumper: Man, Caretaker: Man, Woman

Peter pulled on the restraints that kept him tied to the wall of the Jolly Roger's hold, succeeding only in irritating his wrists. Footsteps sounded and Peter froze in terror.

All children, even Peter Pan, grow up. The legend, however, is not entirely false. Peter did remain a child for centuries, a teenager for just as long, and will be a young adult for the rest of eternity. In human beings, once the body and mind reach maturity, the aging process begins. But, of course, Peter is not a human being. No one knows exactly where he comes from, not even him, but what is certain is that the concept of growing old does not exist in him, nor does that of death.

Such a power was bound to arouse some jealousy. One person in particular wanted to harness his ability by any means necessary. His name was Captain James Hook. During one of their many fights centuries earlier, Hook had wounded Peter and, as he licked the blood from his blade, had felt a wave of power flow into him. His eyes, the color of a forget-me-not, had taken on a red tint, and he understood that he had found the key to stealing the child's immortality. This was shortly before Peter cut off his right hand and threw it to the crocodile, thus mixing the captain's envy with hatred towards the one he now considered his sworn enemy. Peter was only a child then, unable to comprehend all this hatred. To protect his mind, his brain had transformed it all into a game, a great heroic adventure to share with his friends.

Hook had tasted his blood many times since then, and each time his eyes had become a little redder and his lifespan had lengthened. Peter had become an adult and the protective fantasy had gradually faded, giving way to the cruel and bleak reality. He was therefore desperately aware of the seriousness of his situation, now that he had fallen into the captain's trap. Peter's heart skipped a beat as the captain stepped into the hold, an evil gleam in his now entirely red eyes.

"Hello, Peter," he said, his voice dripping with honey and poison. "I've been waiting for this moment for so long. Your immortality is mine, and you will pay for what you did to me."

He showed his silvery hook while pronouncing these last words. Peter felt the anger rising in him, and he could not help but retort:

"What *I* did to you? I was a child, and you attacked me. I didn't understand what was going on, all I knew was that I was hurt, and I was scared. And now you dare to blame me for defending myself? If you didn't want a crocodile to eat your hand, all you had to do was leave me alone."

The captain grinned wickedly and crouched down in front of him.

"You've always had a sharp tongue, but no matter. There's no reason for you to keep it anymore. And when it grows back, I'm going to have a lot of fun starting over."

Peter shivered and curled up against the wall, wishing he hadn't spoken. He knew that not being able to die was as much a curse as it was a blessing, and that angering the captain was about the worst thing to do in his position. Hook grabbed his jaw violently and clenched it, forcing Peter to open his mouth. The captain pierced the young but not-really-young man's tongue with his hook and pulled, then with his left hand he grabbed a knife hanging from his belt and sliced it off. The pain was so intense that Peter's vision blurred for a few moments. The metallic taste of blood filled his mouth as it flowed out of his lip and down his chin. He instinctively tried to speak, but only managed to make a gurgling sound and spit out more blood. His heart was racing as panic overcame him. In his many years of life, and despite the many perils he had faced, he had never felt so powerless, so helpless.

"There, that's much better," the captain mockingly said.

Hook ripped off Peter's leafy shirt and plunged his hook into his now exposed chest and down to his navel, tearing flesh, bone, and muscle in an abominable feast of agony.

Peter screamed in pain, fear, and despair.

The captain laughed.

"So how does it feel to be at my mercy? Do you regret cutting off my hand and offering me this beautiful hook? Oh yes, that's right, you can't answer. Well, enough with the fooling around, it's time to get down to business."

Peter was now shaking violently and his whole body was covered with cold sweat and blood. He squeezed his eyes shut, trying to escape back into the imaginary wonderland of his childhood, but the pain kept him firmly nailed to the damp floor of the hold.

The captain used his hook to slice open Peter's carotid artery and collected the blood that was gushing out in small, steady streams into bottles. Peter felt less and less pain. He felt dizzy, numb, and cold, as his consciousness left him along with his blood, guiding him towards a welcoming darkness.

Peter woke up without knowing how long he had been unconscious. His head was pounding, his mouth was pasty, he felt weak, and he just wanted to get back into the arms of the darkness, but the darkness didn't want him anymore. The blood that covered him had dried, and he could feel that his wounds had largely closed. His tongue had not yet grown back, but it was no longer bleeding.

He knew he had to find a way to escape, a plan, something, but he was so tired, his mind hazy, and he didn't know what to do. If only he could call his friends, let them know where he was, they would know how to help him. A commotion broke out above him on the ship's deck. He could hear screams and metallic clanking, but his brain was too exhausted to make sense of it. The commotion finally died down and Peter heard footsteps coming towards the room he was tied up in. He cowered, terrified of seeing the captain again so soon, but when the door opened, it was Tiger Lily who stepped in. She rushed towards him, followed by the Lost Boys, some fairies, and several members of her tribe.

"Peter! We went looking for you as soon as we saw you weren't coming home! Everything is okay now, we'll get you out of here."

The words didn't register in Peter's mind, but the presence of his friends, her voice, it was enough for him to know that he was safe. He cried with relief and weariness as the young woman undid his restraints.

About the Author

Aiden E. Messer doesn't exist. According to one of the children they work with, if they were a teacher, they would be as tall as a human. They are not a teacher. They have studied psychology, and have always had a penchant for horror and the macabre.

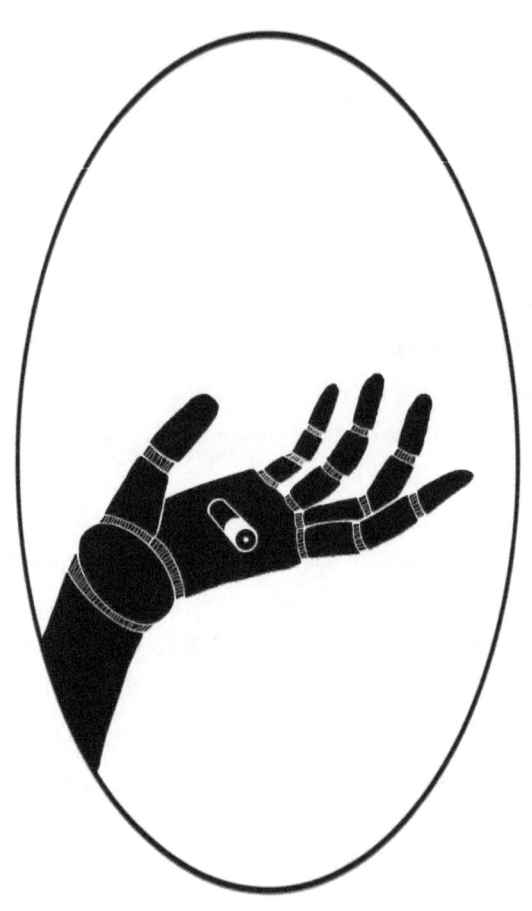

The Little Android

Ruth

CW: Passive suicide/suicidal thoughts, android whump, outcast whumpee, forced labour, neglect, self-neglect, disabled whumpee, sadistic whumpers, artificial pain

Whumpee: Nonbinary, Whumper: Man, Caretaker: N/A

The android sits down against the wall of a crowded metal walkway, box of batteries in its hand. One arm is made up of loose wires and artificial nerve endings left when the attachment was ripped from its socket, and as they brush against the wall, they send a jolt of pain through its systems, almost causing it to drop the box. If only its owner had deactivated its pain circuits after the experiment was completed, but he thought they would be useful to control it. And as a synthetic life form, it does not have the right to deactivate them itself.

It needs to sell these batteries. Oh, they look so tempting, they could power it for the day it's sure, it would have constant heating and a properly working voice and its power wouldn't flicker out so often. But it'll get credits if it sells them, and it's therefore less likely to end up on the scrap heap.

It tries for eight point seven hours, but it doesn't make a single credit. Passers-by barely give it a second glance. If it's lucky. Some step around it with a wide berth, giving it dirty looks and whispering behind their hands (sometimes not even whispering, it doesn't matter, it's not a human after all). A few teenagers make a game of tugging at its exposed nerve endings to see who can make it scream the loudest, and nobody stops them, they just look annoyed at the noise. It's moved on by security more than once.

Finally the lights in the station switch to night mode, dimming and turning slightly orange, reducing the blue light. Usually the android would adjust its vision to compensate so it could keep working with ease, but that function no longer works.

The place it was last moved along to, where it is now, gets almost no night traffic. There are no shops or clubs or living hubs, there's no reason to come here unless you're maintenance staff, who can't, or won't, buy from it anyway. There's no point staying.

Except if it goes back to the shop with no credits again, it will be deemed useless and stripped for parts. Maybe even without its pain circuits being deactivated first.

Its power flickers out for a few seconds. When it restarts, the android is on the floor. It doesn't know how long it was out, which is unnerving but common recently.

Maybe just a little boost of battery power. Just to keep it going.

It chooses a battery, unwraps it with stiff, creaky fingers, and plugs it into a port on its side.

The power zaps around its body and it feels a simulation of warmth for the first time in so long. It's almost comfortable.

In the distance, it sees its makers' workshop. They're laughing and joking together as they start up the charger, preparing to test parts that the android knows are custom-made. It used to help with the more dangerous parts of the job, before they ran out of money and were forced to sell it.

It feels so warm and cosy, and as the light envelopes it, it opens its mouth to speak.

The light disappears. The warmth disappears. The android tries to hang on but it must have had a power surge in its decision-making module.

It feels even colder now. Any warmth is gone, any semblance of care from someone else. What does it have in its life, really? No one does anything except order it around and stimulate its pain circuits. Nobody even interferes when the pain is malicious. Not anymore.

It takes out another battery. If it's going to be scrapped anyway, it might as well make it worth it.

As soon as it's plugged in, the station disappears. It's inside a charging station, one of the ones for VIPs and their androids. It had a job cleaning these, once. Mobile charging packs, as much premium oil as the android can drink, oiled joints, comfortable places to stand or sit... it has dreamed about them, sometimes. It was allowed to drink the last dregs of oil and it really was premium.

This one is busy with humans in fancy clothes and the latest models, so much more advanced than itself. No one is paying attention to the android, and it walks through the central aisle, approaching a serving station. It reaches out a hand for an oil can, wires jittering in anticipation at the taste, the feel of its body afterwards—

The illusion fades.

The android is left cold and alone on the floor of the space station. There's not much use for softness for androids but oh, how it wishes. It's been so long since it had oil, only getting just enough lubrication to stop it from rusting entirely. It doesn't deserve anything more until it starts to be useful. But it won't be, and it just feels empty.

It's startled out of its reverie by a *beep beep beep* of warning. Its power is depleting even faster than normal. If it doesn't get to a charging point soon, it'll power down for good.

Surprisingly, the android finds itself not caring overly much anymore. What does it have to go back to, after all?

The android plugs in another battery.

It's on a starship deck in night mode. The observation deck. It's always wished to be stationed on one of these. It's charging against a wall, sitting down, and it can see the stars.

They're bright spots against the darkness, mostly, but in the distance it can see nebulas, colourful clouds of dust and stars. That's when it realises its vision is fixed. It can see properly, for the first time in years. Who bothered to fix that?

Then reality hits it. Nobody did. The android here, the one with the fixed vision and someone who cares and such a good posting, it doesn't exist. This is a dream. An illusion. Something it'll never get.

It touches its reflection in the glass, feeling a pang from somewhere inside that shouldn't exist. It's been fixed, like a patchwork, different colours and textures of paint-work, but it's more than it will ever really have, more than it deserves. Engine oil leaks slightly from the edges of its vision sensors. Good quality oil too. It really is getting the best on this dreamship.

It can feel itself fading. Its consciousness is fading. And it's nowhere near a power socket really, so it'll deactivate permanently this time.

But it doesn't have anything to lose. There's no one who cares, no one who won't take it apart for scrap as soon as it returns with no credits and barely any batteries. No one will mourn it if it stays here. Someone will take the batteries and someone will take its parts and they'll sell both but they won't *care*. What's the point?

The android sinks back down, leaning back against its comfortable charging wall. It closes its eyes for the last time to an exploding supernova.

The science doesn't really make sense. But it's far too tired to care.

About the Author

Ruth is a British writer and artist who enjoys swordfighting and putting characters in situations for their own and others' amusement.

The Dragon Mark

Lif L.

CW: Character death, torture, gore, captivity

Whumpee: Man, Whumper: Man, Caretaker: Man, Woman

Prologue

Cold sea air whistled about the general's command tent and curled its way inside through the canvas flaps he'd let open to cool himself. His lanterns, already low on oil, sputtered, and the papers he'd weighed down fluttered in the breeze. Still, even in the low light, he struggled on through the reports he was reading. He'd heard tell of healers claiming this would damage his eyesight, but at the moment he didn't care; there was work to be done. His army in Julu had been ready to join the ones in Dong, Ru'nan, and Nanyang to strike for the capital of Luoyang, but had fallen under attack. This missive had come a few days late, but word traveled fast on the North China Plains, so he was expecting to hear of the battle's outcome any day now.

Julu would be a loss. If the Eastern Han reclaimed that territory, then even his position at Pohai Bay would be disconnected from other land the rebellion had conquered. Of course, there were already a few singular bands—the Shu and Wu—that were greatly separated from the main territory of the rebellion, and they were doing just fine. Their locations surely had some play in that, though, as they were less of a threat to the new capital.

In total, if he disregarded the possible fall of Julu and the loss of life that would come with it, he had almost as many men as the Eastern Han.

Perhaps something smaller than taking the city would be needed without Julu.

An assassination, he thought. *A coup.*

Spies had let him know of General Yuxuan's return to the capital for the Summer Solstice Festival, so if he was correct, that meant the entire royal family would be at the palace. Could it be done?

His spies weren't trained to fight as a group, but what they lacked in that area they made up in numbers.

He thought of calling a messenger boy to give word for his brothers to join him in planning. Zhang Bao would most likely be furious since he was either with some city girl, or he was asleep by now. Zhang Liang was probably awake, reading as he liked to in the evenings.

As he was about to rise from his cushions, a man dressed in black walked out of the night. The general didn't recognize him. He was short and thin, almost too thin. Had he been a famine victim like many of his soldiers? His hair was ragged and worn loose without a top knot. Dark eyes—darker than any he had ever seen—stared out at him.

He carried nothing but a small knife at his belt and a gourd. Noticeably, he was missing the yellow sash that all the soldiers wore.

Guards were stationed nearby. Had they just let this man walk in?

The general rose, glancing at his broadsword he'd left on his dark wooden stand. Could he get to it in time? It was then that he remembered the gifts he'd been given from Laozi. They were still so new that they often didn't come to his mind as a first option.

The man didn't bow, and he walked right into the tent and over the furs that made up the floor.

"Who are you?" the general asked, trying his best to make the words a demand, but his voice shook somewhat. Zhang Bao would've laughed at him were he here, having always lectured him on taking some of the classes that his spies did. For all his gifts and what he was supposed to achieve, he wasn't a very good politician. "You can't be here."

"Oh, but I can," he purred, voice low and oddly soothing.

"Who sent you?"

"I believe you'll find that question is hard to answer. Let's just say I'm a friend."

The man reached for the knife at his belt.

The general closed his eyes, and let senses other than eyesight take over. There was the rustling of canvas, and whistle of wind, a shifting of the man's robes as he reached for the knife. The lanterns brought their heat and light into the dark night, and he could smell the sea, the clean, salt scent, and, even from this distance, hear its waves lapping against the sand or crashing against brown cliffs. He felt his feet against the floor, and pushed his connection out farther, into the grass, the yellow soil, and sand. The sense of the camp rose up around him: horses nickering from where they were hitched to their posts, the creak of leather, men talking, campfires crackling, metal armor being oiled and polished, the tiny pushes of needles through cloth as clothes were mended, the crisp, delicious smell of cooking meats and boiling noodles, men snoring or rolling over on their pallets. Everywhere there was life, energy, and yet, this man seemed different. There was a muted ness about him.

He realized belatedly that his guards were missing.

The general drew in energy from the air around him, from the ground, from the motions of his men going about their night.

When he opened his eyes, he pushed his hands out, releasing heat and light: flames. They were a brilliant blue as they left his hands and shot towards the man who now had his knife in hand and was charging forward.

Somehow, the flames didn't catch on him.

He should've been burning! The horrid smell of burning hair and skin should already be in the air with how hot the general's fire was.

Blackness flared against the flames, even sucked them inwards, as he closed in.

The general gasped, and fell back on the kung fu he'd learned from Laozi, wanting his sword but seeing it was too far away to grasp. He had learned fighting as a boy, but what the legendary figure had created and taught him was superior, something that his muscles understood now.

He let out flurries of kicks and punches that were either blocked or deflected.

The knife—he could see now that it was a skinning knife—slashed at his leg. The general let out a cry. He wanted to fall back, wanted to crouch down and press his hands to the wound, as if holding it, hiding it, would stop it from hurting so, stop it from being real. Hours of training, and the knowledge he'd been gifted within his body and spirit, kept him from doing so. Putting more weight onto his uninjured leg, he struck out with his arms.

As he reached for the man's wrist, planning on disarming him, something strange happened. The man seemed to blur, and next thing the general knew he was right in front of him and a pressure had punched against his throat.

For a moment, his body still came forward as it planned to fight, falling into the attack, practically into the arms of the strange man. This close, the general could see now that his eyes were entirely black with no whites at all. This was no man.

The thing smiled, and pain struck the general somewhat belatedly. Blood was running down the front of his robe and staining his yellow sash he'd tied around his neck.

The knife was in his throat.

He tried to breathe, to perhaps say something, or scream in agony, but he choked. Blood, hot and metallic came up in his mouth.

My brothers. The rebellion ...

The general collapsed as all spiraled away and went dark.

***

The demon caught the general's body as it fell, and they pulled the knife free. Blood spurted onto their clothes and face. They savored its heat and wished they could taste it. They had wished to be the demon to possess him, but sadly, they were not old enough, and there were many who ranked above them. (They had not even been gifted with a name yet.)

They knelt, gently turning the body in their arms so they cradled it, its back to their front.

For now, they dropped their knife, promising to retrieve it later, and grabbed the gourd that was shaking impatiently against their hip.

"Yes, yes, I know," they muttered.

They released the wooden stopper on the gourd, and black smoke flew out, fast, raging. They recognized the eagerness with which the smoke took in the general's body. It began to fill this empty vessel, the general's spirit having fled, continuing its journey to the next life

.

The smoke was gone, all inside of the body now. They released it and watched the new general rise, wounds stitching themselves closed.

They bowed before them, head down and resting in the blood on the floor.

The new general turned about, taking in the tent and the mess that had been made.

"Clean this up," he ordered, the snap in his voice making them bow even lower.

"As you wish."

He went to the low table with the maps and reports. After glancing over some of the papers and scrolls and a copy of the *Dao De Jing*, he said, "And when you've finished, send for my brothers, Zhang Bao and Zhang Liang. We have many plans to discuss."

Longwei

Longwei didn't usually pay attention to his father's attendants, seeing as they were numerous, but the ones that accompanied him in the Hall of Supreme Harmony this night looked a little different. Had he just gotten new attendants and Longwei hadn't noticed? He was contemplating this, somewhat bothered by it, as his father, sitting upon the Dragon Throne, lectured him yet again for supposedly flouting his royal duties. Longwei was kneeling before this massive and beautiful creation that he could only ever see his father upon, having previously had his head and hands pressed to the golden floor in a deep bow. A frown passed over his face as one of the attendants smiled at him. Were they too close to his father, walking past the bronze animals and dragons, closing in on him?

Next thing he knew, a wickedly sharp *jiuhuandao*, serrated teeth glinting in the lantern light, was taken out and slashed straight through his father's neck. Perhaps it was just Longwei's imagination, but he swore he heard the awful scrape of blade against gristle and bone. Blood, dark in its large quantity, spurted as the body fell, staining bright blue robes of elegant silk, marring the mouths of dragons, and the head thumped down the jade steps of the dais, trailing more blood and viscera. The crown with its many jeweled beads clattered against the floor as it fell off his father's still-rolling head. Finally, its roll ended right before Longwei, the dead, lifeless eyes staring up at him, his face still set in tight lines of disapproval. Now that disapproving stare would be forever.

There wasn't time yet for shock to take hold, adrenaline kicking in first. It shot through Longwei's body so strongly he almost felt like he was floating, or perhaps like he was just going to tip over right where he knelt. High from it, skin tingling, Longwei jumped to his feet.

The assassin with the *jiuhuandao* charged at him as the others took out *duandao*—short sabers that they'd had concealed under their bright yellow and black robes. Guards in red armor pulled *changdao* from long sheaths. The large, double-handed swords had a single edge that curved all the way up to a wickedly sharp point. Some of the guards ran to meet the assassins in battle while others surrounded him.

Before some of the guards could meet their foes, they were slain by others in their ranks—more assassins! Rebels, surely.

Longwei eyed the guards surrounding him warily. Were these all men who worked for the Imperial family? There was nothing to distinguish the well-hidden assassins from them, save for who were the ones getting cut down in the surprise attack. It was now that he hated how he was always supposed to be unarmed in the throne room.

One of the men rushed him, the tip of his *changdao* reaching way too close to Longwei before he was able to react. Adrenaline could be good in short bursts, but in a battle it would leave you unwieldy, clouding the mind, and having you forget your training. He'd been told this time and time again in the lessons he'd had since he was a child, and had sparred for possibly hundreds of hours, yet none of his training was coming to him. It was all too easy to depend on nothing but strength with adrenaline coursing madly through your blood. He considered it sheer luck that he was able to dodge the first thrusting attack.

Breathe.

The voice in his mind wasn't his own, but that of the late General Feng, who had taken over his military lessons once he'd gotten older.

Sharp steel glinted in his vision, the assassin making another pass at him.

Longwei tried to gain control of his breaths, to time them with how his body moved, as he'd been taught. Part of his mind surrendered, hours and hours of training taking over. As he moved away from the blade, his stance widened, and he easily slipped within the assassin's guard. He knew many ways to fight without a weapon, but against armed and armored opponents he'd be near-helpless. He managed to knock the assassin down, and claimed the *changdao* for his own.

The assassins didn't seem well-trained as a group, and it was all too easy to duck and swerve and let them take out some of their own. But there were still too many.

One of the surviving guards yelled, "Prince Liu Fei, follow me!"

He responded to his public name, ignoring the guard breaking protocol by not calling him *Your Imperial Highness*, and went to follow him down the hall towards the main doors.

The thick Nanmu wood doors burst open, more guards entering, but there wasn't time to feel any relief because they took out short bows and immediately fired upon Longwei's loyal men.

The guard before him took two arrows to the torso, yet managed to push Longwei towards one of the massive golden pillars that ran along the sides of the room before he collapsed, blood on his lips. Longwei took in the space around him, and assassins from both the north and south ends of the room were trying to get to his position. As he popped his head around the side of the pillar, an arrow *pinged* off of one of the many dragons decorating it. He dodged back, safe behind this pillar for now.

If he could get to the door behind the throne, then perhaps he could get out safely. The halls weren't as wide through there and it'd be easier to take on his enemies one at a time.

Yet he realized this might not be a battle to win. Fleeing was possibly his only choice.

His dark eyes alighted on the body of his father, and for a second shock tried to take hold, to chill him and catch him in the disbelief of the moment. His heart twisted, a deep pang in his chest. For all his father's faults, even as a ruler, he had loved him. There had been no one else to love in such a way.

My brothers.

They were surely in danger too!

Longwei had three brothers, two older than him, but without the Imperial birthmark that would give them the right to rule. That was Longwei's, but not his alone. His younger brother bore the birthmark as well.

Were his brothers safe? Had the assassins gotten to them? They must've. This was well-planned, something that had probably taken months to organize, otherwise the guards and attendants wouldn't be so well infiltrated.

Had they watched him, day after day, learning his every move? They must have. He shuddered to think of his enemies being in the palace with him, of them helping him with bathing, with dressing him, combing his hair. And same with his family.

He had to get to them—his brothers. They had their own training—his oldest brother Yuxuan was one of their greatest generals. And he was here, in the palace, having come home from a campaign in the mountains to celebrate the Summer Solstice.

Longwei's path to the dais became a blur of too many close calls on his life. Guards came to protect him, but were mercilessly killed for their efforts, causing guilt to rise up in him, as choking as the thick stench of blood. Others he only realized were assassins at the last moment, and he killed them right before they could kill him. There were too many close calls; by the time he made it to the steps he'd earned a few cuts along his body for his efforts. Most were superficial, save one that went deep into his right shoulder, making his stolen *changdao* unwieldy.

He climbed the steps, keeping his sword raised as high as he could, but it shook and faltered, not even high enough to protect his head. At the top, he turned and cast around for another weapon he could use.

Yellow flared in the corner of his vision, an arm raising. Longwei ducked, barely missing having his head cut off by a *duandao*. The sword did cut into his topknot, but to his luck, the full swing stuck the blade in the mouth of one of the dragons.

Still, the assassin was close and had a hand free. Rather than trying to retrieve his weapon, he threw out a jab straight for Longwei's throat. Longwei raised his sword, just managing to cut off the fingers coming at him. He could've sworn one bounced off his robe, but he ignored it, dropping his own sword and kicking out at the screaming assassin. He leveraged himself on the *duandao* stuck in the dragon's mouth, and the assassin fell to the floor.

Longwei freed the sword and hid behind the throne just as well-aimed arrows came for him. The ricochet of one caught him in the thigh, and the angle had it go up rather than in. A small mercy. He screamed through gritted teeth, head tossing back and hitting the gold of the throne.

Soreness took hold of his leg, a soreness that also lived in his shoulder, but he had to keep going. Snapping off part of the arrow sent a stab all the way up to his left hip, and he did his best to hold in his scream, but it joined the sounds of men dying around him.

With no time to bandage his injuries with strips of silk that could've been made from his robe, he painstakingly got to his feet, one hand on the back of the throne, the other using the *duandao* as a poor makeshift cane. He took his first limping step, holding in a cry. He took another step, and another. The pain worsened somewhat, but he realized once he got going that he could still walk.

He could do this. He could survive the throne room.

He heard orders shouted by one of the assassins behind him not to let him escape.

Turning to face them, he backed towards the hall behind the throne. Two came at him from either side. Longwei parried their blows and retreated.

With less room, this would make the fighting one-on-one, and the assassins seemed a bit apprehensive to go after him.

A big man in guard armor came up behind them, but Longwei didn't even dare hope that he was one of his men. The guards had seemed to have all been killed, lying dead, too surprised and taken off guard by this attack to get the upper hand. Longwei was sure he was only alive through their valiant efforts and sheer luck. Karma perhaps, a blessing from his previous life.

The big man pushed one of the assassins forward, shoving him into the hall. Longwei wished to dart towards him, to impale this man on his sword, but that would bring him closer to the other assassins.

He didn't take the bait and instead continued backing up. He had to make it to the Imperial quarters, to his brothers. Were they even alive? Were they fighting just like he was? Were they injured? Could he even help them?

Longwei found he could barely breathe with all these questions going through his head. His chest ached, and his wounds speared pain deep into him.

Gods help me.

Longwei did his best to dodge blows as he retreated, and he killed one of the assassins following him.

He got to the end of the hall and sealed the door just as the owner of a *changdao* tried to cut through the thick, strong wood.

After barring the door with a heavy chest that had caused him to let out groans of pain as he moved it, he went on his way. Assassins hadn't seemed to infiltrate this part of the palace—at least not yet—but he left behind the sounds of frustrated men trying to get through the door.

Longwei nearly collapsed as he tried to get to the Imperial quarters, the strain of his injuries too much.

He looked at his shoulder, his bloodied clothes. Cursing, he leaned against a pillar to start creating makeshift bandages out of his ruined robe of midnight blue. His shoulder was difficult, and he had to put in a wad of silk first before tying strips under his armpit. With his thigh, the best he could do was tie around the broken arrow shaft sticking out of him. Part of him wished he could remove it, but he knew he'd lose more blood that way.

Wounds now bandaged, Longwei gritted his teeth and went to find his brothers.

As he neared Yuxuan's quarters, dead men in guard and attendant uniforms littered the golden halls.

There was a dead man pinned to the door with a spear, and Longwei took out the spear, shoving him aside. He had to press against the door to get it open, dead bodies surely blocking the way. Already his shoes were heavily bloodied, and with his injuries he worried that at any minute he was going to slip.

Lanterns lit the expansive room, dead men here and there, and a few who were still alive, but had wounds too grievous to be of any trouble.

Heart seeming to freeze, worried tears already pricking his sinuses and swelling up his throat, Longwei searched for Yuxuan. And he found him, dead on the bed, a *changdao* pinning him to the mattress.

Longwei's world seemed to shatter just a bit more.

"No. No, no, no, no, no."

Dropping his short sword, he got to the bed as fast as he could with his awful limp. He pulled the sword out of Yuxuan, almost throwing up at the sucking sound his older brother's body made as pressure changed. More blood flowed. Longwei held him to his chest, as if maybe he could hold off the pain he felt, the shattering of his heart. Yuxuan's brown eyes seemed to look up at him, pleading for help.

Help hadn't come.

He was ...

"Dead," Longwei panted. His eyes squeezed shut, face screwing up, as if he could ignore the awful scene before him, could ignore the way his brother lay limp in his arms, never again to raise a sword, or to shoot an arrow, or laugh or dance; never again able to help Longwei navigate the difficulties of being heir to the throne. Never again would his brother smile at him.

"Xuan-Xuan," he cried.

He wanted to stay there with his brother, make promises of giving him a funeral of great honor, but there was no time. Yuxuan was dead. What of Da-Fu, and the younger, Jiao-Long?

Fear for their lives had him moving, sobbing through apology after apology to Yuxuan as he left him there, left him amongst dead foes. Sword in hand once more, he searched for the rest of his family.

Similar scenes were found in his brothers' rooms. Da-Fu was dead, partially decapitated. Longwei did throw up then, tears and spit running down his face. Sobbing, retching, he found Jiao-Long.

Longwei's eyes burned at the evil of it. There Jiao-Jiao lay, a boy of just barely sixteen years. Dead.

Longwei collapsed by Jiao-Long's body, wishing he was dead like him, like Xuan-Xuan and Da-Da. Would he then rejoin them in the Heavens? Had they made it to the Heavens? Maybe if ... Maybe Longwei could show them the way, take their hands and join them in death, and lead them to luminous clouds of pure white, towards the Celestial Dragon Tianlong guarding the jade gates and the beauty beyond.

His shaking hand holding the short sword betrayed him, because as much as he wanted to, he couldn't do it.

With a cry, he tossed the sword aside.

No, he had to live.

He was the last one left of his line, the only survivor with the dragon birthmark.

I have to get out of the palace.

Longwei realized he'd have to disguise himself. Getting to the attendants' quarters unseen was surprisingly easy, but changing clothes became the difficult task. He'd have to rip off the bandage he'd so painstakingly tied around his shoulder, and what if he got blood on these other clothes? Would someone notice? Would the assassins find him?

Hurriedly, he slid open the doors to one of the closets and found neat cotton robes and even sturdy shoes he could switch out with his bejeweled and bloodied ones. Longwei saved his shoes for last, deciding to first take off the bandage. Already blood had seeped through it, and it was sticky as he undid it, and he pulled out the wad he'd shoved into the wound.

Nausea curled in his stomach, and he grew hot and light-headed, his entire body breaking out in a sweat. He cursed as he almost fell and had to brace himself against the light-colored wood of the frame of the closet. Blood gushed out, and his eyelids fluttered.

Can't pass out. I cannot pass out. I mustn't.

Longwei tried to pull himself together, and decided for now that if he sat it was okay. The assassins didn't know where he was (but what if they were on their way here?). He was safe for now.

As safe as one could be in a palace with assassins hunting them down and bleeding from two serious wounds.

Longwei untied the sash on his outer robe and tried to pull it off of himself. The world seemed to go in and out as he pulled his right arm out of the sleeve. He decided undressing further was too much, and possibly too dangerous for his wound, so he left it at that. Hot breaths puffing in and out of him, stomach fighting its very existence, Longwei did his best to staunch some of the bleeding, holding his robe against the wound before re-bandaging it.

Once he was done with that task he could breathe a little better ... until he saw the wooden shaft sticking out of his thigh.

He'd never been injured this seriously before. The most he'd gotten from training were bruises, sprains, and fractures, some nicks and cuts as well, but nothing that was this incapacitating. Or nearly this painful. Longwei decided he'd rather break a rib again, or have his back muscles get so inflamed his shoulder blade got stuck in them. Yes, that'd be easier to deal with. Less painful.

Breathing deeply, he pushed himself to his feet. He chose a dark robe and shoes for himself, hoping the color would hide any blood. He found it shameful how many times he almost collapsed pulling on the robe and changing his shoes, but finally he had the sash tied around his robe and he was ready to go. He wondered if he could perhaps liberate a staff of some sort from someone.

No, that'd take too much time.

But can I even walk? And where do I go?

Longwei figured he had a few options, the most obvious being leaving the palace through the southern gate and hiding out in the city. But that wasn't far enough from danger, and if he remained in the capital, the manhunt that would ensue would surely end shortly. And he'd live under rebel rule. That wasn't precisely what he wanted, though before this night, he had harbored sympathies for them.

Now, he wasn't sure.

His father had been a cruel ruler, too secure in his position and lacking compassion for his suffering people.

But he was dead. His brothers were dead.

The rebels had killed them.

Red nearly seared his vision, and he had to stop himself with these thoughts, this anger that was boiling from somewhere deep inside him, coalescing in all his veins till he would become nothing else.

He could escape by the river, flee west to the old capital. If he took the western gate, he could get to the docks. He knew if this was more than just a coup that the gates could already be overrun, all those leaving the capital being checked, but he had to try somehow. Longwei refused to let this dynasty end, to let himself fail, to lose what little honor he he ld.

As he made to leave the quarters, he caught a look at himself in the mirror. His heart faltered as he saw the ornament adorning his half-up top knot: gold dragons, heads up to the Heavens, mouths open as if ready to roar, secured by a fine gilded pin, sharp enough to draw blood. The ornament of the crown prince, passed down through dynasties before his, centuries old.

It was a sure giveaway. Anyone who looked upon it would know his identity. Heart heavy, throat seeming to swell, eyes almost blurring with tears, he removed the gold from his hair. Longwei hid the ornament in the quarters, in a place he told himself he'd remember, a place he'd come back to. If he came back.

I must.

The palace would have to be reclaimed for this, for his brothers. For his people. Maybe even for the rebels as well.

Longwei turned from the chest he'd hidden it in and limped out of the quarters, ready to make his way to the docks.

He fiddled with his hair as he limped, even as he was on the lookout for more assassins. He realized even his hair made it clear he'd been in a fight, and could give him away. He untied the blue ribbon he'd chosen for that day, letting the ruined top knot cascade down his back. Or, more to his shoulders. This way it looked rowdy and unkempt.

Perfect.

Longwei stuck to the shadows, and kept his head down as he passed others. He clutched his borrowed robe, making sure to hide the arrow in his thigh, the blood that was still trickling down his pant leg, making it stick to his skin.

Somehow, he made it to the docks, to a boat, and as he lay in a hammock, swaying gently as the boat departed, he let his tears flow.

Lixin

After two days on the river, smoke rising from the city, Longwei reached the old capital. By that time he had another name to go by: Lixin. He hoped he would remember it.

Though, he couldn't remember much. He was weak and shivery, wracked with a fever, and he swayed with each limping step.

He had the vague thought of needing a healer, but wasn't sure how to find one.

Soon, thoughts of finding one fled as he found himself collapsed outside a stone building not far from the docks, not even inside the city walls. The whole place smelled of fish. But he was sure he smelled worse. If he turned his head over his right shoulder there was the clear stench of infection. His leg probably smelled the same. It was all swollen, the arrow still in his thigh. He wondered how hard it would be for it to get taken out at this point since everything around it was swollen.

Longwei—no, no, Lixin—wondered if perhaps he should just die. The rebels surely held the palace, and maybe they'd do better than his father. Why wouldn't they? They'd formed because they were sick of famine, sick of not receiving any help for the flooding that had ruined their crops. His father just … hadn't cared.

I can do better. I have to.

Long—Lixin tried to stand, reinvigorated by his resolve. The world seemed to fade out, his body not even real anymore. His vision went black. There was a loud noise, like someone dropping something heavy on the hard-packed dirt. Before he could figure out what that was and what had happened, he knew no more.

***

Voices faded in and out, a smoky sky no longer above him, but a rough, tiled roof. His eyes didn't want to stay open, his body wanting to sleep and sleep. And perhaps die.

"What's your name?" an old voice croaked; a woman's voice.

"L-Lixin." He wasn't sure how he got the name out. Was that his name? It didn't sound right.

***

"Do you know what this means?"

"Ignore it."

"But—"

"It means if we don't work quickly, we'll be letting the crown prince die."

***

There was a fierce stinging in his shoulder, and Lixin wanted to yell, to feel at what was doing this to him, but he could barely move. Wetness was on his forehead, a cloth, cold water, perhaps.

With his eyes cracked open a sliver, he saw he was in a room dimly lit by a couple of lanterns, and it had rough stone walls and wood floors, and screens with rents and tears in them. A closed window with colored window-paper was directly to his left, with no light peeking through, so it must have been night. A door. There was a door to his right, on the far end of the room. If he …

He still couldn't move, and already sleep was dragging him back down.

Lixin—what was so odd about that name?—shivered, and the darkness took him again.

***

"Hold him down."

Those words couldn't be good.

There was a body resting on his upper half, thankfully avoiding the fire in his shoulder. But still—

A jolt of pressure was the only warning he got before something was ripped out of his thigh.

Lixin came to his senses enough to scream. Fire shot through him from his hip almost to his knee. There was liquid heat gushing against his skin, and pressure was applied where he hurt the most, making him scream louder.

"Keep him quiet, Bo!" that old woman cried.

"Apologies, Your Imperial Majesty," a timid, yet smooth and kind, man's voice said, and then a hand was covering his mouth.

"Bo, you know better than to call him that."

Lixin wanted to agree for some reason he couldn't remember, but he couldn't speak, could only let out muffled and struggling sounds of pain. Oh, dear heavenly immortals, it hurt so much he almost wanted his leg to be disconnected from him somehow.

There were some clucks of disappointment, and through sweat and tears, he saw an arrow shaft get held up by a thin, gnarled hand; a hand that was surely strong, because the other one was still pressing against his thigh like a rod of iron.

"This one splintered. The inflammation really held onto it. I'm going to have to get in there and look at it."

Lixin did *not* like the sound of that one bit. He tried to struggle, but found that he was weak, his body aching, and stars sparked in his vision.

"What should we do for the pain, Yīshī Chao?" Bo asked.

Ah, so Lixin was with a healer. Someone must have found him.

Before he could panic about some of what he'd heard, and what he knew must have happened, that people knew who he was, he was lost to the pain again. Sparks exploded in his vision. He struggled against Bo's hand over his mouth, feeling like he was going to puke.

Lixin did his best not to listen as they continued speaking, not really wanting to know what they were going to do to him; he already felt so sick.

"Aiya! Bo, are you paying attention to him? He's going green! Get a cold cloth for the back of his neck."

The hand left his mouth, and he was breathing in ragged, shallow bursts. He opened his eyes all the way, even as he wished he could fall back into that darkness that had taken him. There was a diminutive man in a green robe, long hair surely pinned up under the round black hat he was wearing, and Lixin only saw his back as he went to a wash stand and basin. Directly before him, by his thigh, was an old woman in brown, long white hair held in thick loops away from her face. There was a kindness to her eyes and dark, wrinkled skin, but a strength there as well. So this was Yīshī Chao.

"Deep breaths, child."

Lixin ignored the *child* comment and tried to do as he was told. Yīshī Chao went through the breaths with him, demonstrating that he had to breathe out through his mouth. Bo came back with a wet washcloth, and gently lifted his head from the pillow, moving his sweaty and oily hair aside and putting it to the back of his neck. Head resting back down, Lixin felt better almost immediately. Well, he was still in pain, but he no longer felt like he was going to be sick.

"Are you finally with us?" Yīshī Chao asked.

Lixin licked dry, cracked lips, and answered haltingly with a dry mouth and throat, "Yes. I think so."

"Someone found you and brought you to us. We took care of your shoulder, and applied medicines for the infection. Your thigh, however ..." She shook her head in disapproval, as if this was somehow his fault. "There are splinters left in from the arrow. I will have to operate."

Lixin frowned at her. "And you know how to do that?"

"Bah, just because I'm not some doctor for the royal family doesn't mean I don't know what I'm doing. I've been practicing medicine longer than you've been alive, boy!"

If he could, he would bow to her in apology. Shame colored his cheeks red.

"Bo," she ordered, "get him a cup of *ma-fei-san*, and quick!"

Bo left the room, closing the sliding door behind him. Well, at least he would be unconscious for surgery, he supposed. Lixin had heard tell of barbaric surgeries done by the peasants of his realm, but perhaps that had just been Da-Fu trying to mess with him.

His heart twisted at the thought of his brother, and things started to come back to him. Lixin cried, and he let Yīshī Chao think it was from pain.

When Bo returned with the awful smelling drink, he was all too glad to swallow it down.

Resting his head back, Lixin waited to fade out again, and part of him hoped he wouldn't wake up.

***

"Where—Where am I?" Lixin asked. The words were difficult to get out. His mouth was dry and had a terrible taste in it, and he felt like it'd been stuffed with cotton. His eyelids were heavy, and at the moment, he really didn't want to open them.

But then panic took him.

What if he was still in the palace, with the assassins?

I have to run.

Lixin tried sitting up even before opening his eyes, and it wasn't till he had his right leg off the bed, skin bare, that someone came to stop him.

He wanted to scream, to fight. He tried to push them back in one of the many ways he'd been trained, but he was weak. So weak.

Too weak to save his father, his family …

"Please, lie back," a slightly familiar voice said to him.

Hands pushed at his collarbones, and Lixin was ashamed to hear himself whimper.

Before he knew it, he was lying back on the bed, chest heaving as his breaths puffed in and out of him, barely granting him the air to breathe.

"Yīshī Chao!" the voice called—a man's voice. "He's awake."

Things still didn't seem to make too much sense, and he wasn't sure how he wasn't in the palace. But he vaguely remembered stolen clothes, a boat, an old woman.

That very same old woman entered the room through a sliding screen door.

"You like to sleep," she commented.

Lixin frowned, still trying to figure out everything that was going on and how he wasn't dead.

I'm supposed to be dead.

His breathing seemed to even as he looked upon her face, as he looked at the man whose hands were now leaving him.

Bo. Right.

Trying to get his thoughts together, he was speechless as Yīshī Chao went on to explain how the surgery had gone. Some of his recovery had been explained to him as well, but he was a bit lost.

Or perhaps very lost.

He realized he was in white cotton under robes that were keeping him warm, and that these robes didn't belong to him. Much of him seemed bare, and he had a sinking feeling that he'd been recognized. Mind still too addled to play back any half-heard conversations, he just gazed at them questioningly. They knew. They had to know. If word of the rebellion seizing the palace reached the old capital, would these two people turn him in? How many others knew? Surely they'd seen his birthmark.

"You're quiet," Yīshī Chao observed. "And you look like you're straining. Don't think too hard. The *ma-fei-san* takes some time to wear off."

Finally, feeling as though he was able to form words, he said, "You know."

A white eyebrow raised, just as Bo (who seemed not as wise as Yīshī Chao but perhaps was on his way there) said, "Know what?"

"My name isn't Lixin," was all he could get out. Longwei. Liu Fei. Crown prince.

Yīshī Chao nodded, but didn't push, didn't even ask him anything about what had happened. While wondering if she simply didn't care about news from the capital, he also was thankful. That night … Lixin wasn't ready to relive it.

"How are you feeling?" Bo asked.

Lixin tried to take stock of his body, but much of it didn't feel real. Somehow he felt like he was floating even while sinking through hot sand. His body wasn't made of flesh and blood, but cotton and exhaustion.

"I'm … not sure."

"Bo, ask him these questions when he's more awake," Yīshī Chao chided.

Lixin tried to rest as feeling and understanding came back to his body. His shoulder hurt, and emanating from it was a clean scent, but also that of pungent herbs. He wondered if his thigh would smell the same way. He remembered infection. Yīshī Chao must have cut out what she could.

A grimace crossed his face at the thought.

Right now his thigh just seemed swollen, awkward against his other leg with thick bandages around it.

Bo opened a window, and early morning light streamed in, some dust motes dancing about in its rays.

Yīshī Chao left to make him some tea, and Bo knelt by the bed he was on.

"What happened at the palace?" he asked. "There's been some news: smoke, people fleeing, but I have been stuck in here, helping you. Perhaps—"

"I don't want to talk about it," Lixin interrupted.

Unbidden, flashes of that night came to him. His father's decapitated head before him, the blood, the lifeless eyes. His brothers, slain in their quarters.

There was so much blood, and he wondered at the pain they had felt. How much had it hurt for them to die? Had they died quickly? Slowly? What were their last thoughts? Did they have regrets, things they had still wished to do? Had they thought of him?

And how were their spirits? Would they reach the Heavens without a proper burial? What had the rebels done to their bodies? Did they desecrate them? Burn them? Put their heads on pikes outside the palace gates?

His country had already slipped through his fingers, and here he lay, in a bed, too injured to be of any use.

Lixin's throat ached fiercely, and it ached even more at having to go by a different name. He wanted to proudly say who he was, wanted to honor his family with his name. If he were stronger he'd climb the steps of the old palace and announce his presence as Prince Liu Fei. He'd tell of the horrors he'd seen, and he'd gather troops to retake his home.

But here he was, just Lixin, no one left alive to even call him by his personal name of Longwei. Perhaps he'd never hear it on another's lips ever again.

As Yīshī Chao came in with the tea, Bo helped him sit up.

The tea was sharp and unfamiliar, but as he continued to sip at it and evade Bo's questions, the growing pain in his thigh started to fade again. Yīshī Chao had sliced it open on the outer side and taken out splinters, infection, anything that might not heal on its own and could spread to his blood. If he lived long enough for it to heal, he figured he'd have a strange, sunken scar for the rest of his life. At least Lixin no longer felt feverish.

His awareness was coming back to him, the effects of the *ma-fei-san* fading.

Yīshī Chao tended to patients in other rooms, and as he realized other people were in this building, he tensed. Did they all know? Or had Yīshī Chao and Bo been the only ones to see his birthmark?

After they got him walking around, testing that he still could, and unfortunately testing that he could urinate just fine, it was announced that Lixin would be staying with Bo. He was surprised they weren't just going to turn him out onto the street; it was dangerous harboring him, surely.

He expressed these concerns, and Yīshī Chao's lips thinned. "Are you mad?" she asked him.

"Excuse me?" He was *not* used to being addressed like this, but he would be hard-pressed to demand the respect his station owed him, especially since it would give him away.

"You want to go back out there and ruin my work? I fixed you up, I saved you. I will not have you acting a fool and getting hurt again."

"But—"

"Yes, I know who you are. No, I do not wish to know what happened. You will be safe with Bo." Then she turned on the other man, and said, "And you, you must learn to keep quiet, eh? I do not want to hear any rumors spreading about a royal heir being in our midst. Keep him safe, or I'll have you here working every night till healing is all you live and breathe. Understood?"

Bo bowed to Yīshī Chao in understanding, and Lixin just gave them a skeptical look. How was this going to end well, especially when he would have to escape their care? Not just to keep them safe, but to take back the palace.

Longwei, Imperial prince of China, and heir to the Dragon Throne, bowed his head, the best he could do while in bed. He appreciated their care, but he would not be able to stay long.

***

Healing was taking longer than Lixin expected. He had to wait almost a full week before he was allowed to walk around unassisted by Bo. His current assistance was a bamboo cane, and he despised it. Despised the weight of it, despised each *clack* as it touched the floor or the ground.

He'd walk in circles in the small enclosed courtyard of Bo's humble home, over and over again till he grew dizzy, trying to strengthen his leg. Always, he nearly collapsed after five laps, his leg too weak and hurting too much, the cane too much for his shoulder he was trying to strengthen as well.

At one point he tore his stitches and Bo sent him back to Yīshī Chao. While Bo brewed medicinal tea for the pain, Yīshī Chao glared at him, her gaze so strong she didn't need to say a word. Each glare was like a strike of bamboo against his back.

And all the while rebels had started pouring into the city; they'd taken the outer walls. Perhaps many just wanted to live peacefully, but the rebellion violence was still in them, violence against his dead father's rule, against any soldiers that might try to rise up and fight out of loyalty.

He heard they were looking for him, but Bo, despite his earlier slip-ups, was keeping him safe. Both of them had somewhat adjusted to the name of Lixin, not to have the bowing and respect his station demanded. Yet he wasn't safe, not in his current condition, and not with the soldiers of the rebellion in the city. From what he'd heard, they'd thoroughly searched the northern half and had started on the southern towards the west. Lixin still had time, time to escape or to fully become Lixin, hide under this new identity.

Well, he'd thought he had time …

For some insufferable reason, even though Lixin was allowed plenty of rest, after a certain point in his healing he still wasn't allowed to be in Bo's home alone. He figured it was something to do with Yīshī Chao and his healing (and his leg in particular); he could even picture a lecture with a pointing finger that he was too dangerous to himself and idiotic to be left alone, which was quite insulting. For the times Bo had to go to the inner city to purchase food or sent on errands for collecting herbs, Lixin was usually dumped back in the old woman's care and too-watchful eyes for an hour or two.

However, as he found the cane easier to use, and as his shoulder no longer needed packing, Bo and Yīshī Chao began to get many questions about him and why he wasn't out and about. Why could this tall and stately stranger not be found striding about the markets? (Or perhaps hobbling.) What was his name? Where was he from? How did he get hurt?

Most questions Yīshī Chao waved away with her innate stubbornness, but his presence still began to grow in the minds of the citizens, if only in this small corner of the city.

On one of the days when Lixin was being brought to Yīshī Chao, a rebel soldier arrived before Bo could leave. The man was short, but wide and well-built. Rather than wearing a cap as many citizens chose to within the city, he had a yellow sash tied about his head, directly marking who he was and what he stood for. The rebel took stock of all those in the front room with a solid gaze before Lixin could be hurried into the back room, or even a closet of some sort.

Lixin figured that he himself was still in shock from the coup at the palace, so his reactions were slow and muted. Still, he was sure the soldier had noticed the slight widening of his eyes, the stiffness to his awkward stance, the white-knuckled grip on his cane.

"I require every man in this room to disrobe," he said in a rumbling voice, his piercing eyes surveying those of the other male patients of Yīshī Chao's, and Bo as well.

Before Lixin could say anything, or possibly think about running or fighting, Yīshī Chao stepped forward, arms crossed and chin lifted. She was a short woman, but clearly not one to be trifled with. Bo stood beside her, but maybe a few steps behind, clearly not used to taking charge. He wrung his hands, and Lixin swore he could feel the mental struggle of Bo trying not to look at him. Meanwhile, Yīshī Chao ignored him completely, her mental faculties quite strong.

"And why should they be asked to do such a disgraceful thing?" she asked.

"I presume you're the healer?"

"And I presume you're a trouble-maker. I respect your wishes and those of the rebellion, but I don't take kindly to someone giving orders in my hospital."

The man put a hand on his sword hilt. Lixin's grip on his cane somehow tightened even more, so much so that he was surprised no one heard his knuckles cracking or the bamboo creaking in protest.

"I'm following strict orders for the rebellion. If you want to help us, step aside, and let these men disrobe."

"What are you looking for?"

The rebel's brows drew low. "I don't see how that's any of your business."

"They're my patients. It *is* my business. And I suggest you leave, unless there is some healing you require."

Lixin idly thought that if he was well enough, he could make this man need healing.

The rebel gave them a grim smile, showing his teeth a bit, more of a warning than anything. He drew his sword from the sheath, about an inch, more of a threat than before.

Lixin felt sweat beading on his brow.

What was he to do? Surely he'd be killed if he was found out to actually be Liu Fei, crown prince of the Empire. But he couldn't put these people in danger. They were his subjects, whether they acted like them or not. Even Yīshī Chao was, her sympathies for the rebellion meaning nothing while he was still alive. The Dragon Throne would not remain in the hands of the rebels. Perhaps …

No, capture could be too dangerous. Surrounded by enemies, how was he expected to take back his country? His only allies were an old woman and an anxious, but well-meaning, man.

Lixin sighed. He knew what to do to protect these people. He would not let them take injury or die for him.

Jaw clenched, teeth nearly grinding, Lixin hobbled forward, cane *clack*ing against the floor.

Yīshī Chao put out an arm before him but did not turn to look at him.

"Leave," she commanded the rebel.

The rebel now eyed Lixin, and Lixin returned his gaze, even as his heart beat like a wild bird trapped in a cage, his blood thrumming through him.

Breathing heavy, he loosened his robes, and then revealed his collarbone and right beneath it. There lay the dragon birthmark in red on his skin.

"Foolish child," Yīshī Chao muttered, head lowering.

Bo gasped.

The rebel's eyes widened, and he drew his sword.

Lixin—no, for he was now Longwei once more, or perhaps Liu Fei as he was known to his people. His royal name.

Liu Fei stepped before Yīshī Chao, the whole affair a clumsy business as he tried to move her arm to get around her. Their eyes locked, and he thought he saw a deep compassion in hers, and maybe the starting wetness of tears. He bowed his head slightly: apology and thanks for her care. Lip trembling, she did something completely unexpected: she got to her knees before him and bowed with her head touching the floor. Liu Fei's breath was stolen from him, and he eyed the rebel again, wondering what punishment this brave and fierce woman would receive for her actions.

The rebel growled, "How dare you bow before this filth! Do you know what his family has done to this country? In the north, parents starve to death while they give what little food they have to their children. Homes are destroyed in floods. And what have they done? Nothing! *Nothing!*"

Yīshī Chao lifted her head, fire in her eyes as she said, "He is the rightful Emperor, whether we wish it or not. We cannot change the flow of the workings around us, only heal what we must." This last part felt like it was for Liu Fei as much as the rebel. Yes, there was a lot to heal, too much. Could it be done?

"And yet you claim to believe in the rebellion?" As the rebel soldier said this, his grip tightened on his sword, face reddening, nostrils flaring.

"I believe in your message, *not* your methods. And ... I believe in him, His Royal Highness."

The rebel let out an angered cry, and Liu Fei tried to get in front of him as he saw him rushing towards Yīshī Chao, who was still upon the floor. The rebel shoved him aside, and even gripping and tearing at his clothes didn't work. Liu Fei fell hard, bruising his tailbone with a bright flash of pain so deep he didn't know how to respond to it. *Ignore it, ignore it. For them, you must.* He couldn't breathe, his heart in his throat, as this scene played out before him. He was on the floor, helpless, only an observer. Nothing. Liu Fei was nothing, even as he tried to lunge forward—

—while the sword came down on Yīshī Chao's neck.

Blood spurted and got everywhere as her body and head fell. It splashed upon Liu Fei, upon Bo. Bo, who was getting sick, and then crying, rushing to her corpse, her head, and trying to put her back together again. All Liu Fei could do was try and swallow back his t ears.

As Liu Fei struggled to his feet, his cane snapped with the effort, making him stumble and slip in the hot blood that belonged inside a living body, not all over the floor. He cried out, "How dare you!"

The rebel grabbed him by the collar of his robes, cleaning his sword off on the stained green before sheathing it. Liu Fei tried to fight him, and this earned him a hand around his throat, thumb pressing in so hard he worried something in him would give and that he would die.

The rebel was filled with a righteous hate and anger.

"You're coming with me, filth."

He was thrown down, and then his hands were tied behind his back with a silk cord, the knots so tight he was already losing circulation, hands tingling.

Liu Fei tried to hold in his tears, his hatred, his grief, his *disgust*.

"I'm so sorry," he mumbled to Bo.

And Bo, that peaceful, loving soul, looked upon him with hatred.

Liu Fei turned his gaze from him, even as he thought perhaps he deserved that hate.

"I'm sorry," he said again as the soldier grabbed him and forced him from the hospital.

The rebel had to drag him somewhat, as his thigh was still unusable, but Liu Fei didn't fight him anymore. What was the point? The people who had cared for him had paid the price, and that price was far from deserved. They deserved high honors and nothing less than that. But how could you truly honor someone who had been killed because of you? And perhaps there was no honor left in Liu Fei.

Liu Fei

Liu Fei was thrown into a sturdy cart drawn by two mules, with no care for his injuries. He clenched his jaw, teeth grinding, as he tried to hold in pained cries. His hands were re-tied with rough rope, rope that soon covered his ankles in sinuous knots. One length of it was secured to the cart, another was left for a guard to attach to his belt. Along with this menacing and large man who wore a sleeveless vest of some sort—the better to show off his bulging arm muscles—two guards with spears and *duandao* at their hips were placed behind the cart, to watch him the entire journey to the river. As the complement of men readied to set out, blood began to color Liu Fei's pants a deep maroon; clearly some of his stitches had torn.

***

The journey to the river was arduous. They often went off the road to avoid travelers or take short cuts, and the ride was bumpy. They rode and marched fast, surely trying to get him to Zhang Jue, their leader, as quickly as possible.

It rained for half of one day. They did not stop to make camp.

Soon Liu Fei's clothes were soaked, and he was shivering, muscles tensing and clenching in ways that made him more aware of his cuts and bruises. His thigh bled for a whole day before one of the rebels noticed and they wrapped it so tight he couldn't feel the rest of his leg. He wondered if it would've been better to just let him bleed.

He was in and out of consciousness, yet found the one night they did stop sleepless. All he saw were rolling heads: his father's, Yīshī Chao's. Would those images ever leave? Was he to be splattered in blood his entire life?

Liu Fei wasn't sure what the worst part of this journey was. The rough treatment? The jeers? The shivering and cold and aching? And he was hungry. All he'd gotten to eat was part of a steamed bun one of the rebels had already bitten into.

Perhaps the worst was when he had to be untied and watched by a guard as he urinated or defecated. There wasn't much of either, especially since he was only given water sparingly.

By the time Liu Fei was hauled onto a ship run by a captain and deckhands with yellow turbans, he wasn't sure what was real anymore. He was tossed into a small room below deck, and then darkness closed in on him.

***

Yuxuan, Da-Fu, Jiao-Long. Dead. They were all dead. Even his father who he'd often quarreled with. Liu Fei wasn't just the inheritor of a broken empire, but of a family dead and gone. His mother had died while giving birth to sweet Jiao-Jiao, and he had no partner to call his own. At court, friends had been fleeting. Either they used him, or he found himself wanting more than he was allowed. More freedom, more fun. Just *more*. More *life*!

And here he was in a small, dark cabin, alone and aching and ill and yearning. His life before had been far from perfect and quite lonely now that he thought of it, but at least he could walk the halls of his palace, his home, and know he was safe. At least he could laugh with his brothers.

Liu Fei wasn't sure when he started screaming, but he couldn't stop.

Over and over he saw his brothers' dead bodies, and it was as if knives were plunged into his chest until he was a bloody mess.

He was struggling against his bonds, skin breaking and tearing against the rough rope, and he was losing circulation. Still he screamed, and still he fought. He wanted to beat his fists bloody against the walls to show his loss. It was the least he could do. There was nothing now, no way to show his broken love.

Face wet with tears, Liu Fei screamed till his throat ached, till rebels kicked at his door and yelled for him to shut up, till he thought maybe he'd screamed enough for his brothers up in the Heavens to hear him. For *someone* to hear him, to help him, to cure him of this pain.

Yet even as he pleaded for something, possibly for death, it felt like the knives digging into him were trying to tear out his heart. The dead bodies of those he loved cracked his ribs, exposed him, and finally found his broken and bleeding heart.

He sobbed with a tortured voice, pounding his body against the deck, waiting for the torment to end.

His capture had brought this all down on him, while his time with Yīshī Chao (oh, Yīshī Chao) and Bo had pushed it away.

Now he was drowning, and he couldn't breathe. Feeling as if his heart would burst, Liu Fei blessedly lost consciousness.

***

He came to again in that dark and terrible hole.

"Let me go," he murmured, voice cracking. "Please."

The rebels didn't hear him, and even if they did, they would do nothing for him. His father's face was the pure essence of his family's failure. They had hated his father, surely still did even now that he was dead. And they hated him. Liu Fei hated himself too …

… For how he'd failed his family. His country. Now he was just a weak, hobbled man tied up in the deep unpleasantness of a ship wishing for death. He wasn't sure anything of the prince remained.

Did he deserve his name? Did he deserve any name?

Perhaps I'm just nothing, no one.

Liu Fei realized perhaps it'd just be better to be nobody at all.

Yet he wasn't. He had the dragon birthmark, the mark of the true Imperial heir, and that meant something, even if he didn't want it to.

Agonized years seemed to pass down there in that dark cabin.

When they pulled Liu Fei out, he could barely stand despite them untying his ankles and loosening the rough bandage on his leg, and he wasn't sure if he actually had working legs or feet anymore. His arms ached, even his shoulders and wrists, though he couldn't feel much of his hands. Maybe one of his pointer fingers still had sensation?

The rebel with the giant arms on display held him up. He was shoved towards the edge of the boat, and the sight Liu Fei beheld was a grand one.

To the east he saw his home. Lanterns were being lit in the waning light of day, the sky painted in magnificent hues of orange and yellow, like a ripe peach filled with splendor and ready to be bitten into. The lanterns and sunset created a soft glow on the ceramic tiles of each roof. He thought he saw people milling about in the streets, living their lives, albeit differently now with the rebels in control. Perhaps up close he'd see the tense set of their bodies. What worries plagued them? What did they go home to? Where did they find comfort at night? With whom? And what did they think of the rebels lining the streets? The fighting had ended so quickly. Now it almost seemed like the rebels had always been there.

To the north was the palace, a great structure of red and gold with many pillars and arching roofs. It grew into the sky, above the city, something that could not be touched, or shouldn't have been before all this. The gold tiles were set afire in the blaze of the dying sun, and it seemed to call to Liu Fei. Home.

Much closer were the docks, merchant ships, and fishing boats lining the well-built wooden structures. Most had already laid anchor, the gangplanks being drawn in by those staying aboard the ships. Others were surely making their way off to inns or other places to stay the night.

There were soldiers to greet them as they laid out the gangplank. Liu Fei almost fell into the water, and he nearly wished he had, so perhaps he could sink to the bottom, never to rise again. He even imagined the sight, looking up, seeing gold flash across the sky, mingling with the lapping of the blue waters. If anything, it'd perhaps be more peaceful than the end he was sure Zhang Jue had planned for him. His stomach clenched at the thought, and it didn't unclench.

He stumbled, hoping to delay somewhat, imagining knives and hot pokers and poles of bamboo and a sword slowly cutting off his head.

"Move," the rebel behind him commanded, giving him a rough push. Liu Fei started moving in a dragging limp to catch himself, and then he had to keep going.

They made their way to the palace, Liu Fei having to be dragged and shoved almost the entire time. The rebels glared at anyone who had the lack of sense to gawk at this.

Liu Fei didn't look at them, too ashamed. Would they recognize him? Did they hate him too? Had he failed everyone?

Finally, he was brought to the throne room before Zhang Jue, the leader of the rebellion.

Zhang Jue was tall, muscular, and his yellow turban hung around his neck, letting his long hair hang loose, part of it up in a top knot though he was surely old enough to have all his hair up. Where he was clean and well-kept with a long, shining beard, Liu Fei was a mess, soaked in blood and tears and sweat, his hair ragged and oily about his head. Behind Zhang Jue was the Dragon Throne, cleaned of blood, of death, waiting for its rightful r uler.

Surely Zhang Jue had been sitting in it.

"This is him?" Zhang Jue asked in a deep, rumbling voice, descending the dais with his hands clasped behind his back. He wore all black, as if inviting darkness upon him, while his position showed he had brushed it all aside. He was the leader here.

Two ornamented chairs had been erected amongst the golden animals beside the throne, and there Liu Fei saw the leader's brothers, Zhang Bao and Zhang Liang. If he remembered correctly, Zhang Liang, the one who would be at Zhang Jue's left, was the youngest. He squirmed in his seat, something clearly bothering him. The other just watched with a quiet satisfaction, fingers steepled above his lap.

As answer to the rebel leader's question, Liu Fei's robes were torn, even as he strained against such behavior. The birthmark below his collarbone was shown. Zhang Jue came close, appraising it.

A slow smile spread across his face. Something was wrong about it. It wasn't quite human. Liu Fei almost thought it looked like someone pretending to know what smiling looked like, having never done it for themselves before. His stomach dropped to his feet, his legs shaking.

When their dark eyes met, Liu Fei wasn't sure what it was he saw in them. Zhang Jue's seemed … inhuman somehow.

"So, this is the crown prince who has caused all this trouble," Zhang Jue drawled, standing straight, not even nodding his head in deep respect. There was none to be found. "You look terrible."

Liu Fei found it in him to frown.

"No thanks to your men."

"Ah. I would apologize, but … there is work to be done. You would not believe how difficult it is running a country."

That last comment bit deep. It was true. Liu Fei did not know those responsibilities, having always pushed them onto his older brothers while he planned parties or galavanted about the city or explored the mountains and valleys.

But he could change. He could *try*, and he wanted to try. This was his country, wasn't it? It was his responsibility now, and even as that terrified him so much he almost wanted to be back in that wretched, dark ship's cabin, he knew it had to be done. Not just for his honor, but for the honor and well-being of China.

Zhang Jue started pacing. "Now, we have some matters to settle. Some of your family's court survived, including several advisors. They have already bowed down to me. What I need is *you*."

He stopped, staring, clearly wanting Liu Fei to respond.

"Why?" he ground out, wanting to bite his tongue, not wanting to play this conqueror's games.

"My soldiers are coming down from the mountains, others mounting from Pohai Bay—" Liu Fei frowned, aware of how much land these rebels had conquered "—and I no longer want a protracted war. As of now, I have over 350,000 men at my call. My sources say we're almost evenly matched. I don't wish for the destruction of my people or of lands and cities. I want a peaceful transition."

"Oh, is that all?" Liu Fei asked, starting to think of where this was going, even as he had to be held up by two men, and was greatly wishing to sink to the floor. And how he'd said *my people*. How dare he! These weren't his people! He had taken this land, this palace. They were Liu Fei's people. He had to fix this.

Somehow, someway ...

There had to be a way.

Zhang Jue signaled some staff, and they left through a side door that still bore the marks of the coup. Liu Fei swallowed roughly, not wanting to remember any of it: the death, the screaming, the blood, the tears. He'd learned the hard way what it sounded like when a man was stabbed, when a long sword was pulled from his body, the sucking sound of it.

He wondered how Yuxuan had done it, how he'd been able to go through battles, face that death and destruction, and come home and still have a smile for him.

He would smile no more.

An administrator came in, bearing a scroll of thick, creamy paper. He handed it to Zhang Jue, and had a brush and ink ready.

Zhang Jue unrolled the scroll, showing it to him.

It was easy to tell what this was. The neat characters detailed Liu Fei's abdication, and all he would have to do was sign.

Perhaps he should do it. This would stop the army that was making its way to the capital, stop the destruction, save his people. And he knew they were suffering. Why else would they rise up? But there had to be more to it. There were stories about Zhang Jue, ones that made his skin crawl even as he considered them.

This rebellion wasn't just about the famine, the floods, the dead children. It was about Zhang Jue believing he was more than just a man, that he was blessed by the legendary Laozi with the right to rule, with abilities. Liu Fei had always said those abilities weren't real, but now that he had to face him, they came to his mind. What could he do? What would he do to *him*?

His skin crawled, and he looked over the scroll again.

Then he looked up at those dark, glittering eyes.

What was this man?

Liu Fei couldn't sign this, could not let his people be ruled by something other than human.

"I won't do it," Liu Fei said.

He wasn't sure what he'd expected in response, but Zhang Jue rolling his eyes was not one of them.

Zhang Jue looked Liu Fei over again, and handed the scroll back to the administrator.

He said, "Aang, Hongli, let's not be rude to our guest. Make him comfortable."

More of his men left, and when they came back they carried a low table of strong, light-colored You mu wood between them.

Liu Fei was shoved onto it, the sturdy wood easily taking his weight. He struggled futilely, movements weak, as they tied him to the legs. He was forced down onto his back, and the rough hands on him were gripping strong enough to bruise. They tied him with ropes that had survived his rough journey. He tried to hold in a whine as they scraped against the open wounds on his wrists and ankles in new ways, burning, burning …

Blood oozed from his thigh.

He couldn't help but look over at the Dragon Throne and wonder how badly he'd failed. The two brothers, the other leaders of the rebellion, looked back at him, one with grim satisfaction, the other seeming to question it. Or was Liu Fei just making that up? Looking for hope where there was none?

His attention was drawn back to Zhang Jue as he walked over to him.

He put a hand on his head, which made Liu Fei squirm, even as he wanted to hold his reaction in.

"Liu Fei, you will sign that abdication."

"Why don't you just kill me?" he snarled.

"I could. I could so, *so* easily, but how would that look to the people? Surely they'd rise up. Already factions of your army have had to be quashed. A pitched battle is the last thing I need. So, how about you just decide to sign it? We'll let you go after."

Liu Fei looked at one of his bound wrists.

"I doubt that."

"You dare question my generosity?"

"What generosity!" he yelled. "Killing my family? Was that some kind act I'm supposed to thank you for!"

"You should! Without your father the people of China will no longer starve—you would not believe the resources I've found that he had at his call—and Daoism can reign free!"

Liu Fei wanted to spit at him. "You're not a Daoist. Daoists are peaceful, calm. You think you have the power to rule, to kill whomever you want, and who knows what else? Your abilities are *wrong*."

"Are they?"

As much as it hurt to say, as much as it reminded Liu Fei of what he'd lost, he said, "We aren't meant to be immortal."

There was a long pause, Zhang Jue hanging his head, perhaps to hide his expression from him. Then: "I see."

He turned to his brothers. "Bao, Liang, come. And Bao, bring your *chui*."

Zhang Bao stood in a leisurely manner, glancing at his younger brother. Was he worried Zhang Liang wouldn't listen to Zhang Jue? No, Liu Fei was just being hopeful.

He needed hope because the weapon that had laid by Zhang Bao's seat was now being carried over. It was a long, thick staff with a weighted ball at the end. Those weapons weren't used much in battle given the strength needed to wield them, especially since they usually came in pairs, but they weren't unheard of to him.

What were they going to do? Smash his kneecaps? His elbows?

The thought of that weighted ball landing anywhere on his body set him shaking. He felt like he was going to be sick from the horror and the anticipation.

"May I do the honors?" Zhang Bao asked, a wicked grin on his face.

Zhang Liang's jaw clenched, lips drawn in a tight line.

Up close the family resemblance between the three was unmistakable, except Zhang Liang went without a beard.

"Of course," Zhang Jue answered. He then asked of Liu Fei, "Which hand do you hold a brush with?"

Now the shaking really took over, and his heart was pounding so hard and fast it felt like his skin should be broken in more places, the blood flying out of him. His shoulder and leg bled even more.

He couldn't answer.

He swallowed down bile, but kept his mouth shut. He wouldn't aid in his fate. He couldn't. But even as they expected an answer of him, his right hand began to tingle in anticipation of the pain. Liu Fei held a brush with his left hand, and he knew Zhang Jue would want to preserve that, if only so he could sign the abdication.

"Liu Fei," Zhang Bao began, "my brother asked you a question."

"Just smash his left and be done with it," Zhang Liang said. "Most people use a brush with their right hand."

"No, no, please!" Liu Fei got out as Zhang Bao started over towards his left hand. He'd be powerless without the use of his left hand. Any activity would be made incredibly difficult without his dominant hand. "Left!" he cried. "I use my left hand."

"All right," Zhang Jue said, like he wasn't about to torture someone. "Bao, his right hand, please."

Liu Fei squeezed his eyes shut as the *chui* came down on his hand, hoping that if he didn't see it it wouldn't hurt as much.

But it hurt.

He screamed as bones shattered and moved, as tendons surely snapped, as shards of bone broke through skin, as muscles and ligaments tore. The pain went up to his elbow, and it was unlike anything he'd ever felt before. His hand was *ruined*, utterly ruined. How could a healer even fix it?

Liu Fei thought it was funny he was thinking of afterwards because surely they'd kill him once he signed, or maybe they'd just keep him prisoner in a deep, dark dungeon where he'd never find any relief from his injuries.

What did it matter? The pain was *now*, and he wanted it gone. He couldn't bring himself to look, even as he felt blood gushing. The pain was sharp and throbbing, more immediate than anything he'd ever felt before. It was almost like his hand was so tired that it *hurt*. And he started feeling very cold on the right side of his body.

Tears trailed down his face, mingling with the sweat that had broken out all over his skin. He couldn't breathe out of his right nostril, his crying making it too full of snot. Some of that was running down his face too.

He couldn't breathe. He couldn't breathe! Maybe he was breathing, each breath making his chest rise and fall rapidly, but he felt like he wasn't getting any air, like his blood was slowing, and his head was fuzzy.

He thought maybe someone slapped him. His head had moved, and there was a slight sting on his cheek.

Then his face was grabbed, much too hard, his jaw letting out a small creaking sound in protest.

Zhang Jue's cruel face appeared in his vision, and it was all he could see.

"Are you ready to sign?"

A strange, animal-like sound was coming from Liu Fei, and he didn't know how he'd be able to speak.

He tried to shake his head, but Zhang Jue's hold was too strong.

"Fine," he said with a sigh.

Before Liu Fei knew what was happening, Zhang Jue had a hand on his thigh. With a small knife he tore at his clothing, revealing the wound from the night of the coup.

"Hmm, these stitches are coming out," he mused, his tone almost accusatory like it was somehow Liu Fei's fault.

There was a strange tugging sensation in his thigh, and then he was bleeding more. The stitches had been taken out. Before he could so much as complain about it, Zhang Jue had taken the *chui* from his brother and slammed it against his thigh. The corrugated edges of the sphere tore at his skin, even as his muscle was crushed.

He screamed again, thrashing at his bonds, which just made his ruined hand hurt even more.

Liu Fei held his breath, trying to stay still.

"Aiya," Zhang Liang said, having approached to see this as if Liu Fei's torture were some grand spectacle. "Perhaps we're being too hard on him."

"Do you know what he is?" Zhang Jue accused, standing suddenly, showing that he was taller than either of his brothers. "That man is the last of that cursed bloodline that ruined this country. He needs to pay! He's had it coming for him, and you know it."

"He's just a man," Zhang Liang said. "And what if we kill him?"

Zhang Jue seethed, power seeming to emanate from him. Maybe Liu Fei was delirious, but he swore he could see light dimming around him, a darkness bursting forth. His shivers increased in strength.

"Fine. Then we'll just castrate him."

Liu Fei started begging, and Zhang Jue kicked the table. It toppled with Liu Fei on it, falling to its side. He landed on his hand, and he thought maybe he blacked out for a few seconds. Nausea built up in him from the pain, and he couldn't relax, couldn't tell his body not to be sick.

Don't vomit. Don't vomit. Please ...

Inside he was nothing but begging. Begging for this pain to end, for things to not be worse, to be let free.

"You really should sign it," a too-recognizable voice said in his ear. That voice had commanded armies, led people, destroyed lives, built up his household. It was grave, imperious, and so very clear, knowing exactly what power it had.

Brow furrowed, he questioned, "Father?"

"Longwei, you are useless to me. My weakest child. Do you really think you can withstand this? There is nothing in you worth saving. You may have the birthmark, but you cannot serve China. Oh, how I hated to see that birthmark on you, even when you were born. Your mother despised you."

"No, Father, please."

"Maybe they should castrate you. Any child you create will be a disgrace."

"Please, let this unworthy servant make things right."

"Make things right? How dare you think you could do such a thing! China will fall, and it is all your fault."

"Then show me, show me how. Please."

"Don't beg. It's beneath you."

"Then what shall I do?"

"You think I care? Make them kill you. Beg for that, dog."

Liu Fei was sobbing, even as his father's voice disappeared. He was right. Everything he'd said was right. He was useless and pathetic.

The brothers seemed to have been arguing with each other, the youngest now backed against one of the pillars while Zhang Jue had a hand around his throat. Liu Fei couldn't help but wonder what was going on there. Was there something he could use to his advantage?

Even as plans tried to form, they were shoved away, the pain too much. As a reflex, he tried moving the fingers of his right hand. A ragged scream tore from his throat, and then he was gasping, panting, breaths forcing their way in as ugly, broken sobs tore their way out .

Zhang Jue came back over, kicking him in the gut, again and again, till he thought something snapped, till he couldn't breathe, till he was just that awful pain in his abdomen.

As black began to surround him, eyes centering on the empty Dragon Throne, Zhang Jue yelled, "Take him away! Lock him in the deepest dungeon."

***

Liu Fei came to what seemed like only an agonized second later. He was in a dark, dank room, a wooden door with some metal slats providing his only glimpse of the outside. There was a lamp on the far side, casting some light, the oil burning the dust and mold that fluttered into it, creating an acrid scent that nearly had him coughing.

There were other smells. Damp, mold, blood, rotten straw.

He lay on a mat of that straw, his left hand cuffed to the wall. He didn't really see a point in that—what was he going to do, try to escape? With a mutilated hand and an injured leg, and tired and beaten from his terrible journey?

Footsteps sounded outside the door. He was surprised he heard them because he realized moans were leaving him in an endless stream. There was nothing he could do to stop them.

There was some discussion, perhaps with a guard, and then a woman was being let in to see him. She carried a basket, and he smelled pungent herbs.

Liu Fei didn't understand much as she tended to him, just groaned and let out tearless sobs. He thought maybe he heard mention of amputation, which got his heart racing, but before he could make sense of it, he drifted in his pain again.

She left eventually, and he realized his thigh was wrapped, and his hand smelled vile but clean, the bandages like a club around it. Beneath his under-robes there were bandages around his chest, perhaps for some broken ribs.

After, food and water were given to him, but he could barely manage to eat. How could he when he couldn't stop crying? He felt sick, so sick he didn't know how his stomach was still inside of him.

Was this pain the price of his failure? As a ruler, as a son?

And had he actually seen his father? Had he not descended to the Heavens? But if he was here, he'd be a hungry ghost, unable to speak. How ...?

No, the only explanation was that he was hysterical, insane. How could he not be while suffering as a tortured prisoner in his own dungeon?

Time crawled, as slow as a snail.

Eventually the woman came back and made him drink something vile. His pain ebbed, and he fell into darkness.

***

"This is too much," a timid voice said. "Why don't we just kill the poor man? His armies have lost their best general, and we've taken the palace. We'll win any battle."

"There should not *be* a battle. The people need to see that *I* am the rightful ruler."

"Why, because Laozi came out of the sky and granted you mysterious powers?"

"Perhaps if you doubt this rebellion, Zhang Liang, you should join the imperials. Of course, that means death for you. Is that what you want?"

"N-no."

"Good, little brother."

That voice was different, perhaps the middle brother, Zhang Bao.

A groan rent the air, dissolving some of the horrid tension between the three of them.

"I think he's waking up," Zhang Liang said.

"Excellent," Zhang Jue purred. "Bao, the skinning knife, please. And fetch the gourd."

Liu Fei opened his eyes, finding himself in an adjacent room off the throne room, decorated in gold and green. He was on a low, backless couch. Surprisingly, he wasn't restrained, but he found that he could barely move. Where he could sense his limbs they were disconnected, almost unreal. Was he inside his body?

Zhang Liang was at the back of the room, arms crossed, eyes wide with something that might have been horror. Zhang Jue was handed the knife, his dark eyes like cruel daggers deciding where to next strike his flesh. And Zhang Bao was ... content, of all things. Perhaps things were going exactly as he wanted them to.

The small, curved, jagged knife was dangled in Liu Fei's vision, swinging back and forth. His breath hitched as he took in the sharp glint.

"So, here's how things are going to go," Zhang Jue said. "We're going to get rid of that pesky birthmark, and perhaps I might just keep going. Who knows, I might need a new skin eventually, and yours is very nice."

Liu Fei frowned.

He wasn't the only one confused by the statement. Zhang Liang just stared at his brother, maybe also wondering what he was.

Was Zhang Jue human?

Stories of foxes and demons came into Liu Fei's head, but he dismissed them. No, that was impossible. Those weren't real.

Zhang Jue receded, and Liu Fei could see the rest of the room, could see Zhang Bao now holding a gourd with a wooden stopper. It was shaking. All on its own.

His heart seized.

He'd heard of these demons, the ones that stole people's skins, that could be held in gourds until their time of release. Were they going to kill him, use his body to sign the abdication, to pretend he was the perfect prisoner?

Was Zhang Jue one of them?

"This is wrong," Zhang Liang said.

Suddenly, Zhang Bao drew a dagger, and he had it flush against his younger brother's throat.

"Show your weakness one more time, little brother, and I'll cut your throat."

Zhang Jue interceded.

"Let's have none of that. Bao, it's not Liang's fault he can't understand."

"Then why don't we make him?"

A slow dread had been creeping through Liu Fei's blood and now it was filling him, almost till he felt like it would come out of his mouth, steal his voice.

The rebellion leader was a demon, and a fight was about to break out.

The gourd was uncapped, and black smoke rushed out of it so quickly it was like a dam had burst. The smoke clouded the room, even prodded at Liu Fei till he was screaming and wishing he could move his body to bat it away. But he was helpless.

Through the smoke, he heard weapons clashing, yelling, Zhang Liang asking if his big brother was dead.

Zhang Liang was thrown, and he landed against the couch, knocking into Liu Fei.

The smoke—the *demon*—came for them.

Blood gushed down onto Liu Fei and he realized Zhang Liang had a sizable cut near his neck, almost close enough to have killed him. But the blood loss still could.

"Where's my brother!" he screamed.

Zhang Jue approached with black eyes. "Dead."

Zhang Liang threw himself through the black smoke, even as he choked on it, letting out a ragged cry. He launched into Zhang Jue, throwing him back. They knocked into a vase, the blue and white porcelain shattering on the wooden floor.

Zhang Bao ripped Zhang Liang off of him and stabbed at him again. The brother dodged.

The fight continued, a fierce rush of bodies, the thumps of flesh being hit ...

All the while Liu Fei was slowly gaining the ability to move again. He was sitting up now, sweating and panting, terrified of the black smoke. But it seemed to be ignoring him now, trying to seep into Zhang Liang's wounds.

Was Zhang Bao a demon as well? Perhaps it didn't matter.

Liu Fei knew what he had to do.

Slowly, gritting his teeth, cries leaving him, he got onto the floor. He couldn't stand and had to drag himself. A foot kicked him in the face, his neck arching back, body twisting from the blow. Blood began to run from his nose.

He cried out, but still reached, reached ...

He had to get the gourd, he almost could. Just a little farther. It was there, right beyond the fingers of his left hand.

A triumphant cry left him as he grabbed the gourd. He wasn't sure now what to do with it, but he had to do something!

"Demon!" he cried.

Zhang Jue turned to face him, even as the smoke somewhat stilled, writhing in place just before Zhang Liang's mouth, his eyes.

"I am Liu Fei, crown prince of the great Chinese Empire, heir to the Dragon Throne, and I command you to return to your prison!"

All was silent.

Zhang Jue started laughing, a hoarse, rasping laugh—

—that was cut short as Zhang Liang stabbed him in the throat.

He collapsed, skin beginning to slowly peel away, black skittering out from under him. But instead of searching for a new host, this demon seemed to dissipate.

"How dare—!" Zhang Bao began to cry, and Zhang Liang stabbed him as well, a sob breaking loose.

The demon without a body didn't seem to know what to do, but with Zhang Liang the only brother left, and screaming and screaming, it flew back into the gourd.

It was surprisingly heavy, and Liu Fei fell to his knees, nearly dropping it.

Zhang Liang caught the gourd as he collapsed into the blood on the floor, capping the prison with the wooden stopper.

He was panting too, tears streaking his young face. There was blood on him and in his hair.

"Please," Liu Fei begged. "Please let it be over."

Zhang Liang swallowed roughly, nodding, "It's over."

"What do we do?"

Zhang Liang looked at the dead bodies of his brothers, even the one that no longer looked human with much of its skin having fallen off. It was like a slab of meat in ruined, black clothes.

"They—they were the real leaders of this rebellion, but ..." He glanced at Liu Fei's collarbone. "I think I know what to do now."

He helped Liu Fei to his feet and then got on his knees before him, head bowed.

"Forgive me, great Emperor. I will recall the armies. I will do whatever you wish. On behalf of China, I apologize for my wrongdoings."

"Then go. Tell the people that this rebellion is over."

Zhang Liang brought his head to the floor, and despite Liu Fei feeling like he was going to collapse at any second, he realized that it was done. He was free. He was ... he was Emperor.

He stood taller and ignored the hateful words some semblance of his father tried to whisper in his ear.

Emperor Liu Fei stood amongst blood and death and demons, a rebel kowtowing before him. So, this marked the beginning of his reign.

Emperor

Liu Fei's right hand twinged, and he winced, shifting his arm about on his desk. He put his brush down to reach for his hand, but it wasn't there. That was something he still hadn't quite gotten used to in the few months since the end of the rebellion. His hand was gone, yet he still had phantom pains. The healers said it was normal, but it was still grating.

With a sigh, covering the stump of his wrist with his long, billowing sleeve, he got back to work. Responsibility had been difficult for him to fall into at first, especially with the small rebellion sects that had not heard of their surrender, but now he took it up gladly, trying to chase away the pain in his heart, the grief.

The weather hadn't been kind in the months that had followed. Many farms had dried up under the heat, crops not yielding, and now there had been the early rains that signaled the coming of winter. There had been floods, mudslides, deaths, famine ...

This time though, rather than ignoring it all, Liu Fei was working on yet another bill with Zhang Liang's help that would have his soldiers aid any they could. There were even search parties amongst the destruction from the rivers. It was hard work, and the month before, Liu Fei had gone to one of the camps that had been set up. Delivering food had been difficult with one hand, but he couldn't just sit by while his men did all the work, while he saw bodies that were ruined from hunger.

His reign began with many difficulties, and there was a lot of work ahead of him, but Liu Fei was willing to do it all, willing to prove his father wrong, to show his brothers that he was honorable, and worthy.

And sometimes, he imagined his brothers with him, not as hungry ghosts, but somehow as themselves, standing beside him while he tried his best to fix their once-beautiful country.

There was loneliness, an unbearable ache that kept him up most nights, but he dove into his work, into living for his people.

Emperor Liu Fei would bow to them as they bowed to him, always their servant, and he vowed he would bring them great honor.

About the Author

Lif L. is studying screenwriting at SNHU, and has loved writing for years. She started writing to one-up her twin brother, but eventually realized she should do it for herself, which she began to do in 2016. She lives with her twin and their two beloved cats, Alley and Loki.

The Huldra Hunter

Amie

CW: Character death

Whumpee: Man, woman, Whumper: Man, Caretaker: N/A

The trees were rotting in the ground after the mild and wet winter. The woodland the men had planned on logging was useless. They spent a day or two moving farther up the side of the valley, at last finding an area where the temperatures had been low enough to give the trees a fighting chance come spring. It was still cold up here, and their horse would have to work twice as hard to bring the logs down into the valley again, but it was all they had.

Anders, being the youngest and most foolish, had the task of limbing the felled trees of their branches after the rest of the men had taken them down. It was an easy job, reserved for clumsy younglings such as him. Felling required skill and experience and wouldn't be his field for a few years yet. Even having turned freshly eighteen, he was skinny and barely looked his age. That was why he didn't mind spending hours alone, limbing the trees one by one with his little axe. The other men never hesitated to poke fun at him wherever they could.

As the sun started to drop lower in the western sky, Anders decided he could finish a couple more trees before having to break for the day. As he started hacking at a particularly gnarly branch, it was as if the little ax slid out of his grip on its own, the sharp edge slicing effortlessly through the skin and flesh at the pad of his thumb. He winced and gripped his hand, trying to gauge the severity of the wound as he bit his lip to suppress a swear.

It wasn't very deep, but it bled like it was. Anders looked around but couldn't see the other men. He could see where they had gone, though, by the strip of felled trees they had left behind forming a wide path that led around a hill a couple hundred yards away. He frowned, but figured he might as well return to them for supper. It would be dark soon. He knelt down to pick up the axe he'd dropped.

He startled when a pair of naked feet stepped into his field of vision. As he quickly grabbed for his axe with his good hand, he looked up, and his eyes fell on the most beautiful woman he had ever seen. Young and old at the same time—skin as smooth and pale as the early morning clouds, yet almost translucent like an old woman's, and bearing the scent of wildflowers and the forest ground after a rainfall. Her hair was loose and long, falling around her face like a great waterfall, like the flaxen mane of a horse, waving slightly now even when there was no wind. The apples of her cheeks were perfectly rosy, matching the frosty night they had woken up to this morning. The most prominent feature of her round face were her eyes, large and piercing, the color of ... of everything. Anders saw the green forests, the yellow flowers who were the first to peek out after winter, the clear blue sky and the stormy gray sky, a laughing bright creek fresh with melting water from the mountains, the shining, reddish fur of a fox in the sun, the licking orange flames of a bonfire burning in the night. Her eyes, rimmed by pale lashes, held everything.

"You are hurt," she said. He blinked at the voice, which seemed to come from inside himself. Her perfect pink lips had moved, but it was as if the sound reverberated from the walls inside his head.

He had forgotten the bloody wound when she appeared. With some difficulty, he tore his gaze away from her wonderful beauty and looked down at his hand, resting in his lap.

"Yes," he agreed stupidly.

"I can help you." Her ethereal voice floated around him as she carefully stepped closer, her bare feet making no sound on the soft moss.

"Yes."

He wanted to say something intelligent and charming to her, but it was as if all other words had left him, as if he was unable to do anything but agree to her propositions.

"These trees, they aren't always friendly," she said, as if she was apologizing to him on their behalf, like the trees had a soul and could choose to hurt him. Maybe they would choose that. He did, after all, mutilate their bodies with his axe. Her hands, pale and delicate and bearing no signs of such hard labor, glided along the straw and the bilberry shrubs as she moved closer. Her body was like fluid, each joint disconnected from the next, like the head of a bird. Anders found it mesmerizing. He could not help but stare.

"Let me see."

The woman held out her open hands to him. She bore no weapons. Her wrists were so skinny and frail that he could reach around twice with his own hand. She was no threat to him. Gently, he lifted his own injured hand from his lap. His crimson blood dripped from his knuckles and down onto the forest floor.

"I don't want you to get blood on your dress," he managed to say, his eyes fixed on hers. He couldn't look away. Her presence filled every spare space within him, heart and mind, warmed him up despite the still-cold April air surrounding them both.

"Oh, this thing?" she ventured airily, almost laughing as she tugged at her pretty blue skirts, belonging to a dress which seemed too thin to be her only garment. "I have dealt with blood before, you dear."

Something moved just at the edge of his field of vision—something small and light peeking out from under the hem of her skirts, but he couldn't find it in himself to care about anything but her everything-eyes. He sat, still and trustingly, as she reached out for his hands, and—

"Vanish, Hulder!"

Something flew through the air and buried itself in soft forest ground at Anders' feet. Before he could react, the woman had turned on her heels and disappeared into the forest, a faint shriek following her, as if she hadn't made the sound, but it had just risen from the ground around her. The last Anders saw of her was a little tuft of flaxen hair down by her feet, swinging in time with her leaps into the woods. It looked like ... the tail of a cow—but that was impossible, surely.

"Begone!" Karl bellowed at the top of his lungs after her. Anders whipped his head around, coming to face his superior, mouth agape. The burly old man was furious, bushy brows drawn down over his eyes and his toothy mouth looking more scowly than usual. Still, as he raised his hand to draw a cross in the air with his fingers, Anders could see his hand shaking.

"What—" he breathed, not entirely sure what had just happened.

"You foolish boy!" Karl rumbled, striding over to him with a vigor not fit for a man over sixty. "Did it touch you?"

"I—she—"

"Did it touch you, Anders!"

"No!" he yelled back, still utterly confused. He turned his head again to look for the woman, but she was long gone, having disappeared amongst the spruce trees.

Karl grumbled something indecipherable as he grabbed hold of Anders' injured hand, roughly turning it over to look at the wound. Anders winced at the sudden movement.

"Did it do this to you?"

"No! She didn't touch me!"

"Nasty thing ..." Karl muttered to himself, still furious, as he tore his handkerchief out of his pocket and tied it tightly around Anders' hand, stopping the blood flow. Anders looked between the rough patch-up job and the place in between the trees where the woman had run off to.

"Who was that?" he asked Karl, ignoring his nasty scowl. "Why did you yell at her?"

"It, not her." Karl finished the knot on the makeshift bandage and bent down to pick up his knife, which was the object he had thrown with great force into the ground between Anders and the woman. The silver blade was grimy with dirt, and he wiped it off with his wool shirt. "Never, ever meddle with the Huldras, boy," he grumbled to Anders as he worked to clean the knife and put it back in its sheath.

"Huldras—!" Anders sputtered, widening his eyes. "Was that a—!"

"Yes, you fool." Karl took him by the shirt collar and tugged him up to his feet, a surprising amount of strength still left in his wiry body as Anders was forced to follow. "And don't you forget it, either."

"She was going to help me!" he exclaimed as he stumbled after Karl down the bare-ly-there path, managing to snatch his axe at the last moment.

"It was going to do no such thing!" Karl answered curtly, not leaving it up for discussion. "It would have tricked you. It already was, judging by the stupid look on your mug." Abruptly, he turned around and faced Anders, his eyes still storming furiously. "Faeries eat men, Anders. Especially foolish men like you." He grabbed a handful of yellowing straw from the side of the path and tugged at it, gathering the chaffy ends to stick out of his fist. Much like the end of a cow's tail.

"But she wasn't—"

"Listen to me, boy!" Karl shouted. Anders wisely shut his mouth, letting Karl continue.

"They bear the mark of beasts. That's how you tell them apart from the other women in the forest," Karl informed him dryly, shoving the handful of grass up to his face. "If it seems too good to be true, it probably is."

Neither man said anything for a moment, Karl letting his admonishment sink in and Anders too frightened to break the silence.

In the end, Karl straightened back up.

"Come along," he said as he turned around, heading towards the clearing further down the hill where the other men were working. "We're breaking for the day. Mikkel and Sigurd will teach you how to fell tomorrow."

Anders was too young and had too little experience to learn felling just yet, and he knew it. He suspected Karl no longer trusted him alone. He looked over his shoulder, gazing back at the dark spruces where the woman—the Huldra—had disappeared.

Maybe for the best, he thought, as a sudden gust of wind blew through the trees and made him shudder. He hurried after Karl down the path.

They were sitting around the fire, all five of them, all with their own wool blankets bundled over their shoulders, as close to an approximation of comfort as possible on the April mountainside. The horse, a trusty old steed with no particular name, was peacefully napping tethered to a tree nearby. Sweat marked the places on his shoulders and flanks where the harness had rubbed during the day's hard labor. Through half-lidded eyes, Anders watched how the light from the fire created sharp and dramatic contours of the reddish animal against the dark forest behind it. Now that most of the snow had melted away, the nights were extra dark, like it was October all over again.

"Anders will join you two halfwits tomorrow," Karl said as he lifted his dented tin bowl to his mouth and slurped up the last bits of the watery sheep stew they had boiled for supper, fixing his stormy gaze on the two thirty-somethings on the other side of the fire. Mikkel and Sigurd both looked and acted the same way, more often than not being mistaken for brothers. Now they both leered at Anders from across the fire, evidently more than ready to spend tomorrow tormenting the youngest of their little logging group.

Karl shifted his gaze to meet that of Elias, the last of the five, sharing a knowing look with him as Mikkel snickered lewdly at something Sigurd had said to him. Karl and Elias fell into talk of which areas they should begin felling tomorrow.

Anders didn't know how much the others knew of what had occurred earlier, or if they had heard anything at all. Sound doesn't travel far in the forest, the tall trees and dense underbrush making sure of that. The rest of the group had been a ways away, down around a hill, when Karl and Anders had rejoined them. In any case, none of them had asked him about it—although he had seen Karl mutter something to Elias earlier as the stew was being prepared.

A deep baying far away disrupted them all, throwing Anders off his train of thought. The horse abruptly raised his head, ears swiveling around to listen better. Mikkel and Sigurd for once shut their mouths and looked up towards the mountains, where the sound had come from.

"What on God's green earth ..." one of the idiots muttered. The baying was moving closer to them now, still far away, but the way the sound jolted off the bare stone walls across the valley revealed their direction.

The dogs—they had to be dogs—were moving towards them.

"No one should be hunting in April," Anders said, thinking of the deer and moose who soon would have little brown calves following them around. Hunting was for autumn, not spring.

They all sat quietly for a moment, merely listening and trying to gauge how far the dogs were and how fast they were moving, when suddenly, something—no, someone – burst through the underbrush, almost running straight into their fire before stumbling to a halt, catching them all by surprise.

Anders recognized the flaxen locks of hair immediately. And she must have recognized him, because she clasped her palms together in front of her heaving and not insignificant breasts, fixing her everything-eyes on him.

"Save me!" she pleaded, staring at him with true desperation written all over her perfectly shaped features, sharp and soft in just the right places. Her vivid expression tugged at something deep in Anders' chest.

But before he could muster together enough of his mind to utter any words, Karl had risen to his feet, now brandishing his great felling axe as he bellowed, "Begone, she-devil!"

Mikkel and Sigurd, ever the imitators, lunged for their own axes, and Elias gripped the handle of the knife he bore at his waist. The horse stomped the ground nervously, tugging at his tether. Anders did not move at all.

"Dear humans, save me! Let me stoke your fire so that the hunter and his dogs may pass me by!" Her voice was like a frantic, sharp breeze, sounding nothing like the pleasant tones she had served Anders earlier that day. He could see movement down by her bare feet, and there it was—the flaxen cow's tail, swishing violently back and forth under her skirts. Anders opened his mouth to say something, but again Karl spoke over him.

"Flee from here, Hulder! We will not help you!" he yelled, his voice echoing through the valley.

"We need to help her!" Anders suddenly managed, and immediately Karl turned to him, furious.

"No, fool! Do you remember nothing!"

"Listen to him!" the woman shrieked, looking over her shoulder into the forest from whence she came, where the baying still sounded. "Help me now, and I will protect you later. You have my word!"

"A demon's word is worth nothing!" Karl yelled at her, swinging his mighty axe in the air as if to scare her away. Her breath caught in her throat as she flinched back.

It looked as if her entire being pulled back into itself slightly, only to swell back out, into a version of herself that at first glance looked the same but was not the same at all. "Fine, senseless mortals!" Her voice morphed into a warped gargling, louder than any human could produce, stinging in the loggers' ears. The horse whinnied loudly and pulled hard on his rope, terrified. The woman's face warped as well, her delicate features sharpening and her eyes darkening. Anders understood then what Karl had meant. This was no ordinary woman. This was no woman at all.

She started to say something, but the words disappeared in a maelstrom of screeches and howls erupting from her twisted lips as she took off running again, rounding the loggers and their fire and disappearing in between the dark spruces.

She was gone in an instant, leaving behind nothing but a faint smell of rot. Karl put his axe down again. None of the five said anything for a few minutes, too shocked by the whole encounter. Then, abruptly, the previously faraway baying appeared to have moved much closer. Now Anders too pulled his knife, just in time to see two great, black dogs leap out of the forest, barking in long, drawn out howls, frothing at the mouth. It looked like they were heading right towards the fire and its keepers. Anders thought that the five of them might be able to handle two dogs, even with how big these two were, but before he could make a reality of that plan they too angled their bounding and followed the exact route the Huldra had taken across the clearing, disappearing as quickly as they had appeared. Their baying continued all the while, this time growing fainter and fainter.

Again, none of the five moved, as they stood and stared at the spot where the dogs had left them. They had been too massive to be regular dogs, Anders decided, thinking about how they seemed to reach him to his hip and then some. The Huldra was not a woman, and those were not dogs.

And the next shadow who appeared from the forest must not be a human, as he towered two heads over all of the men around the fire. Anders saw him first in the corner of his eye, causing him to whip his head around and let out a gasp at the massive size of the figure. Over his broad shoulders he carried a rifle, its barrel glinting menacingly in the moonlight. The rest of the loggers turned too at Anders' exclamation, and Karl did not say a word as he raised his hand and pointed to where the Huldra and the dogs had disappeared. The man—the Hunter—looked at him for a second before he set off at a brisk walk after his beasts, his legs covering ground as quickly as they had. Soon he too was gone.

They were all silent and still for another few minutes, as if gauging by ear whether or not another being would appear from the forest. But none did, and soon they all sat down around the fire again. It seemed Karl and Elias were able to act like nothing had happened, and the dumb duo followed suit, but Anders could feel his hands shaking even after he had rubbed them in his wool blanket and held them near the fire.

As Elias went to calm the horse, who still seemed incredibly alarmed, Karl turned to Anders as he shook the grass and straw out of his blanket. "The first time is not easy," he muttered to him, and Anders thought an explanation was underway, but all Karl did was put another few logs on the fire and lay down to sleep. Anders could but do the same.

None of the five said anything when a gunshot sounded sometime later, far, far away.

Anders had just barely fallen into a light slumber when something yet again made the branches on the trees of the far side of the clearing rustle. He sat up, leaning on his elbow as he blinked and waited for his eyes to adjust to the low lighting. The others were still sleeping soundly. For a long while, everything was still and quiet. Anders convinced himself it must have been just a bird and was about to settle back down, when one of the dogs appeared. This time, it trotted along peacefully, slightly wagging its tail when it saw Anders. The other dog came too, and they looked nothing like the furious beasts who had chased after the Huldra. For a moment, Anders was afraid they might come closer, but they stayed on the outskirts of the clearing, occasionally stopping to sniff or look back.

Behind them, the Hunter reappeared as well, strolling almost peacefully now. Anders could hear him whistle a short melody as he ambled after his dogs.

The pleasant sound of his music was a sharp contrast to the body of the Huldra, which he had slung over his shoulder. Her flaxen hair was so long it reached the ground, the strands catching on the bilberry bushes. One lock fell away to reveal a bloody hole on the side of her neck. Her pretty blue dress was bloody and torn where the dogs had gotten to it.

Anders couldn't move or speak, he could barely breathe, as he watched her cow's tail, following the tuft of hair swinging in time with the Hunter's steps.

About the Author

Amie is a 20-something student who in between midterms and exams finds solace and joy in reading and writing whump.

Three Times Over

Zi Trone

Scene One

The day had begun early for almost everyone. The rooster called, commoners rose, both inside and outside the Lord's lavish residence. On the inside, they hurried to prepare breakfast, to get the Lord's clothes, to clean, to work in whatever ways they were expected to, knowing well that the day of the market was a day that had to be perfect. On the outside, people were soon arriving and setting up their stands, trying to contain their animals or organizing their pots by shape and size.

Lord Döbrögi was the last to wake. He had nowhere to be, not yet; he just had to slip into his prepared clothes, lazily eat his prepared breakfast, then walk out to the stables and fetch his prepared horse with ease.

The market held on the lands he controlled wasn't necessarily famous, no. But it attracted enough merchants and peasants from the area for it to be an interesting occasion, perhaps even for a lord. It certainly attracted some with stock he was looking to acquire, so to say, in any way he deemed fit. Because it was his land, and what he wanted was law. Justice was elusive, justice was pliant and mouldable, justice was whatever he wanted it to be that day. Justice was nothing more but a term to describe any situation the Lord found pleasing.

He trotted around in the market, with not a care for where the soles of his horse's hooves landed. He was gracious enough to keep the pace slow, so people could get out of his way in time, and that was as much as he was willing to do for them. The broken bones of a peasant were less than an inconvenience in his mind; he wouldn't even need to stop to help, the rest could take care of it while he moved on.

The merchandise was expensive everywhere, and the Lord couldn't stifle a smug grin. The poor fools, trying to make a living with nothing but pottery and some sick pigs. Oh, but they were "award-winning pigs, the best pigs of the lot," he'd heard the seller argue when someone tried to buy them for less than the original price. He almost burst out laughing at that. *Award-winning pigs.* That was exactly what they were, the lot of them, standing behind the stands and desperately screaming at the passersby to come closer, take a look at the goods, spend some money, all to keep them alive. *His* award-winning pigs. *His* work horses.

Of course, he didn't care much for the prices. Not only would he have been able to buy several whole stands without making a dent in his fortune, he didn't actually plan on *buying* anything. It was his land, after all, and it was his market. Any and all things and creatures on sale were his by default; he simply didn't need all of it. The unwanted could be kept and traded between the peasants, for all he cared.

As he walked his horse along the dirt road, he soon spotted a younger-looking boy with at least fifteen geese around him. He looked to be around twenty years of age, with eyes and hair dark as the night, in a loose, white linen shirt and a matching pair of pants. Lord Döbrögi had no real reason to suspect him of any sort of mischief, other than the odd feeling in his gut when he looked at the boy. He decided it was better to buy his geese and have him leave before he had a chance to wreak havoc—hell, he'd even ask for the price once they were close enough to talk. He could be generous to someone so young and, well, until proven otherwise, innocent.

"Whose are the geese, boy?" he asked, and the boy's head snapped to him in an instant.

"Mine, sir, all twenty of 'em," came the dutiful reply, already mocking him. Sir? He was a lord, lord of everything this boy could see if he'd just bothered to look around, lord of the castle, lord of the vast forests all around, the lake, the sea, the most likely pathetic house he and his family lived in, held together by rope and luck.

"Do you know who I am?" he demanded, wholly unsatisfied when the boy didn't even seem fazed at all. "Do you know whose market you brought those geese to? Do you know whose land you stand on?"

"My sincerest apologies, m'lord," the kid finally said, with not an ounce of regret in his voice. At least he didn't need to be spoon-fed the exact name and title. "I've never seen you, it's my first time visiting your wonderful market."

"Stop with the antics, boy. Just tell me the price."

His eyes lit up with excitement. "Three silver coins, m'lord, for all twenty."

The lord huffed at the sheer audacity. Three silver coins for those geese? He was about to do the boy a favor. "I'll give you half, and you get to be back home by dinner."

"Three coins it is, m'lord," he replied with a faux-serious look on his face, the mark of a boy who was having fun posing as a serious man. "Wouldn't give it cheaper to the soul of my late father."

"It can't be helped, I suppose," the Lord sneered, turning his horse around. "Three coins it is, then. Get the boy and bring him after me."

The people around them seemed to finally take notice of the events. The Lord could see them pointing at the boy as he was seized, whispering to each other, and he would've lied if he'd said their visible amusement didn't make him want to perform a bit more. Why not show all these peasants who he was and what the consequence of disobedience would be?

While his personal guards tied the boy's hands and secured the other end of the rope to the saddle of the Lord's horse, Döbrögi raised his leather purse, letting all the silver and golden coins rattle around inside. He picked out more than enough to cover the price of the geese, then nonchalantly threw all of it on the ground to scare the birds away.

The surrounding people immediately jumped on the opportunity; men and women rushed to get at least one of the coins, making all the geese scatter and run in every direction of the wind. The boy was even yelling something, cursing the money-hungry villagers for not catching his feathery fortune, unaware that the Lord would've ordered his men to turn each and every one of them into a feast for him anyway. But there wasn't much time to cry over the birds as the horse began trotting up towards the castle, pulling the fool along.

Laughter and cheers followed the group as they made their way across the market, insults raining down upon the apparently not-that-innocent boy. Lazy, trickster and thief were just a few of the names that were thrown their way, and the Lord relished every second of it. He thought he was merely exercising his power over the less fortunate, making an example of someone new who hadn't yet learned how things usually progressed. If he managed to catch a thief, however, then the reward would be even sweeter. He wasn't about to become a lord of terror, but a hero to all of these empty-headed vessels of blind hate and mockery.

Upon arrival, he got off his horse and called for the commissioner, who hurriedly met him outside the castle gates. His decorative and expensive clothes, indicative of high status and respect, clashed severely with the way he carried himself in the presence of the Lord. His trembling couldn't be hidden even by the thickest of fabrics, nor the way his voice shook as he asked what the matter was.

"Count for me, dear commissioner," Döbrögi said cheerily, motioning towards where his men had already taken the boy's shirt away, and one of them had even acquired a hazel cane to carry out the punishment. "You're the man of justice here, after all."

The commissioner straightened his back when he realized that the punishment wasn't for him, rather the struggling young man not too far from where he stood. "Yes, my lord. How many should it be?"

"I say fifty, that ought to be enough to make him learn."

And fifty it was. Lord Döbrögi laughed with every pained cry, reveling in the sight of the red welts scattered across the boy's back. Lashes were delivered harsh and sharp, from just under his shoulder blades down to just above his knees. Every whistle of the cane was followed by the angry snap of wood on bare skin, an agonized cry and the commissioner's count.

Before the Lord knew it, the number had reached fifty, and the boy was released from his restraints. The men threw his clothes on the floor in front of him, which he quickly pulled back over his head, wincing as the linen made contact with the fresh wounds. Crimson spots bloomed on the back of his shirt within moments, creating a pattern of suffering, complemented by the two clean streaks of dried tears cutting through the uniform dust coating on his face.

"I thank you for the payment, m'lord. With God's help, I shall repay it three times over," he said with his head held high, black eyes boring into the Lord's own, who met this kind of empty arrogance with nothing but the stone-cold confidence of an established noble. What were the choked up words of a peasant boy against a castle and armed guards? "Write it on the gates, m'lord, so you won't ever forget!"

He could barely finish the sentence before the Lord's guards got a hold of him once more, punching and kicking him until he could barely crawl. Döbrögi watched the scene unfold from the comfort of his chair, a smug grin on his face as the thief still found the energy to look back and utter, "Three times over, m'lord," prompting another round of laughter from everyone who heard.

Scene Two

It had been years since that frankly ridiculous encounter with the commoner boy. Lord Döbrögi had moved on long ago. He was much too preoccupied with the construction on his land and the improvements that were being made to his castle. Everything was going quite well, all to his liking, coming together as well as he'd imagined.

That was no coincidence, of course. He'd hired the best of the best, skilled workers who had studied in far away lands, only to then come back home and offer their services to the richest lords and ladies.

The Lord liked to watch the workers. He liked taking strolls around the property, seeing his place of residence be polished and upgraded. The walls were looking immaculate, and the wood they had gathered from his own forest looked like it was going to make the perfect roof. A worthy final touch, fit for a masterpiece.

But then he spotted another person walking along the cobblestone roads, touching the walls of his new home here and there with a pitying smile. He especially seemed to have a problem with the wood, the wood the Lord had been so immensely proud of! The wood from his own forest! He didn't waste a moment going up to the man, his tone already accusatory.

"What might you want here at my home?" he asked in a rather hostile manner, prompting the visitor to bow his head a little with an apologetic smile on his face.

"Oh, nothing, absolutely nothing, my lord. I was merely taking a walk in the area, and I couldn't help but notice this magnificent building. You see, it's very clear to me that the stone-mason has done an impeccable job, but the roof, oh my ... I wish I hadn't seen the roof! I certainly hope you don't plan on using that sort of wood to finish this majestic palace, my lord."

The Lord scoffed, feeling conflicted about accepting the flattery. He felt insulted, of course, but the other half of him was quite intrigued by who this stranger might've been, someone brave enough to critique the work of the finest craftsmen. "This wood is directly from my own forest, where only the most beautiful trees grow."

"Oh, certainly, they are beautiful ... maybe for smaller houses, or a little cottage, but not for a castle like this, my lord. Has your lordship ever seen the work of the Italian masters? Oh, Italy is famous for the gorgeous roofing on top of its many palaces, and I have been lucky enough to see them firsthand! I have worked on the mansions of princes, and I can tell you, my lord, it is impossible to construct a proper roof from this wood. One that would fit the home of a lord like yourself." The man looked at the pile again, condescension written all over his face. "But I'm not here to belittle anyone. I'm sure that the people who have been tasked with finishing your lordship's castle are fine men of the trade. I shall get going right away, so I don't disturb the work."

Mansions of princes? Döbrögi imagined himself as a prince, in all the finest clothes, embroidered with golden thread, lounging about on a throne all day. Commanding armies of tens of thousands instead of the hundreds he had under his control. Yes, yes, he needed a home that would reflect those aspirations, that power, that luxury.

"Hold on, my friend," he said before the stranger could turn on his heel and leave. "I haven't made a deal with any one carpenter yet, you see." He grinned wide, ushering the man towards the part of his home that wasn't affected by the improvements, the one that was neat and tidy, ready to accept any guest. "So you've visited Italy, then? Please, do tell me about your experience, and the kind of expertise you've seen. Have you had lunch today? Perhaps we could talk over some fresh duck, caught by my hunters just this morning."

"I don't mean to offend, my lord, but I would loathe to accept your generous invitation knowing I can't possibly offer my services to you. Your taste in the construction of such elaborate buildings is clearly refined, but I can't live up to those expectations, nor my own tales of the Italian palaces with wood that is simply not suitable."

"My friend, please, let me take you to the forest! You won't find trees of better quality in the whole of the country, I can assure you. Surely, my servants must have chosen the wrong ones, is all."

Soon enough, the Lord was leading the carpenter through the dense woods, bursting with pride and enthusiasm. The forest was vast, and his satisfaction only grew when the man finally seemed to recognise the magnificence of it. He'd picked out one tree after another, until all the workers they'd brought were busy, and it was just the two of them walking along the narrow path.

"I just wish I'd one more," the man said wistfully, and Döbrögi was quick to respond with utmost confidence.

"If we walk a bit more, I'm sure you will find tens and hundreds to your liking." He pointed to one that resembled previous picks, eager to seem knowledgeable. "How about that one, my friend?"

"A very good pick, my lord, if only a little thin for the purpose." The man stopped to think for a moment, then took out a piece of braided rope from his pocket and walked over to the tree anyway. Döbrögi followed, interested to see what that tool might be for. "I'm looking to see whether your lordship could get his arms around this tree. If yes, then it is indeed too thin."

Döbrögi didn't need any more encouragement. Of course his pick was right, he had been walking with the carpenter in the forest for quite a while now, and saw all the trees he had marked good enough. How hard could it be to pick one out himself?

He pressed his chest against the trunk, reaching around and stretching his arms as far as they'd go. Even then, he couldn't feel his fingers brush against each other in the slightest; what he did feel, however, was the bite of that braided rope around his wrists, tightening and securing him to the tree. He pulled against it in a panic, trying to free himself, but it was no use.

By the time he thought to cry out for help, cry for the servants they'd left far behind, the carpenter had already taken some moss and shoved it in his mouth as a makeshift gag. He tried to spit it out and get rid of the feeling of all the little bugs crawling around on his tongue, but the man kept getting moss by the handful, pushing so much inside him that he thought he'd be forced to swallow it entirely.

And then, when he was silenced and immobilized, only then did the man speak again, answering his muffled questions. "I have to confess, my lord, I'm no carpenter. I'm the mere peasant boy you stole from all those years ago."

The Lord's eyes widened in recognition, and he screamed profanities into his gag. The useless, the thief, the unruly, unkempt, mischievous boy from that day on the market. Now that he grinned at him like that again, he could tell, it was the very same cocky look from when he'd told him that he wouldn't lower the price, no matter who asked. He tugged on his ropes again, part from fury, part from debilitating fear.

"You ordered me to be beaten, and you took the geese raised by my mother," he went on, grabbing a branch and pulling it down to a level where he could easily cut it off. It was a thick branch, thicker than the hazel cane the Lord's men had used on him. "I told you then, and I'm telling you now, my lord." He walked back around the tree, leaving

Döbrögi's field of vision, and making the powerful Lord tremble in nervous anticipation. "I shall repay it three times over."

Nothing could've ever prepared him for the torment that a single hit would already cause. The agony coursed through his body as if he'd been struck by lightning, and he bit down on the disgusting plants in his mouth to stifle a scream. The second hit was even worse, and the third unbearable, and yet they just kept coming, raining down on him like the most vicious storm, the sound of thunder echoing through the forest each time the branch came down.

The Lord had lost count long ago, dazed with pain and humiliation by the time the vengeful man finally stopped. His legs had given out, and he was half-kneeling with his head resting against the tree and arms stretched above his head. The trunk was thicker towards the roots, and the rope was tight around his wrists; when he allowed himself to slide down, his arms got caught, putting way too much pressure on his shoulders. Yet he just couldn't muster up the strength to get back up, not after his attacker had removed his boots and delivered quite a few lashes upon the soles of his feet, taking advantage of his weakness.

He barely registered the feeling of hands in his pockets, removing some of the coins he'd brought along. Thief. Thief, he was nothing but a thief, a lowly, dirty—

"For the geese, my lord," the man taunted, and Döbrögi couldn't stop himself from flinching away.

Scene Three

Lord Döbrögi hadn't been found for hours after the lashing. He tried to spit out the moss still in his mouth and call for help, but no one seemed to be around. And of course they weren't, when that damn criminal made sure they'd be spread out in every corner of the forest except this one.

Bugs were crawling across his feet and back, lapping up the leftover blood. The branch had torn his skin open in several places, even under his shirt, and every creature on God's green earth wanted a taste of the aftermath. The Lord didn't have the energy to shake them off, instead forced to deal with the feeling of tens and hundreds of little feet pattering across his body.

The minutes ticked by, and the Lord's thoughts slowly started to shift. At first, he was angry. How dare a man like that tie him to a tree and make a mockery of him? Once he got out of his bonds, he was going to go after him. He was going to send all his people to hunt him down like the geese he had been so protective of. But as the wounds continued aching and the silence of the forest engulfed him, he started to worry.

What if he wasn't going to be freed? What if his people had already left, thinking he'd go back by himself? What if the commissioner saw this as the perfect opportunity to just leave him and settle into his life as the new lord of this land? Was he going to die of thirst and infection alone, in a dark corner of his own luscious forest?

Eventually, after what must have been hours, the Lord heard voices. Voices calling his name, calling for their lord, and he tried to answer, but all that came out of his dry throat and mouth still filled with moss was a weak grunt. Someone finally called for the commissioner, and soon after, he was surrounded by a small crowd.

At that moment, crushed under the weight of his own helpless body and the stares of his men, he wished he'd never been found.

His servants cut the rope and helped him get rid of anything green stuck to him, giving him robes to cover up his own expensive but torn ones, asking what had happened. The Lord could barely choke out the words, the story of that boy they'd beaten years ago, all while clutching the waterskin he'd been given like his life depended on it.

"We'll catch him, my lord. We'll send the men right now—"

"Don't! Oh, don't, just get me home! I'm dying, I can feel that I'm dying, I can barely move!" The Lord's word was law, and the people jumped to accommodate him. They brought him back to the carriage in their arms, putting anything soft under his aching back and legs that they could find. The commissioner instructed the driver to go as slow as possible to minimize the jostling of their lord from the bumps in the road, and all the servants spent their night wide awake, waiting for any and all whines and sighs from the master bedroom.

The next day, the Lord felt well enough to finally give the command to the commissioner for the capture of that damn boy. Day after day, while he was lying on his bed motionless to relieve some of the pain, he had to deal with his men coming in one by one and saying they weren't able to find him. There was no trace of him anywhere, and they didn't have a lot to go off of. After a couple of weeks, Döbrögi told them to just leave it, he didn't care anymore. All he cared about was that his back was still on fire, and his feet still hurt too much to stand on.

"Get me a good doctor!" he cried. "Get me one that can finally cure me! Can't you see that I'm in agony? Will I be bed-bound forever because of your incompetence? Get me a doctor that knows what he's doing!"

The servants were rushing up and down, in and out of his room. Different doctors tried different medicines, different techniques and approaches, each one worse than the other. It all hurt, and the Lord wasn't used to coping with pain, much less for an extended period of time. His cries for the most skilled of doctors became cries for anyone who was willing to offer his services.

One day, the judge of his village rushed into the palace, carrying news that might've been met with cheering before, but was now met with skepticism and impatience. He'd told the Lord that a combat medic was traveling through the area.

"Bring him in," the Lord groaned. "God knows it can only get better."

"I would, my lord, I would, it's just—he says he doesn't have the time for a stop like this. He's a very busy man, my lord, and—"

"I said to bring him in!" he boomed, making the judge shiver. Even in this state, when he couldn't even stand, Döbrögi was a frightening man.

"If you'd be so generous as to offer some silver, my lord, I'm sure that the dear doctor would be more than willing—"

"Ask him how much he wants, and then double it! I want that medic here! Send my best carriage, send whatever you think will get him here, but get him to my room!"

The judge nodded and left the room, leaving the Lord alone again. He hissed in pain as he tried to shift to a more comfortable position, agitating the black, blue and purple bumps on his back. The thief must've broken bones, that was the only explanation he could think of.

Alas, there was nothing left to do but wait. And wait. *And wait.*

The doctor arrived at his doorstep the very next day, and the Lord hurt himself again in his excitement. He wanted to explain everything all at once, the rope that must've hurt his delicate wrists, the bugs, the moss, the hours and hours he'd spent in that awkward position, the lashes, oh, the lashes with that horrible oak branch, and the vengeful little bandit who dared humiliate him.

The doctor listened to the story intently, not a single twitch of his facial muscles betraying what he thought about his present condition. That made the Lord desperate, and his tale turned into frantic begging to be healed.

"It is quite apparent why the pain won't go away, my lord," the doctor said eventually, and Döbrögi let out a sigh of relief. Finally, someone who knew what to do. "How is your memory, son?" he asked the closest guard, who straightened his back and swore that whatever the doctor said, he would tell the staff downstairs, word for word.

The Lord listened to the doctor call for a warm bath, rattle off tens and tens of different herbs, explain what each of them were for and what they looked like. His staff ran to comply with the orders, and he just lay there on the bed, imagining how this concoction was going to rid him of this horrible pain.

"I myself have come prepared, upon hearing your respectable judge's retelling of the events." The doctor walked over to the bed, taking out an ordinary piece of cloth. "I have soaked this in some medicine to heal your lordship's mouth."

"Could it have gotten infected, doctor?" he asked worriedly. "Must I have my mouth cleansed even weeks after that happened?"

"It's best to be safe, my lord. It will take only a minute."

The Lord opened his mouth for the doctor to place the cloth inside, thankful that at least the medicine he had spoken of didn't taste too foul. When a second piece of cloth was secured over his mouth, however, he suddenly felt his stomach sink. He tried to get away from the doctor before he could tie it at the back of his head, but the pain was too great, and he could only utter muffled threats and, eventually, pleas.

"I have to confess, my lord," the man started in a low voice, and Döbrögi knew, he already knew what he was going to say. "I'm no doctor."

Don't, don't, not again, not when he was still in so much pain. He screamed into his gag, the sound of his own mindless panic drowning out the other's monologue entirely. The man seemed to sense that, the fact that he wasn't listening, but he also seemed well aware that the Lord knew what he had done and what he was paying for.

'You ordered me to be beaten, and you took the geese raised by my mother.'

Words couldn't describe the feeling of having his torn up, swollen back beaten again, just as ruthlessly as his men had done to the boy before. He couldn't think, couldn't be angry, couldn't hold onto a single thought or emotion to save himself from experiencing the blinding agony.

Stop. *Stop.* That had been more than fifty. That had to have been more than fifty. Fifty was even too much, fifty would kill him, he couldn't take a single more hit.

But he did. And he took the next, and the next, and the next, until the man he'd wronged finally finished and dropped the wooden rod he'd brought along. His entire body was one throbbing wound, from the nape of his neck down to the soles of his feet. It felt like all of his bones had been shattered, it felt like he'd just fell out of the highest tower of his castle and landed on the cobblestone road, it felt like he'd been mauled by a bear.

His tears soaked both his gag and the pile of pillows underneath him, and he didn't dare make a sound as his assailant rummaged through his drawers for the three silver coins he'd refused to pay that day and more. "For the geese," he said once again, grinning. "Really, your lordship should be grateful I'm not dragging it out forever. With God's help, I'll be back very soon for the third and last time, and I'll consider my debt paid."

Scene Four

Real doctors had been called to the castle to treat the half-dead Lord. Laws were being made specifically against that one, fretfully clever man, warnings and wanted posters were sent out with no luck due to how well he disguised himself, and all the geese were killed around the area so Döbrögi wouldn't have to see a single white feather.

His physical injuries had healed over time, but the icy fear gripping his heart hadn't subsided. He knew, he'd been told three times now that he should expect a third visit, and no matter how many men he'd stationed right outside his bedroom door and around his person whenever he left, he couldn't erase the feeling. Every noise, every sudden movement, every unusual occurrence sent him spiraling.

He didn't even look like himself anymore. He was too paranoid to let his own servants into the bedroom, and especially to leave and go down to the kitchen where every bite was a disaster waiting to happen. Who knew which cut of meat had a hidden contraption in it that would unfold and gag him once more? Who knew whether the mashed potatoes had poison in them or some kind of potion that would make him faint? He didn't trust his own cooks, and he didn't trust the maids who were supposed to bring him the food. His coats and shirts hung off him oddly; his pants couldn't be tied tight enough at the waist not to drop. The tailor was in an endless cycle of fixing everything up to suit the Lord as he wasted away by his bedroom window, watching the cobblestone roads for any sign of the man.

Everyone had to be searched before entering. They had to make sure that no one had anything on them that could work as a rod, a cane, anything of the sort. The guards and servants whispered amongst each other, wondering whether the Lord was even fit to govern his property anymore. Döbrögi pretended not to hear the gossip, until he couldn't anymore and ended up snapping at a maid and ordering her to be caned.

But then, oh, then he changed his mind. He knew very well how vicious the cane was, how it bit into the flesh and left nothing but mind-numbing anguish in its wake. He'd ordered so many people to be publicly humiliated and beaten in front of the very castle he was standing in, but now, as he saw the maid be dragged away by his men, on *his* orders, he felt his stomach churn.

Yet he straightened his back and followed his men outside where the punishment was about to take place. This was exactly what he had to do to take back his power, to show that unhinged, vengeful snake that he didn't care, and to show the entirety of his palace, all the servants and cooks and guards, that he was the very same lord from before.

In the back of his mind, he was aware that he was still letting that man control his decisions, if only now pushing him towards the other, crueler end of his spectrum of behaviors. He knew he was looking for that ever-changing face in the crowd of acquaintances, friends and strangers, he knew he wanted to see the helplessness, but was afraid to see him show up and look at him with that unshakeable arrogance.

He wouldn't see the thief here. He wouldn't dare come so close to the place of a caning, not after his own fifty lashes had left him bloody and weak back then. He wouldn't. *He wouldn't.*

The Lord watched in silence as the woman was punished in front of him, with the commissioner counting once more. In the end, the experience did nothing but make him sick. He stumbled back inside the castle, sending away every single person who tried to help as he slowly made his way back up to his bedroom.

It was unthinkable that a lord like him would feel bad for mere peasants. That their screams would move anything inside of him, be it heart or just stomach contents. He cried out in frustration, throwing one of his books against the wall across from him, followed by another, and a third, eventually causing one of his expensive paintings to fall off its nail, face first onto the floor. The frame had clearly cracked, Döbrögi could see that even from where he was standing, and it only made him angrier.

He walked over and brought the heel of his boot down on the wood, breaking it farther apart, and then stomping on the canvas when that wasn't enough to satisfy his craving for destruction. He grabbed it from the floor and tore the fabric apart, the sound of ripping cotton filling the room. He couldn't rest until that lowly thief was caught, he couldn't sleep, he couldn't eat, he couldn't *breathe* without feeling like at any moment someone could grab him from behind, cover his mouth, and beat him with a rod again.

Phantom pain echoed the memories of the first two visits, and the Lord punched the wall next to him several times to make the haunting sensations go away. He needed another type of pain, something else to focus on. He couldn't sit inside and rot away in the protective circle of his maybe-not-so-loyal servants. That was exactly what that commoner boy wanted, along with his idiotic geese.

He needed to go outside.

Luckily for the Lord, the perfect opportunity was just around the corner, with the national market being held on his property, in the village just by his palace. He decided then and there that he had to attend, no matter how many guards it took to ease his fears about being ambushed. That viper wasn't going to get a single glimpse of even his baize coat.

A couple days later, after getting himself together and eating a generous amount for lunch to fill out his clothes a little better, he called for his carriage. Just as the horses came to a stop in front of him, however, he hesitated.

"My lord?" The driver turned to look at him, as did the commissioner, waiting for an order or some movement. "Is everything alright?"

"Yes, yes." Döbrögi willed himself to step into the carriage, happy to at least be seated. If he fainted out in the open, in front of every one of those peasants, he would never show himself in the royal court again. "Let's go for a bigger round, shall we? Towards the forest, and then back to the market. I would really like to breathe some fresh air first, away from the crowd."

His wishes were fulfilled as the driver turned the horses around in a half-circle, trotting down the hill on another road than originally planned. The Lord let out a sigh of relief as they left the castle and the market behind them. He knew there was a big chance that the demon was in there somewhere, mingling with the crowd, disguised as someone else; he also knew that he was both an easier and a more difficult target in the midst of all those people. It was better to avoid it altogether for the time being, until he calmed down enough to think with a clear head.

They had just reached the edge of his forest when he heard yelling, and his eyes snapped to the stranger now riding next to his carriage. There he was. There he was! He wasn't even disguised. He had the gall to catch up to his noble ride and trot alongside it like he was some kind of prince, telling the driver to slow down and listen!

"Do you know who I am, my lord?" the man asked them with the insufferable attitude of his past assailant, and Döbrögi couldn't be quick enough to scream for his guards to finally catch him.

This was his only chance, now that the thief had become so arrogant. He'd slipped away two times before, but now there was no chance of him escaping, and the Lord just shouted and cried for his guards to go, go, finally catch him. He seemed to be as elusive as ever, and Döbrögi finally yelled at the driver to go on, get his horse and go after him as well! Clearly, the guards weren't trained in horse-riding, or at least not enough to catch some peasant! "I'll pay a hundred golden coins to the one who catches him!" he added, spurring on the servants even further.

This was it. The end of his painful nightmares, the end of the pest that had made his life a living hell for the past weeks and months. He watched with equal parts glee and anxiety as the horses disappeared deeper into the forest, clutching the side of the carriage so tight that his now-bony fingers turned entirely white. If those horses were just a little faster, just a little more agile—

"What's the spectacle, my lord?" came a voice from right behind him, and he spun around to see who could've possibly dared approach him in such a manner. The blood drained from his face when he realized he knew that grin, and he'd made a grave mistake sending everyone after the rider from earlier. "They won't catch him, no matter how hard your lordship stares. Besides, he's not really me."

Döbrögi couldn't utter a single word before he was dragged out of his carriage, landing in the dust and mud with a heavy thud. Each of his muscles that hadn't wasted away yet locked up, paralyzed by the overwhelming terror at the sight of the man standing above him. In his weakened state, without any of his guards, he was helpless to be yanked up and fastened to the saddle of his former victim's own horse.

"It's only a shame that the commissioner is so busy! I'd love to ask him to count for me!" the man said cheerily, prompting his horse to trot right back towards the market, pulling the Lord along, no matter how much he stumbled and tripped.

One moment they were at the edge of the forest, and in the other, they seemed to be right in the middle of the market, and the Lord had no recollection of ever walking there. He couldn't pick out a single face from the crowd, all of the commoners blending together into one mocking, taunting entity, pointing with their dirty fingers.

This entity was there on that fateful day as well, sneering at the unfortunate boy who had been ordered to be beaten and whose geese were stolen. Ordered by him, Lord

Döbrögi, now standing in front of the great majority of the villagers from his own domain, stripped not only of his shirt, but his dignity.

Fifty lashes. The last of the three times this man would pay him back for his crimes he'd committed while laughing, then tried to deny and run from them.

The rod came down for the first time, and he heard the crowd chant,

"One!"

About the Author

Zi Trone is but a humble fear enthusiast with a passion for writing. An undying love for scared and crying characters has been the driving force behind hundreds of thousands of words already written, and hopefully many more to come.

Worse Than Death

Ari (withalittlebitofwhump)

CW: Sickness

Whumpee: Man, Whumper: Woman, Caretaker: Woman

He was retching before he was even awake, the nausea fighting with the headache for control of his consciousness.

His face was against something soft and wet. Moss?

He convulsed again. Cold fingers tugged through his matted curls and a woman's soothing voice murmured nothing in particular, the sort of drivel used to comfort children.

Delirium, then. He was in bed. He took an unsteady breath and resolved to settle in until the fever broke.

A bird shrieked above him. It was too real. The sounds, the dead leaves against his jaw, the smell of mud mixed with vomit—whatever was happening to him, it was real.

He wiped bile from his mouth and coughed wetly. "Who are you?" His head throbbed with the effort.

Fingers caressed his cheekbone. He could see her wavering outline now, her hair piled up in the old style, the thin, red line of her lips. "Your rescuer," she whispered. "You've had a fall." She snickered. "That'll be the story, anyway. Now, young one, will you give me your name?"

"Tamlin." Tam's voice was hoarse, and he tasted blood. Something was deeply wrong here, but he was dying.

"Tamlin," she said, cooing like a farmer over a prized piglet. "You won't die, you know."

Had she heard his thoughts?

"Not yet, anyway. I have things to show you, Tamlin." She spoke a word and cupped his cheek with her hand. Instantly, his headache abated. It was too quick, some part of him screamed, the relief too complete. Her hand moved down to his chest. Something inside of him snapped back into place and he grabbed at her arm, gasping.

"Oh, love," she said, looking his bedraggled body up and down. "We have so much to fix. Come on, then. Up." She towered over him, taller than any of his father's men, her hands extended. "Come to Faery with me, Tamlin."

Tamlin, who was beginning to realize he didn't have a choice, went.

END

About the Author

Ari is a writer, educator, and hanger-around of the Tumblr whump community for the better part of a decade. Ari is the head editor of Wince magazine and author of Fancywork, a sapphic h/c novelette, and their short stories and microficiton have been published elsewhere under an alternate name.

In Search of Shadows

Jayde Layne

CW: Medical abuse, institutionalization, ableism, referenced self-harm, attempted sexual assault

Whumpee: Woman, Whumper: Man, Woman, Caretaker: N/A

"You don't want her, sir. She's mad and half-feral besides. She looks calm now, but that girl's got the Devil in her and no mistake."

She looked away from the snow falling from the white ceiling and cast her eyes to her cell door. There was only a small opening to look through, covered with bars, and she couldn't see who was speaking to the orderly in the hall.

"Excuse me," scoffed another voice, "but I haven't come to your charming asylum by mistake. Mad is precisely what I'm after."

She frowned to herself and tilted her head, listening. That accent was familiar to her. It summoned memories of warmth, itchy lace, the rich taste of butter—she dragged her fingers over her lips, trying to hold the flavor hostage, but it fled as quickly as it had come. Pity. She missed butter.

"Well, er, yes, I suppose, but you know what the papers said. Killed her family, she did—I have plenty others that are tamer and won't fight you, sir."

Her fists instinctively clenched in the fabric of her ratty gown. It always made her angry, that accusation; it always felt wrong, but if the police and everyone else thought so, then it must be true. She couldn't refute what she couldn't remember; she ground her teeth, the familiar buzz of frustration settling under her skin like a swarm of hornets.

"I won't get coherent answers from the catatonic and comatose. I need a subject who can speak to me. Preferably in full sentences."

Ah, so he was one of those. Another "doctor" straight out of school, trying to prove themselves to their esteemed colleagues, and came looking for someone less fortunate than they to test their pet theories on. Must be an asylum-type doctor then. The body-doctors just took corpses. She'd heard all about it from Thomas down the hall, who swore up and down that he'd seen one such test subject stand up and walk out of the dissection room despite most of his organs sitting in glass jars not three feet away.

"Right. Well, better than her rotting in here and taking up space. You might like to stand back, sir." There was a soft jingle of the orderly's keys; for the first time in the conversation she sat up, and the snow that had been falling from all directions, padding the walls and floor with their fluffy white protection, hung still in mid-air. "There's no telling when she'll have a fit."

The door slowly creaked open. She sat very still in her corner as the man stepped inside. He wore a nice, well-fitted coat and neatly pressed shirt, a top hat held loosely in one of his hands. It was on the taller end as far as top hats went, though she knew someone with a hat even taller, so tall he probably wouldn't have fit into this room.

"Hello, Alice," he said primly, chin held high so that he looked down his nose at her. His eyes were a strange hazel behind his gold-framed spectacles. "My name is Doctor James Gordan. Your guardianship and treatment will be transferring to me to assess your fitness for experimental treatments for madness and hysteria."

Alice narrowed her eyes. Doctor Gordan was a strange man. Most doctors didn't bother to explain anything, just did what they wanted and left her to try and figure it out. He was being congenial on purpose, perhaps to ensure her cooperation, but she wouldn't be fooled so easily. The man had just bought her like a new teapot, after all.

Doctor Gordan's careful smile fell. "You do talk, don't you?" he asked brusquely.

Alice's fists tightened. There it was. It was easier and quicker than she thought it would be to see past the mask.

"Yes," she said, her voice cracked and rusty. "When I want to."

The smile returned, this time with a spark of excitement in the Doctor's eyes. "Excellent. I'm sure we'll have many interesting discussions. Come along, now." Her eyes darted to the orderly, not wanting to get her ears boxed for moving without permission, but he only nodded and gestured towards the Doctor. "Go on then, 'fore he changes his mind."

Gingerly, Alice slid off the edge of the rickety bed. It had been a while since she was last allowed out of the room, since her last fit where she apparently tried to put Malachi's eye out with a spoon, but she didn't remember it like that. She remembered a touch on the hand that held the spoon, an unwanted one that made fire roar up her arm, and then she was standing at the edge of a warm red waterfall, letting it drip down that same arm with the sun warming her back.

She hadn't seen the sun since, and there were still dried brown flakes stuck to the fine hair on that arm.

Anxiety twisted in her gut as she crossed the room. Almost immediately, she was distracted from it by the sting of cold around her ankles as she waded through the snow that covered all of the flat surfaces in the room, the flakes still suspended mid-air. When she reached him, the doctor looked her up and down and nodded.

"Yes, you'll do quite nicely."

***

"Where are you from?"

Alice licked her lips. Blood was welling up where she had been biting and picking for the last hour of jolty carriage travel. "Shouldn't you know? You said you read my records."

Doctor Gordan frowned and scribbled something on the book perched on his lap. He used a fountain pen, hefty and sharp.

"I did. I want to hear it from you."

"London. I don't remember where exactly. There were a lot of trees."

Her mouth was too wet; she had too many little wounds. She wiped her mouth with the back of her hand and it came away smeared with brown, making her feel only more out of place in the fancy carriage with her soiled asylum gown and bare feet. Being out of the asylum for the first time in Lord knew how many years felt like breathing fresh air, but the obvious way she stuck out in the world she'd been locked away from made that air taste toxic.

"What do you remember besides the trees?"

She turned to the carriage window. They were still trotting through town, though they had left the grimy center where the asylum was—now they moved past rows of identical brick homes and pointed iron gates, trails of ivy climbing the walls towards peaked roofs. Something about them was familiar, but there were no trees here.

"I remember the shadows."

She wasn't looking at him, but she heard the frown in the Doctor's voice. "Shadows?"

"Shadows lived in that house." She could still see them if she tried. Faint and flickering against the bright green wallpaper in the firelight. Looming tall, far taller than she, stretched thin towards the ceiling. She blinked and shook herself free. "They're what made me mad, you know."

Doctor Gordan leaned forward over his notes. "That's when the hallucinations began?"

Alice watched him warily from the corner of her eye. Doctors were always interested in their patient's delusions at first, when they were still fresh and new, perhaps to be used in some study or another to boost their reputation. But then, once the profit has passed, they grow bored.

Still, she'd been mad for a long time, and would be mad for as many years as she had left. There was no point in holding back.

"No. I'd been to Wonderland before the shadows came. But they crawled inside my head, tainting and corrupting everything they touched. It's not such a happy place anymore."

"Ah, yes," said the Doctor, scribbling away. "That's what you call it. 'Wonderland.' Tell me—"

The carriage jerked to a stop, making the Doctor's pen skate across the page and eliciting an angry sound from his throat. They had stopped in front of a house in the center of a row, tall and thin, built of dark brick, the curtained windows staring over the street like stern, hooded eyes.

"Here we are, sir," said the cheerful carriage driver as he opened the door. Doctor Gordan grumbled to himself as he perched his hat atop his head, packed away his pen and notes, and began to clamber out with his ungainly limbs. "Just in time for tea, sir, if it pleases you."

The Doctor merely grunted at the man and handed him a few coins. "Come along, Alice."

Carefully, she climbed out of the carriage. The stone beneath her feet was rough and cool, a light breeze brushing her cheek, and as she blinked against the sun at the house, the eye-windows blinked back. The mouth of the house opened, and behind its teeth stood a woman with gray hair restrained under a cap. She wore a housekeeper's uniform, though the ramrod line of her spine, pushed back shoulders, and lift of her chin made her look like a queen. No, not quite a queen—there was a pinched quality to her face that made her look too bitter to be a queen. Perhaps a duchess, endlessly longing for more than she had.

"Doctor," she said with a slight dip of her chin.

"Mrs. Greenway," he greeted as he mounted the steps. "Please make our new patient presentable and have Maryanne serve tea in my study."

"At once, sir." Her eyes landed on Alice, a cold, pale brown that reminded her of a windswept heath in winter. "Don't dawdle, girl."

Alice hesitated a moment more. She could feel the eyes of the house glaring, its teeth bared as its maw hung open, hungry and dark. It wanted to eat her alive. But when the housekeeper gave a sharp jerk of her head, she remembered that she didn't have any other choice. So she put her bare foot on one step, then the next, and climbed into the beast's jaws.

The thing's throat was papered in bright green with a strange jagged pattern. A long red tongue unfurled from the stairs and ended at the door—somewhere in her mind she knew it was a carpet, not a tongue, and yet the texture was still slimy and unpleasant under her feet. The door closed behind her, and the house swallowed them all up.

The Doctor was ahead, handing off his coat and hat to a young woman with fair skin and red hair. She looked nervous, not meeting the Doctor's eyes, and only caught Alice's for a split second before they darted away again.

A hand prodded between her shoulder blades. "Upstairs," said the housekeeper shortly. "Before you track filthy footprints all over the carpet."

The Doctor was already ducking through his study door. He gave no indication that he heard Mrs. Greenway's words, but Alice supposed it didn't necessarily matter. He probably didn't care what the housekeeper said to the mad girl; it sounded like a bad joke.

There were few women working at the asylum, but those that did struck more fear into the hearts of the inmates than any of the orderlies. The men could be violent and unpredictable, dealing out blows and pain with glee, but in the end it was all just bruises and cuts that would heal and cease to ache. The women weren't rash; they were cruel, and they searched for reasons to be. They kept a score in their minds of who had broken a rule and how they might use it to their advantage later, they were strict with food and rest, and their words cut deeper than any wound an orderly could inflict, though the women could inflict those too, should they choose.

The Duchess reminded Alice very much of those nurses. She was in charge and had the master of the house behind her—she could do whatever she wanted, and she reveled in it.

Good thing Alice had prior experience.

She went up the stairs, evidently not quickly enough for the Duchess, who continued to poke and prod her all the way up into the next hallway, where she shooed her through a door and into a small bathroom.

This was the house-creature's stomach, Alice decided. The walls were papered in what appeared to be the leftover scraps of the paper from downstairs, and the pale yellow tiles under her feet put her in the mind of bile. But it was small, only large enough for a tub, vanity, and looking glass; the house-beast was so large, it surely must have other stomachs.

The Duchess pushed past her and turned on the brass tap of the tub. "Quit daydreaming and get undressed," she snapped at Alice. "You won't be wearing that filthy thing around here."

Having been naked in the asylum many times, Alice shrugged out of her stained shift without hesitation. Waiting for the tub to fill, she found her eyes drawn towards the clouded looking glass where it hung on the wall above the vanity, the edges of the gold frame just beginning to tarnish.

It had been a long time since Alice had seen her own reflection. She knew she had grown and changed over the many years in the asylum, but in her mind she still carried an image of herself as a small girl, rosy-cheeked and plump with ribbons woven in her long hair.

That was not the image she found in the looking glass. The Alice in the fog was tall and skeletal, dark hair cropped close to her skull to be sold by the orderlies, her green eyes too big and bright and strange for her paper-pale face. If she lifted her arms she could count her ribs, and her collarbones jutted out from her like blades.

How strange it is, she thought to herself, *to look in a mirror and see a stranger.*

Her reflection dropped her arms before she did and turned to face Alice head on. Her lips spread wide into a smile, teeth tinged red, and when she turned her palms face up, they were coated in the same deep shade.

Alice just sighed and shook her head. She knew she had blood on her hands. There was no need to remind her.

Her reflection flickered like a sputtering candle. When it returned, she was no longer alone in the mirror; now there was a shadow behind her, tall and thin and sharp, and the mirror-Alice had lost her smile. The shadow reached out a hand and rested it on the reflection's shoulder—both she and the real Alice shuddered at the touch—and more red flowed over her skin.

A sharp pinch on her arm snapped her attention back to the scowling Duchess. "Stop daydreaming and get in the bath, girl."

When she glanced back at the mirror she saw only her normal reflection. Damn shadows.

Alice climbed into the tub before the Duchess could pinch her again. The water wasn't warm, but it wasn't freezing either, which to her was more than luxurious. She sank into it, but before she could tilt her head back to soak her hair, the Duchess was grabbing a washcloth in one hand and Alice's shoulder in another.

"Filthy," she hissed again as she began to scrub. "I'll never understand why Doctor Gordan insists on getting his patients from places like that. You've all got nits and lice and Lord knows what else." To be fair to the Duchess, she wasn't wrong. Alice was covered in dirt and the remnants of dried blood from her last fit, and she wouldn't be surprised if she had lice in her short hair—lice were always finding a way into the asylums. Fleas, too.

The Duchess scrubbed at her until she was bright red and stinging all over. Only then did she allow Alice to wet her hair, then she scrubbed at it with equal violence, like Alice was a stubborn stain that needed to be scrubbed out of existence; or perhaps this was the first step of being digested by the house, and the Duchess was an agent thereof.

How long does it take a house to digest, she wondered.

"There," the Duchess spat as she tossed the washcloth aside. "That's as clean as you're going to get. Even the best soap can't scour a soiled soul."

Alice let the words slide off of her. That was the trick with women like the Duchess: if you didn't let the claws of their words sink into you, they became just another person who beat you for being mad, the same as everyone else.

"I thought it was my mind that was soiled," said Alice, standing up from the water. The droplets made lovely music when they fell from her and into the tub, like the gentlest of rain on the surface of a pond, or tears on a quiet cheek.

"It's both," scoffed the Duchess. She tossed a rough towel at Alice's chest. "I'm going to fetch your dress, and you'd better be dry by the time I get back."

Alice's body obeyed the order on its own. Meanwhile she considered the Duchess' words; it was an interesting concept, the idea that the shadows had corrupted her soul as well as her Wonderland. Some of the doctors at the asylum believed that delusions were caused by immoral behavior and a lack of faith. Others claimed it was her gender, or her upbringing. One, who was more of a priest than a doctor, had declared her possessed.

But if this was true, which came first? The stains on her mind, or on her soul?

The door opened again. In her arms the Duchess held a simple blue dress that had clearly been worn many times before. If she looked closely, Alice could see where hems and sides had been raised or lowered or let out or tucked in to accommodate all of the different people who had worn it. Her suspicions were correct: Doctor Gordan had done this many times before. How long would it be before Alice's delusions grew stale and he tossed her out with the bathwater?

"You still know how to dress, I assume?" snapped the Duchess. Alice took the clothes from her arms without a word, which only made her more cross, but Alice was expecting that.

The dress sagged off of her shoulders and hung limp to her knees. It was too big, or perhaps Alice was too skinny for it, but either way the Duchess didn't seem inclined to do any more needlework on it.

"Well, it covers you," was all she said before pushing Alice out of the bathroom door. "Doctor Gordan is waiting for you in his study. For God's sake, don't forget to knock!"

She had been given stockings, but no shoes, and the polished wood floor was slick. She descended the staircase more carefully than Everest, not daring to touch the banister or the walls after she tried once and the house-beast growled at her, which was fair enough. She wouldn't want someone touching her insides either.

It was strange. This was the first house she'd been in since being sent to the asylum. From the corners of her eyes she could see ghosts, echoes of happier times past, little girls sliding down banisters for fun and running to greet their fathers at the door. One such ghost ran right through her middle as she stood at the door of Doctor Gordan's study, where she waited for an answer to her knock.

"Come in."

If the bathroom had been a stomach, Doctor Gordan's study was in the heart of the beast. It was all dark wood paneling and neatly arranged bookcases, the walls expanding and contracting with each dim beat that thundered in Alice's ears—how he could focus in here with that din, Alice couldn't fathom.

"Ah, Alice. Please sit," said the Doctor with hardly a glance up from his paper and pen.

She took a step forward and felt her toes squelch. There was a puddle of black ichor on the floor, with more scattered around the room, and rivers slowly oozing down the moving walls. A house, of course, wouldn't bleed red. Still, it was rather unpleasant when it stuck to her stockings on her way across the room to the chair the Doctor had indicated.

She sat. The Doctor's desk was in front of a large window, the pale light rendering him a faceless silhouette in front of her.

Doctor Gordan finished his sentence and signed at the bottom of the page with a flourish. Then he set whatever it was to the side and picked up the same notebook he'd had in the carriage.

"Now that we're settled, we can get some real work done. Where were we ... ah yes, Wonderland. When did you first go there?"

Alice chewed on the inside of her cheek as she tried to remember. To her it had felt like her entire life, but that couldn't be right.

"I think I was four," she said when the Doctor started tapping his pen impatiently. "I went to a marvelous tea party with the Hare and the Dormouse and the Hatter."

"And these are characters of yours?"

"You could call them that," Alice said, squirming uncomfortably in her seat. Once she had called them her friends, but nothing had been the same since the shadows.

"Why don't we start at the beginning?"

So, feeling like a butterfly pinned in a display case, Alice recounted the day to the best of her memory. Her mother, a faceless figure in wide skirts, had taken Alice along when she went to a garden party. Alice had chased a rabbit wearing a waistcoat to its hole and fallen down into the earth, where she found herself at a table so long it spiraled up into the air, and the Hatter and the Hare and the Dormouse had to run up and slide down it when they switched seats. And Alice had laughed and laughed, clapping her little hands.

What she didn't mention was how she'd already seen the waistcoat-ed rabbit in her dreams long before she fell into the rabbit hole. The good Doctor hadn't asked about dreams, after all.

"And how did you return from Wonderland?"

That gave Alice pause. She swung one of her legs, her foot grazing the surface of the ichor pool that had formed under her chair.

"I don't remember."

Doctor Gordan frowned fiercely at her. Alice blinked, and when she opened her eyes he had a shadow of his own draped over his shoulders. A shadow with familiar yellow eyes and bright white teeth.

"Be careful, Alice," the cat cooed. His shape was cloudy and black, scratchy around the edges like an ink drawing, and his teeth were blunt and human, with only two sharp fangs at the front. "The sun casts its shadows everywhere." His tail grazed the Doctor's cheek, but he didn't react to the touch as he kept talking, saying words Alice didn't hear.

She huffed to herself. The cat was never as helpful as he thought he was.

"Alice."

She jolted, eyes snapping back to Doctor Gordan, whose gaze was running her through like frustrated daggers. The cat smirked one last time and vanished in a cloud of black that lingered like ink in water.

Doctor Gordan didn't say anything at first. He just regarded her with narrowed eyes for a long moment. Then he scribbled something in his notebook, set his pen down, and opened a drawer in his desk.

"Do you know how to write?"

"Somewhat," Alice answered. It had been years—she wasn't allowed near pens after the fit several years ago when she'd plunged one such implement into her own wrist. That's what they told her, at least, and she had the scar to prove it, but she remembered it quite differently: someone had asked her to write something down, something about her old house and her family, and a strange buzzing drone had filled her ears. The light changed, growing brighter, and when she blinked the sunspots away she was in Wonderland, stabbing a beehive with the intent of killing the insects that buzzed under her skin whenever someone asked her about that night.

"Good enough." From the drawer, the Doctor produced another notebook and a second pen. "I want you to write down everything you can remember about Wonderland." He slid the notebook across the table. Alice took it and the pen, resting them in her lap as she slowly dragged her fingers over the leather of the cover. It was identical to the one the Doctor was using—how many of these did he have?

"Before the shadows or ... after?"

Doctor Gordan tilted his head thoughtfully.

"They're very different places," Alice tacked on.

"Both," said the Doctor, and before Alice could say anything else, he rang a little bell that was sitting on his desk. A moment later the study door opened.

"Maryanne, will you please show Alice to her room?"

There was a barely audible, "Yes, sir," and with another pointed look from the Doctor, Alice stood up, shuddering as the ichor flowed over her toes. As she turned towards the door, she caught an ever-so-slight glint of a yellow eye, winking at her.

The red-headed serving girl led her back upstairs. The girl was coiled tighter than the springs that the Hatter wore down his back, but who exactly she was scared of Alice couldn't tell. She kept her hands clasped tightly in front of her, huddling in like she didn't dare to touch the walls—perhaps she was frightened of the house-beast too.

"This will be your room," said Maryanne when they reached the door at the end of the hall.

It wasn't much: a small bed, a dresser, and a whitewashed desk with a matching chair and oil lamp. "There are some more dresses in the drawers for you."

Alice stepped inside. "Much nicer than the asylum," she said with a smile in Maryanne's direction.

The other girl didn't smile back, but her eyes did lift from the floor. She took a short breath, as though steeling herself, then asked softly, "Which asylum were you from?"

Alice's eyebrows rose. Not the question she was expecting, but what was the harm in answering? "Saint Margaret's."

Maryanne nodded. After a moment's contemplation: "My mother died in an asylum. Humphrey's." Then, before Alice could answer, she looked back at the floor and muttered, "I have to help fix dinner." She quickly fled, closing the door behind her.

What a strange girl.

Alice shrugged it off. She sat down at the desk, opened the notebook to its first blank page, and picked up the pen. Then she stopped, rolling the wooden body of the pen between her fingertips.

Where should she start? She didn't remember much of her old Wonderland. Sometimes that version felt like a dream, and the Wonderland she had now was how it had always been. But that wasn't true, she knew it. She didn't remember that night, but the shadows were there. They crawled in through her eyes and bled through the earth and air and water, thick and black like the ichor that dripped down the study walls a few minutes ago, and she'd felt it as Wonderland began to twist.

She remembered all of that, but she couldn't remember what had really happened to her parents.

A shudder went down her spine. This wasn't what she was here for. The only thing the Doctor cared about was Wonderland. As far as anyone else was concerned, the deaths of her family were already solved. It didn't matter.

At a loss for what else to do, she simply wrote 'Wonderland' at the top of the page. The letters were shaky and awkward, but legible enough, she hoped. Then she sat there another moment—there was so much to Wonderland, where should she begin? More importantly, what did the Doctor most want to read? She'd tried explaining Wonderland to so many doctors at the asylum, but none of them really cared about the specifics, they just wanted to know how many leeches they needed to stick to her this time around. Perhaps she should start with the things she saw outside of Wonderland …

Alice blinked. There was a pawprint on the page that hadn't been there before. The ink spread through the fibers of the paper like tree roots searching out water, saturating it with black, growing from edge to edge. Alice stared into the ink, waiting patiently until the page was entirely black.

She let herself fall into it.

She fell through a void, surrounded by spirals of parchment and scrolls, past waterfalls of ink that seemed to have no source or end, through flocks of flying quills. One of them pecked impishly at her arm and drew a dot of blood as she plummeted ever downwards.

She wasn't afraid. She knew that eventually—ah, yes, here it was. Her descent slowed of its own accord. Alice leaned back until she was falling vertically, and the skirt of her borrowed dress poofed up around her waist like an umbrella. It made her heart warm; she hadn't had a proper fall in a long time. During her fits she skipped the whole ritual and went right to somewhere else. This was much gentler, and the dress reminded her of when she used to visit as a little girl, as the asylum shifts had been too loose and shapeless to make the skirt poof out like this.

Eventually her bare toes brushed ground. Or rather they brushed rough parchment, as though landing on a page. At her touch, ink billowed out, ripples on the surface of a pond, and drawn ink shapes sprouted all around her: trees, shrubs, flat little tufts of grass, and a waterfall that she could somehow still hear despite the water being stationary.

Alice giggled to herself as she settled her feet. Stationary. The Hatter would like that one.

"Something you find amusing, Alice?" The purring voice came from behind her. She turned to find the cat, sprawled out on a rock like an ink-blot with only the faintest suggestion of a proper shape.

"Just a silly joke," she responded.

"All jokes are silly," countered the cat. "That's what makes them jokes."

Alice rolled her eyes. "I haven't missed your needling."

The cat blinked his yellow eyes at her and slowly revealed his wide grin, still pearly white even when the whole world was yellow parchment and his body was black ink.

"Just a bit of fun. You know the twins are much worse than I."

"Ugh, don't remind me." A pause, then: "When you spoke to me in the study, about shadows, what did you mean?"

"I would think it was obvious." The cat stood and bowed into a stretch, yawning and showing off his two sharpest teeth. "The sun casts shadows everywhere, not only in one house in London."

Suddenly her throat felt tight. "You think there are shadows in the Doctor's house, then?"

"Certainly. A beast can devour its prey, but nothing can digest a shadow, as you know all too well."

Alice folded her arms across her chest. Looking into the inked shadows of the parchment trees now came with the icy touch of dread down her spine, and her doubts from earlier returned with all of their cavalry.

"Cheshire, do you know what happened the night the shadows came?"

The cat, who had been busily licking his paw, stopped and flicked his ears back. "The shadows came. That is what happened."

"That can't be all of it," Alice argued back. "The sun can't make shadows on its own. What cast these ones?"

His tail thrashed. "You should be more careful, Alice," he hissed with an arch to his back. "The shadows are short here, but they can grow long." As if to prove his point, one of the tree shadows suddenly stretched across the page of the ground towards them, ending in a threatening sharp edge by the cat's rock.

"Why don't they want me to know?"

"Some things are not worth knowing."

Lord forgive her, Alice stamped her bare foot like a child. "Should I not be the one who decides what is worth knowing? They're my memories. What gives them the right to keep them?"

Before the cat could respond, the shadows began to grow deeper, longer, and when Alice looked to the sky, she found the parchment sun slowly being filled with ink.

"You're out of time," said the cat. The shadow crept across his body, leaving only his eyes, blinking yellow in the dark. "But if you insist on suffering, I will find you again. You made this choice. Don't be late."

Alice jolted back into her body still sitting at the desk, her hands covered in ink, a full page of writing in the book before her, and a small dot of blood on her arm.

***

Alice was served supper in her room, which she was perfectly content with. She certainly didn't remember her table manners, and the way she devoured the food after years of asylum fare would've caused a polite lady to faint.

Her favorite part was the bread and butter. Oh, how she had missed butter.

That night she lay awake, watching bread-and-butterflies flit around her small room, waiting for the cat to make an appearance. The house-beast shifted, creaked, and growled as the hours passed. It still didn't like her.

Eventually she could keep herself awake no longer. Her eyes fell closed, and she slept.

Bang bang bang. "Time to wake up, missy!"

The Duchess is feeling shrill this morning.

"There won't be any lying about in my house, you hear me?"

This time she was summoned to the kitchen to eat her breakfast. She went, wearing another worn dress from the dresser, this one in a yellow that had probably once been cheery before all the fading.

The color felt out of place in the sooty kitchen. The cook was already hard at work snapping at Maryanne and preparing the Doctor's breakfast. Alice was handed a plate with toast and jam, which she ate eagerly. The jam was sweet and sharp and tangy, a fruit that she couldn't quite discern.

The Doctor took his breakfast in the dining room, during which Alice was ushered upstairs to make her bed, then she returned to the study and sat in the same chair as the day before. The ichor pool underneath had grown; she now had to keep her feet pressed against the legs of her chair to keep them from sinking into the muck.

Doctor Gordan took his time going over what Alice had written the day before. She had already read it, worried that she had subconsciously transposed her conversation with the cat, but that wasn't what was on the page. Instead the words described her first true fall into Wonderland at the garden party. The Doctor scribbled a few notes in his own notebook, then began the questions.

Dozens and dozens of questions. How many times had she been to Wonderland? (Too many times to count.) When did she usually go there? (When she was upset, overwhelmed, in pain.) Did she only hallucinate when she was in Wonderland? (No.) What kinds of things did she see when she wasn't there? (All kinds of things, like the house-beast. That one got her a vexed frown and more scribbles in the Doctor's book.) Did she choose where in Wonderland she appeared? (No.) Were any of the creatures or things there threatening? (Yes.)

He didn't ask about the shadows, which Alice found more vexing than she cared to admit. For her there were two Wonderlands: before and after.

Before was a lovely place. Strange and frustrating to understand, but beautiful, and it never stepped outside of its own bounds, leaving her waking world untouched.

After was dark and dangerous. Beautiful in some places, but in a way that made her stomach drop. The shadows leaked out of it, slithering out into London, staining everything they touched. The first morning she woke up in the asylum it was to a ceiling full of knives dripping blood onto her face and her hair and the dirty sheets.

But Doctor Gordan didn't seem interested in the differences or the causes thereof. He muttered words to himself as he wrote his notes: *hallucinations, delusions, dissociation, hysterical fits.* All words Alice had heard before. Most of them didn't mean much to her. They were just words, stuck to her like signposts, things other people used to navigate her like she was a twisting, rocky road.

Eventually, as the clock in the hall struck eleven, the Doctor closed his notebook. "We'll do our first experiment this afternoon," he announced. "I want to ascertain whether your dissociation can be triggered deliberately."

"You want to send me to Wonderland on purpose," she translated, and he nodded.

"Precisely."

That was ... hm. On the one hand, it was worrisome—who knew where or with what she would end up without Wonderland choosing to pull her in? On the other, maybe it would make the cat cooperate in a more timely manner.

She found herself nodding. "Very well, Doctor."

Doctor Gordan gave her a sharp grin. "As if you have a choice, Alice."

***

For all his talk of experiments and new treatments, the one he chose first was one Alice had endured many times before: hot water.

After lunch she was brought back to the house-beast's small stomach, escorted by the agent of digestion herself, the Duchess. She turned on the tap for another bath, and Alice stood still as instructed, staring at the mirror. This time no shadows or other Alices appeared. There was only her, frowning at her reflection until steam clouded the glass too much for her to see.

"As the Doctor ordered," said the Duchess, drying her hands on her apron. "Piping hot. In you get, you little wastrel."

Alice, having already shed her dress in the growing heat and humidity of the room, stepped into the tub and winced. The water was indeed piping hot, too hot to be comfortable, stinging her skin everywhere it touched, but she made herself submerge anyway. It wasn't the first time she'd had a hot water treatment.

"Now stay there. If you get out, I'll give you a whipping." The Duchess snapped a towel for emphasis, then swept out of the door. Alice heard the lock click behind her.

Letting out a slow breath, Alice tried to relax into the heat. It was better than the cold, but it did feel disconcertingly like really, truly being digested by the house-beast; the air was practically water itself with how much steam had risen, and beneath the surface Alice's skin was beginning to turn red.

It didn't take long for her lungs to start struggling. Her short, heaving breaths made ripples spread across the surface of the tub, mirror ripples of heat rolling across her skin underneath. Alice leaned her head back against the edge of the tub and stared up through the steam. *Breathe slowly,* she told herself, but her lungs didn't obey. *I always give myself such good advice, but I very seldom follow it.*

Her hair was soaked and sticking to the back of her damp neck. She rubbed her wrinkled fingertips against her thighs, searching for sensation as her breaths turned to gasps. She knew better than to try to get out—she'd had plenty of beatings from the orderlies, and didn't particularly want to know how the Duchess compared—and the steam was close and thick like the smoke from Caterpillar's hookah. She hadn't seen the Caterpillar in a long while. Perhaps he was in a cocoon somewhere. That would be better than being twisted by the shadows like the Hatter and the others.

A new scent rose in the steam. Leafy, herbal. When she opened her eyes and looked down, the bathwater was blooming with a new color: thin brown.

"It's a bit early for tea, isn't it?" she asked aloud. The cat's voice laughed in her ear.

The world did a dizzying flip. One moment she was staring down at her tea-filled bath, and the next she was back in her yellow dress, sitting at a table with a full teacup before her. The air was just as damp and close it had been before, and her feet dangled, not touching the floor.

The reason became obvious as soon as she peeked over the edge of her chair. Neither her nor the table were sitting on anything solid. Instead they were floating dozens of feet high, buoyed by the steam rising from the massive vat of boiling tea below them.

"Don't worry." Alice's head snapped back up to see the cat sitting on the table to her left. Lazily, he dipped a paw into a teacup sitting beside him and licked it clean. "You won't fall. So long as you don't fidget."

Before she could snipe back at the cat, her attention fell back on the circular table. It was covered with a blue lace tablecloth, fully set for a high tea fancier than any Alice had ever seen (not that she had been to many, mind you). Opposite her sat a figure in a red velvet top hat.

For a moment her heart caught in her throat. Her last visit to the Hatter hadn't ended well, him screaming about her terrible table manners after she pointed out how grotesque his body was now, jammed full of bloody clockwork, but to her relief it wasn't him at all. It was a little automaton in his top hat and atrocious green jacket.

"The Hatter isn't so sociable these days," the cat explained. "It's just as well for us. Shadows cling to him everywhere he goes."

Alice's eyes darted up and around. There wasn't much to see; the steam from the tea below blotted everything else out in a white cloud, and the table dipped and rose in a steady rhythm like a ship at sea.

A soft *click* reached her ears, and the automaton sat up straight. It had no face, just a head full of gears that were now whirring away as one of its arms extended. It had no fingers either, only a strange clamp for a hand that snapped around the handle of the teapot in the center of the table and lifted it.

Alice tilted her head curiously at it. The pattern on it was so familiar, a gathering of sunflowers in the center, with more yellow blooms ringing the lid and handle, but before she could get a good look, the automaton jerked it back towards itself. Its hand detached halfway from its wrist to tilt the teapot, pouring more tea into its already overflowing cup. Brown spilled over the sides, filled the saucer beneath, and ran out onto the blue tablecloth.

"Not a very good automaton, is it?" Alice sniffed, unimpressed. The cat chuckled and batted a biscuit from one of the tray towers onto his plate.

"As a tea server, no. As a simulacrum of the Hatter? It's perfectly unnerving."

The automaton stopped pouring, extended its arm again, and let the teapot fall back to the table with a jarring *clang*. From somewhere in its clockwork, a rasping voice came. "Time for tea!" it chirped before grabbing the pitcher of cream and repeating its pouring.

Alice shook her head at it. "Why am I here, cat?"

He blinked at her, biscuit crumbs on his black whiskers. "You asked, Alice. Don't you remember?"

"I don't see what a terrible tea party has to do with the shadows."

"Look closely."

She swept her eyes over the table again, and again the teapot snagged her attention. Something about the vibrancy of the sunflower petals. She reached out, curled her fingers around the handle, but before she could lift it even an inch, the automaton suddenly started making a terrible ringing noise like an alarm clock.

"No!" exclaimed its mechanical voice over the ringing. "I am serving! I am serving!" Its hand sprung out of its socket. Alice barely had time to retract her hand before it landed in a metallic fist, right on top of the teapot, shattering it into tiny pieces.

"You idiot!" Alice shouted back. Her face felt hot, her hands shaking as she stared at the broken china. The stupid machine didn't know what it had just done. "That was my mother's!" She remembered her mother bending over the table, pouring tea into her father's cup. She remembered ...

She remembered.

The teapot tilted. Her father's face was anxious as he scoured the newspaper in his hands. Then a flash, and a knife, and the teapot smashed against the floor.

The tea in her cup was red. Alice stared at it, trembling, while the automaton went on ringing in the background and smashing more of the china.

The cat padded closer to her. "Well, Alice?" he asked with his wide grin. "Was that what you wanted?"

She didn't get a chance to answer. A deafening creaking and clanging suddenly filled the space, so piercing that Alice clapped her hands over her ears. Staring down, she saw what was making the noise—a wrought iron crane, swinging something large and dark and flat. Metal shrieked, and the steam began to dissipate as a lid was pulled over the boiling vat below.

She screamed as the table plummeted.

***

She came back to herself laying on the bathroom floor, naked as the day she was born. The air was clear of steam, now sharp and cold, and the Doctor's face hovered over hers, the Duchess' annoyed one in the background.

"Welcome back," the Doctor said, sitting back with his stethoscope around his neck. "Mrs. Greenway pulled you out just in time. We thought you had drowned."

Her lungs did ache, come to think of it. Alice coughed a couple of times, feeling liquid in the back of her throat, tasting tea on her tongue. Neither the Doctor nor the Duchess moved to help her up or fetch her clothes.

"Did you go to Wonderland?" the Doctor asked with an eager glint in his eye.

Slowly, Alice levered herself upright. "Y-yes," she stuttered out around more coughing. "Wasn't—terribly interesting—I'm afraid."

"Nonsense." Doctor Gordan stood and gestured at the Duchess. She handed him a towel, which he draped over Alice's lap. "This is very interesting. Very interesting indeed. Once you're dressed again, I want you to write down what you experienced as you did yesterday. We'll go over it this evening."

Without waiting for Alice's answer, the Doctor turned on his heel and swept out of the room; after all, why should he wait for an answer that didn't signify anything to him?

"Get up," snapped the Duchess, hauling Alice to her feet by her arm and leaving her to scramble for her towel. "You've spent enough time lazing about in the bath."

"I was hardly lazing," Alice responded without thinking. The exhaustion settling into her bones was proof enough of that, but the Duchess clearly didn't feel the same as her hand came down across Alice's cheek.

"And no talking back! I don't know how things were run at the asylum, but in this house you will keep your place."

The inside of Alice's cheek smarted when she ran her tongue along it. The taste of metal mixed with that of tea in a nauseating combination.

Still, the asylum had been worse. A voice floated through her mind, delicate as spider silk, and her heart ached at its familiarity.

Count your blessings, Alice.

**

Alice sat awake much longer than the rest of the house. Even the beast itself seemed to be asleep with its steady creaking, so Alice quietly paced back and forth across her small room, mind spinning.

The Doctor was disappointed with her visit to Wonderland. Apparently a tea party on a floating table with a talking automaton wasn't outlandish enough for him. But it had given Alice plenty of things to think about.

She ran the memory through her mind over and over, like a child tonguing at the space where a tooth was missing. It didn't run smoothly—they were isolated images, the teapot, her father, the knife, her mother's back, the teapot on the floor. From all the years at the asylum she knew what the official story was, what was splashed across the newspaper headlines: *Mad Child Murders Parents in Cold Blood.*

She knew her parents were stabbed. She knew she was found holding the knife. This memory didn't really reveal all that much, except for one significant thing.

She could remember.

Alice paused before her small bedroom window and pushed back the curtains. Her room was at the back of the house, so it didn't reveal much, just the tiny sliver of a garden behind the building before the back of the next row began. It was late enough for all yellow light, electric or oil, to be out and all the city was bathed in silver. She drank it in eagerly; her cell in the asylum didn't have a window.

Across the garden, something moved on the opposite roof. A dark splotch broke off from the long shadow of a chimney and slid down to the gutter, then leapt gracefully down to the top of the wall separating all of the gardens from each other, and trotted across to the Doctor's house. Alice wasn't afraid as the shadow leapt up onto her windowsill. The bad shadows only walked on two legs.

She obligingly slid open the window when the cat appeared. "Good evening, Alice." His teeth shone even whiter than the moon.

"Hello, cat. Twice in one day—to what do I owe the pleasure?" Back in the asylum Cheshire rarely appeared to her outside of Wonderland.

"A warning." His tail swayed in the air behind his head, twitching with agitation despite the wide smile he still wore. "The shadows are displeased. If you keep pursuing this quest, they are sure to pursue you as the fox pursues the hound. Your next visit will not be as easy as today's."

Alice didn't bother to correct him. Many things were different in Wonderland, foxes and hounds included. "I expected as much. If you've come with the intent to talk me out of it, it won't work."

"Oh, I know full well how stubborn you are. But be careful. Only one of us has nine lives."

"You're down to seven, as I recall."

The cat laughed. It sounded loud in her ears, but there was no answering echo off of the bricks. "You remember correctly."

Alice paused. "Cat, why haven't the shadows touched you? It seems like everything in Wonderland is different except for you."

"Simple. I am a cat. They can't corrupt what they can't catch."

It was Alice's turn to chuckle. "I do recall the Queen spending a whole afternoon looking for you."

"There are many things you remember, I suspect. All you have to do is find the right key."

"And the right-sized door," Alice grumbled with a roll of her eyes.

"Yes," he said with a long, roiling purr. "The right-sized door indeed." Then he faded into the air, only his white smile and yellow eyes lingering for a moment before disappearing.

Suddenly Alice was very, very tired. Her chest still ached from the almost-drowning, the inside of her cheek stung with the cut the Duchess had left inside her mouth, and it felt as though her very brain was pulsing in her skull.

She stumbled over to her bed and fell asleep, leaving the curtains open.

***

Something was shaking her. A voice said, loud in her ear, "Up you get, you layabout!"

Alice groaned and rolled away from the hands. They followed, giving her a hard pinch on the arm that didn't relent until she peeled her eyes open.

It was the Duchess, as expected, with the thin form of Maryanne standing behind her with a tray of toast and jam in hand. As Alice blearily rubbed sleep from her eyes Maryanne scurried over to the desk to set the tray down before retreating again, and a new figure took her place: Doctor Gordan.

In polite society, it would be unthinkable for a man to barge into a woman's bedroom before she was properly dressed. But Alice was not polite society, and she wasn't even in her nightgown anyway—she'd fallen asleep on top of the covers, still in her yellow dress from the day before. Damn it to hell, her muscles ached.

"Good morning, Alice," he said as he strode into the room. He had a clock under his arm, one that had been on the mantel over the fireplace in the dining room, which he set down on her desk beside the tray. "We're going to try something else today."

Alice reluctantly pulled herself upright. The Duchess stood beside her bed, one eye on the Doctor and one eye on Alice, doubtless waiting for the slightest provocation to strike.

"Today you will stay in this room. I want you to try to go to Wonderland, or if not, write as much as you can remember about it."

One of Alice's hands twisted into the blanket beneath her, mirroring how her stomach twisted into knots. Only the Lord knew how long she'd been confined to her cell in the asylum after her fit with the eye and the spoon. Being left in a room and told to stay there was one thing, actually being locked in was another—but there wasn't much she could do about it. At least this room had a window.

Doctor Gordan turned to her with a stern expression. "I'm expecting much from you today. Do not disappoint me." With that he took his leave, followed by the Duchess, who gave Alice her own harsh look as she passed.

"Maryanne," the Duchess said in the hall, "lock the door, and make sure she doesn't go back to bed. Lazy thing will do nothing all day if we let her."

"Yes, ma'am," Maryanne answered, so softly Alice almost missed it.

Alice was tempted to do exactly that, to lay back down and go back to sleep. But the toast and jam called to her, and Maryanne was still standing in the doorway. Her eyes were on the floor, as usual, but Alice could tell when people watched from their periphery. She did it all the time.

After a few minutes of deliberating, she got up to change her dress, this one a weak, pinkish-red color. It was only when she turned towards the tray of food that Maryanne spoke up.

"Why did they put you in the asylum?"

Alice almost laughed. "Have you been paying attention to the Doctor at all?" she asked, unable to prevent the amusement from coloring her voice. When she first went into the asylum, the story had been all over the papers, and ever since people simply assumed that if she was in the asylum she must be mad, end of conversation. She couldn't remember the last time she'd heard such a question.

But Maryanne remained solemn. "Doctors say a lot of things."

Amusement rapidly melted into annoyance. Why was Maryanne so curious, anyway? Maybe she just wanted to know what kind of lunatic she was forced to share a house with. Well, Alice was used to people fearing and reviling her. What was one more?

Despite her bravado, she still found herself bracing for the look of horror that was about to cross Maryanne's face.

"If you must know," Alice huffed, "my parents were killed. They say I did it."

"Who says?" Maryanne's expression wasn't scared at all. It was merely hard, her jaw set like stone—she hardly looked like the same timid maid that flitted about the house-beast unseen. Perhaps that was purposeful.

"The authorities. The doctors. Everyone, really."

"And what do you say?"

Alice shrugged. "I don't remember." Her stomach churned, and she told herself it was hunger and not the frustration of not knowing what really happened on the most terrible night of her life. Grasping for something else to think about, she asked, "What did they put your mother in for?"

Maryanne's face suddenly darkened. "Nothing," she snapped at Alice. "Nothing at all." She turned smartly on her heel and strode to the door, pausing only long enough to say, "Don't go back to sleep," before closing the door behind her. The lock turned, and Alice swallowed back a spike of nerves.

She distracted herself from the locked door by eating her breakfast. Then it was just her, the notebook the Doctor had given her, and the ticking clock. With nothing else to do, she sat down at the desk and opened the notebook.

Once again, no words came to her. She fidgeted, swung her feet, chewed on her nails, but it was no use; she hadn't written anything since going into the asylum, and she didn't know the words she would need to describe a place like Wonderland. And that damn clock was driving her to distraction!

Tick—tock—tick—tock—tick—tock

Alice cast an annoyed glare at the contraption and stood up to pace. It was an overcast day outside her window, the air thick and heavy even inside the house, all the world holding its breath. All except the clock, ticking on without mercy.

Tick—tock—tick—tock—tick—tock

The sound was burrowing into her, under her skin, into her head, itchy like the parasites that infested every piece of cloth in the asylum. She raked her nails up and down her arms, but the little clockwork bug only buried itself deeper with every passing second.

Tick—tock—tick—tock—tick—tock

She squeezed her eyes shut tight. The ticking and tocking reverberated, multiplied.

Tickticktick—Tocktocktock—Tickticktick—Tocktocktock

She opened her eyes to darkness. Gone were the walls of the house-beast, replaced by dozens of clocks—no, watches—hanging from long chains, their faces twice as wide as Alice was tall and each softly glowing with an eerie silver light, like a hundred full moons suspended in the sky. The moment her eyes opened, the watches all stopped ticking, leaving the sound to echo into the cavernous darkness.

Her breath was loud in her ears. Alice had never been to a place like this before.

From behind her came a voice. "Figured it out yet?" Never before had she felt so relieved to hear the cat speak.

She turned to find him draped on top of one of the watch faces, idly swinging his tail and grinning down at her. "No, I only just got here."

The cat chuckled and lolled his head off the side of the watch, looking at her upside down. "Time doesn't matter so much here."

"And where exactly is 'here'?"

"How should I know? You made it up."

Alice scowled and crossed her arms over her chest. She wasn't relieved anymore.

"Oh, come now, don't pout. Think for a moment—if you remember how." His grin widened, and Alice scoffed, turning back towards the never-ending collection of watches. Perhaps this was part of the Hatter's lands. Lord knew the man was almost as obsessed with time as he was with tea. Probably because time always brought him to tea-time, if only to take him away from it again.

The darkness made her nervous. She couldn't see the floor, even if she knew she was standing on something flat, and spotting shadows would be much harder when she was already surrounded by them.

Well, let's see. Last time it was a tea party with her mother's teapot. What could the pocket watches mean? Maybe just a reflection of the maddening clock ticking away in her bedroom, which Alice was sure Doctor Gordan had done on purpose.

Unconsciously she began to move, strolling in between the watches, her mind spinning as she tried to figure it out. Every so often she would see a puff of black against the silver glow of a clock face as the cat kept pace with her. The watches went on for miles, disappearing beyond the horizon, and as she walked further into the forest of them, she slowly became aware that the ticking hadn't stopped. Or maybe it had, and was now starting up again, soft and far in the distance.

Tick ...

Tock ...

And yet none of the watch faces moved. Not a single hand budged, even as the ticking grew and Alice's nerves frazzled and frayed at the ends.

Eventually she could stand it no longer. Whirling towards the last place she'd seen the cat, Alice exclaimed, "What is making that *confounded noise?*"

The cat's laugh, predictably, came from behind her. "Surrounded by watches and asking where the ticking is coming from?"

"Are you blind?" Alice snapped, refusing to turn and look at him purely on principle. "I'm surrounded by *broken* watches that shouldn't be ticking!"

"You're right," said the cat, "they're not supposed to be ticking. Perhaps that's why they're broken. Or perhaps it's the other way around, and they are broken because they are ticking when they aren't meant to be."

"For crying out loud." Alice was about to turn and give the blasted cat a piece of her mind when one of the watches caught her eye. There was nothing special about it, nothing to signify that it was different from the hundreds of others, yet she found herself padding closer to it. The face was taller than she, and the chain creaked slightly as it swayed in some incorporeal wind. Neither the second nor the minute hand twitched, yet she could still hear the mechanism inside, ticking away like everything was perfectly swell.

Tick—tock—

The watch read 8:27 p.m. When Alice was supposed to be in bed. But she wasn't in her room where she belonged ... where was she?

Tick—tock—

It was 8:27 p.m., and she was looking at the pocket watch. The familiar pocket watch, with the tiniest scratch along the side. She'd made that scratch when her father tried to teach her how to wind the thing he always carried in his pocket.

Tick—tock—

It was 8:27 p.m., and it wasn't in the familiar grip of her father. The watch hung in space, toppled from his pocket and hanging from its chain. Something red dripped slowly down the chain and smeared over the face.

Tick—tock—

Suddenly the sound was deafening. Alice clapped her hands over her ears as a drop of red larger than her head slid over the face of the watch she'd been staring at. All around her the watches vibrated with the sharp, booming sound.

Softness—she looked down to find the cat pressed against the front of her legs, ears pricked up and tail lashing in agitation as one by one the glow of the pocket watches changed to red. From the corner of her eye she caught movement—a sliver of a shadow slipping around the metal back of a watch—and the cat's fur rose all along his back.

"Run, Alice!" he snarled, barely audible over the noise of the watches.

Alice didn't bother to ask where she was supposed to run in the endless maze of timepieces. She turned and fled as fast as she could go without being able to see her feet. All around her shadows were appearing, peeling themselves off of clock faces and slithering down chains to join the hunt, all so eager to drag her back into the darkness, to make her forget the teapot and the bloody pocket watch.

Alice didn't want to forget.

The moment the words crossed her mind, she felt the floor fall away from her feet. She fell, the wind rushing in her ears and a choked scream lodged in her throat, unable to release it as she plummeted into the abyss. She could only pray that the shadows hadn't followed her. The dark swallowed her up ...

And her eyes opened to her bedroom in the house-beast. Heart pounding away in her chest like a steam-hammer, she looked down at the floor, where her feet were solidly resting, and then the notebook on the desk, which once again was full of messy scribbling. After a quick read-over it seemed like she'd described the watch room, but hadn't recorded anything about Cheshire or the shadows.

Curious.

Tick—

Instantly Alice tensed, all of her metaphorical feathers ruffling.

Tock—

The damned clock was still on the desk where the Doctor had left it. Still—

Tick—

—ticking. It echoed in her head like church bells, every—

Tock—

—tock winding her tighter and tighter. Would the shadows follow the sound?

Tick—

Would it send her back to the forest of watches? If she returned—

Tock—

—the shadows would surely catch her.

Tick—

Damn the thing to hell!

Tock—

Alice stood, grabbed the clock off of the desk, and threw it to the floor.

Splinters of wood, shards of glass, springs and gears and mechanisms, all flew about the room with a stunned, offended-sounding *twang!* Alice stood over the remains, panting and victorious, as heavy footsteps came pounding up the stairs.

The bedroom door opened, revealing the Duchess and the Doctor. "Alice!" cried the latter in stunned admonishment.

Ears buzzing, Alice gave them a wide grin. "I shut it up for you."

"Imbecile," the Duchess snapped. Crossing the room in three long strides, she grabbed a handful of Alice's choppy hair and yanked. "The Doctor has done so much for you, taking you out of that asylum where you belong, giving you food and shelter, and how do you repay him?"

She shook Alice, making her scalp smart, but Alice couldn't drop her Cheshire grin. The relief of no longer hearing the clock was still so heady.

"By destroying his things like a child!"

While the Duchess shouted and shook her by her hair, the Doctor stood impassively to the side, notebook in his hands. He tsked and shook his head, even that small sound enough to stop the Duchess in her tracks. He snapped the book shut and tucked it under his arm.

"There's hardly a thing in here," he said disapprovingly. "You've been up here for hours. You really must try harder."

Alice jerked away from the Duchess' grip. The giddy feeling from before was fading, replaced with sharp, crackling frustration. "I'm not exactly *conscious* when I write those, you know."

Doctor Gordan's eyes lit up. "What do you mean?"

Alice huffed and folded her arms over her chest. After so many years, you'd think she would be used to feeling like a butterfly pinned under a microscope, but it never stopped being irritating. "I go to Wonderland like you want, and when I come back, there's writing in the book."

"You don't remember writing it?"

"No, I was in Wonderland."

"Fascinating." The Doctor turned towards the door. "Come, let us use the study. I have more questions for you. That will be all, Mrs. Greenway."

The Duchess' face wrinkled up like a toad's. Alice restrained herself from doing a rude gesture on her way out the door, but only barely.

***

"In general, I dislike hysteria as a diagnosis."

The next morning, the ichor in the Doctor's study was knee-deep. It soaked through Alice's stockings, moving thick and sticky against her legs. Another few hours and it would rise over the seat of her chair and stain her dress. The Duchess would have an apoplectic fit for certain.

"It's far too general. People use it for everything, when a more specific diagnosis would be more helpful. However ..." The Doctor leaned back in his seat, steepling his fingers as he peered at Alice over his spectacles. "In some cases it does apply."

Alice sniffed and pushed her legs through the goop. She hated that word. Nearly every woman and girl in the asylum had been called that at some point, and for many that was the only "condition" listed in their shoddy records. One woman, Grace, had been diagnosed as hysterical for reading a novel.

"Take yourself, for instance," the Doctor continued, ignoring Alice's lack of response. "Many aspects of your madness I would not say are specifically hysterical. Delusional, more like. But these fits of violence that you have, with the clock, for example—those could certainly be described as hysterical."

She frowned to herself. The incident yesterday hadn't been a fit; she always snapped back to Wonderland during a fit and never remembered what was happening in the real world. Smashing the clock was just good old-fashioned irritation. But Doctor Gordan was still talking, not allowing her a word in edgewise.

"So, it stands to reason that if the hysteria was treated, these fits would end, which would make the rest of our trials that much easier to complete, yes? Then—"

"I've been treated for hysteria for the last ten years," Alice interrupted brusquely. "I doubt it would suddenly work now."

Doctor Gordan leaned back even further in his chair, gaze so sharp it felt like it was piercing through Alice's skin and seeing into her skeleton. "Yes, I saw the list of attempted treatments in your records. The documentation is rather unimpressive, I admit, but I believe some of the treatments were not administered correctly."

"I wouldn't be surprised," she huffed back, folding her arms tightly. Truth be told, the thought of enduring more treatments made her stomach twist up in knots. After years of ineffective treatments the asylum had given up on her, merely locking her away when she grew too wild, and though she hated the confinement, she much preferred being left alone.

Of course, treatments being administered "correctly" didn't make them any less awful.

"There is one in particular that caught my attention. Apparently they were going to attempt it, but you went into another fit and had to be isolated before it could be done."

She furrowed her brow. She'd had so many fits it was hard to keep track of them all, but she believed she could remember this one. One moment the orderlies were trying to get her to lie flat on a table and the next she was deep below the surface of the sea, chained in the brig of a sunken Spanish galleon. Near her feet was a half-rotted, waterlogged, barnacle-encrusted wooden button that she kicked at with her heels until it caved in. The chains had unlocked themselves and the galleon rocketed to the surface so quickly it made her bones ache from the pressure change, breaching from the waves like a whale.

When she woke, she was in the room filled with snow, where she would end up after every fit from then on.

"I believe your fits are caused by a buildup of stress and tension in your mind and body. Relieving the tension elsewhere could reduce how many you have."

That didn't sound right either. She had noticed the pattern; the fits came when she was angry or afraid. She'd learned to recognize the swell of frantic rage and panic that rose in her before a fit came on, and once she was in Wonderland, everything melted away into a hazy calm.

"There has been some success in treating hysteria by inducing a paroxysm in the patient. Much like your fits, you will tense up, and then relax as the tension is released. I've read several studies on the subject, and many patients report feelings of calm afterwards, and others note how much calmer and quieter they are."

Alice had heard the word before around the asylum, but always in contexts she didn't understand. She remembered hearing it several times as the orderlies tried to hold her down before she went into her fit. With the word came wisps of memory, barely there, slipping through her fingers as though she was trying to hold a cloud. Hands on her, everywhere, on bare skin, and the phantom touch made her shudder.

The Doctor stood up from behind his desk. His shadow stretched long and thin, casting itself over the window behind him, directly counter to the light, and Alice's breath hitched. She bit her tongue to keep calm as the words of the cat floated through her mind: *The sun casts its shadows everywhere.*

"Come along, Alice. We'll do this in your room."

Alice waited for the Doctor and his shadow to pass before standing. Neither of them seemed to have any trouble moving through the ichor lake, and the reason soon became clear; as she slogged after them through the goop, she noticed the Doctor's hands, for once not wearing gloves. They were soaked, palm to fingertip, with black that dripped slowly, inexorably, off of his hands and into the lake. It was not unique to the house-beast, it seemed—or the Doctor was himself part of the beast. Like those deep ocean fish that had been in the papers with their fleshy lures hanging just before their vicious jaws.

She supposed it didn't matter if she followed the lure. She was already in the belly of the beast.

Alice's chest grew tighter and tighter as they ascended the stairs, but she did her best to quash her dread down. She'd endured many terrible treatments at the asylum, this one probably wouldn't be so bad, but she could still feel those phantom hands. They pressed down on her shoulders, and she got the faintest whiff of—kerosene? That didn't make sense. The Doctor's house had electric lights.

By the time the Doctor opened the door to her room, the smell was thick in her nose and there was another set of hands, these gripping tightly around her right wrist, curling over her fingers to make her hand into a fist.

"Lie down, Alice."

Somewhere in her mind she was aware that she was shaking as she obeyed. The gas and kerosene smell was too strong and her thoughts were muddled. The Doctor loomed over her, his shadow twisting on the wall behind him as though in excitement, and Alice's mind conjured up an image of other shadows cast on faded wallpaper, flickering in firelight.

One of the Doctor's hands landed on her hip. It was long and pale, fingers twitching, like some kind of albino cave spider that no longer had any eyes, and the ichor on his palm smeared over the faded color of the fabric. Every muscle in her body locked up.

"Relax," said Doctor Gordan. His other hand moved up towards her face. A drop of goo landed on her collarbone. The orderlies had been much rougher with her back at the asylum, but she could feel where his first hand was going, leaving long smears of ichor across her skirt as it moved towards the hem. Her blood rushed in her ears so loudly that he must've heard it, but if he did, the Doctor didn't react, and his fingers brushed over her chin.

She blinked, and the room, the Doctor, and the house-beast were gone. Now she sat on a blanket in a patch of tall, soft grass, a picnic basket at her side and a plate in front of her. She was surrounded by blooming hedges, and overhead a willow tree shaded her with its long boughs. The air was filled with butterflies (real ones, not bread-and-butterflies), in an array of colors she hadn't seen so beautifully or vibrantly since the time she looked in a kaleidoscope when she was seven years old.

On the plate was a little peach-colored cake that made her mouth water. It had been so long since she'd had cake. On top, in cursive royal icing, were the words "Eat Me."

She plucked it delicately from the plate and examined it. As much as she wanted to taste, she had to be wary—food and drink in Wonderland tended to have strange properties. Then again, maybe it would be fun.

Slowly, Alice sank her teeth into it, neatly bisecting the words. The cake was soft and yielding, and as her teeth bit through the center, something thick, bold, and metallic spread across her tongue, red filling dripping down her chin and onto her lap.

Before she could finish it off, a familiar blob of inky black coalesced on the other side of the blanket.

"Well, well, here we are again, Alice," the cat said, still with his usual snark, but joined by a strange undercurrent of pity.

"What do you mean?" The filling in the cake was runnier than she expected. The red spilled down her fingers and across her palm, following her veins down the underside of her wrist. She licked at it absently; she couldn't say it was a good flavor, but an interesting one nonetheless.

"You always end up here. Haven't you noticed?"

Oh. Right.

"I'm having a fit," she said aloud, and the cat nodded, grin stretched wide.

"Yes. You always come running back to Wonderland, and it always protects you. Even with the shadow's influence, all it wants is to protect you. To save you from the truth."

Alice frowned to herself and put the second half of the cake back on its plate. Her hand was stained red—when had her hands been this color before? It seemed so familiar, and yet …

"Do you want to know the truth, Alice? It's a hard, cruel place, not bright or beautiful as it is here."

The red on her hands was nagging her. It had something to do with that smell of kerosene and gas, something to do with the shadows and the teapot and the pocket watch. Somewhere deep down it was frightening, but the need to know was stronger than the dread.

"I do want to know."

The cat's grin widened. "That's what I hoped you would say." He turned, tail held high, and set off across the grass at a trot. Alice scrambled to her feet and followed after him, leaving the picnic and the red cake behind.

The cat led her towards one of the hedges. She hadn't noticed from a distance, what with the butterflies and the willow tree and the fascinating cake, but as they got closer she realized there was a green door nestled amongst the leaves. It was just large enough for her to fit through if she knelt down and squeezed, and the knob shone bright and brassy, as though freshly polished.

"The right-sized door?" she asked, and the cat let out a purring chuckle.

"And the right key." His tail vanished into thin air for but a moment before returning, a brass key hanging from a ring on the end. "Think carefully before opening it. Once you go through, there is no turning back."

Gingerly, she plucked the key from his tail and considered it. If she went through the door, she would remember, but the memories would be terrible. If she stayed, it would be safe and pretty until the fit ended, but the events that brought her to where she was would remain a blank space in her mind, never to be understood, only suffered for, and the shadows would forever lurk in the dark corners of Wonderland.

She clenched the key tight in her fist, took a deep breath, and turned towards the door.

"I knew you wouldn't disappoint," the cat said with a pleased purr.

Alice inserted the key into the knob and turned. The lock clicked. The hinges made no noise when she pushed the door open, revealing only darkness ahead, so much like the rabbit hole she'd fallen down as a tiny child at a garden party.

She got on her hands and knees, only slightly cringing at what the Duchess would say about the dirt stains, and wiggled through the door.

At first there was only more darkness. Alice determinedly crawled forward, grinding dirt into her knees and her palms. She kept crawling until her back and neck ached and her stockings were torn. She was about to yell over her shoulder at Cheshire when she spotted a light ahead of her.

"About time," muttered Alice under her breath as she hastened towards it.

When she finally emerged from the tunnel, it was to a small room, the walls and floor alike tiled with white and black marble like a chessboard. In the middle was a four-post bed, but it looked rickety, more like doll furniture than functional—it suited, as the two figures situated on it were clearly dolls despite being the size of Alice herself.

One was a girl in a blue dress, lying on the bed, with long black yarn hair that spilled across the bed sheets like twisting snakes. The other was a man in a top hat, a stethoscope hanging around his neck as he leaned over the girl. The joints were intricate, allowing the doctor to have one hand on the girl doll's waist and the other near her articulated jaw.

Alice circled the room once, twice, but nothing happened or moved. The cat emerged from the tunnel and sat before the entrance with his usual smug smile. Once again, Alice was on the verge of snapping at him to explain when from above her head came a loud, mechanical *click,* followed by the whir of clockwork and a lilting tune. Looking up, she saw a ballerina figurine hanging from the ceiling like a chandelier, slowly turning as the music played, and the dolls on the bed began to move.

Set to the cheery tune of the music box, the doctor doll's hand moved down from the girl doll's waist, down towards her knee, then up under her skirt.

"What's he doing?" she asked.

The cat vanished from his position in a puff of black and reappeared at Alice's side. "Inducing the paroxysm."

Alice tasted bile at the back of her throat. At the same moment, the girl doll moved for the first time. She turned her head, her mouth opening like that of a nutcracker, and bit down on the doctor's hand. The doll reared back, hand now painted red, then the other hand came down on the girl doll's face in a hard slap.

The music box slowly ground to a stop, and the dolls froze.

"This is it, then?" Alice's voice sounded rough even to herself as she tried to swallow the lump in her throat. "This is what happened during my fit?"

"Yes." For once the cat lacked the edge of self-importance in his tone. "I'm sure you've noticed how the fits come when people touch you."

"Not every time," she protested, but the cat merely chuckled at her.

"No, that would be rather exhausting, wouldn't it?"

"The cake ..."

"Yes, that was the good Doctor's hand you were biting into. I didn't know you enjoyed the taste of blood so much."

Alice just shook her head and looked down at the brown stains on her palm. "I daresay he deserved it."

"He certainly did."

"So, what now?" Alice's eyes scanned the room for another door, trying to avoid looking at the dolls. "Another bit of theater?"

"No." The cat walked to a corner and very purposefully put his paw on one of the black marble squares, which sank down at his press, as did the tiles around it, descending into a spiral staircase. "Now it is time for your next choice."

Alice followed and peered over the edge of the floor and down the staircase. All she could see was more darkness and the faintest flicker of firelight. For some reason, a chill ran down her spine.

That light was familiar. Familiar like the blood on her hands. But it wasn't really a choice, was it? She'd made her choice when she unlocked the door in the hedge. She'd made it when she asked Cheshire to show her what cast the shadows. When she went to Wonderland, again and again, and didn't let it take her away into a pointless daydream.

Her stomach twisted up in knots.

"Be calm, Alice, or you'll call the shadows," the cat hissed at her. She couldn't help or understand how her hands shook, but she fisted them into her dress and stepped down onto the first separated tile. Afraid or no, she wasn't going to let the shadows get in her way this time. She wanted to know, and she wanted to know *all* of it.

She descended the tiles. She kept her eyes locked on her stockinged feet, unwilling to look at the light yet, until they rested once again on a solid floor, this time made of deep brown wood. The cat jumped down onto her shoulder, and one by one the tiles floated upward, disappearing back into the ceiling.

"What did the doctor say?"

That voice didn't belong to Alice or the cat, or even the Doctor. It was a voice that she only faintly heard in her dreams, one she barely remembered: it was her mother's voice.

She was at the table, arranging cups and saucers as her father read the newspaper.

Alice's shoulder hit the wall as she staggered. Neither of them reacted to the noise. She was standing in the hall. She shouldn't have been. It was past bedtime.

Her father sighed and folded the paper to set beside his cup. "He said it's likely just a child's vivid imagination, and she'll grow out of it."

Her mother scoffed. "I'll believe that when she stops chattering about mad queens and hatters, which will be the same moment that hell freezes over and London Bridge comes down."

"I don't understand why you're so concerned," her father answered, pinching the bridge of his nose. "All children imagine things all the time."

Thin white hands picked up the teapot, wreathed in sunflowers, trembling lightly in the woman's grip. "It's not natural. Other children run and play, but I've seen her sit completely still for hours, staring at nothing, and then she says she was taking tea in Wonderland!" She shook her head and tilted the pot, beginning to pour the tea into her father's cup. "It's all a bunch of non—"

The kitchen door banged open. Alice jerked back as her parents both jumped, but before either of them could move, a man the size of a factory crossed the space between door and table in one step and plunged a knife into her mother's back.

The teapot fell and shattered. Her father cried out and leapt to his feet, but the intruder had three other men behind him that fell upon him in an instant. Blood dripped down the chain of his pocket watch, and Alice could see it all where she cowered in the hallway.

"Oi," said one of the men, brandishing a club towards the hall. And, she realized with a sinking, cold dread, right at her. "Who's that?"

The biggest man stormed forward again. He clamped a heavy hand on Alice's shoulder and hauled her forward into the firelight. All four men, dressed in rags and rough caps, grew weasley smiles at the sight of her, and the scent of kerosene filled her nose.

Kerosene. The factory. Her father had been an overseer at a factory that made kerosene. These men must have worked there. But why would they—

"It's that mad girl of theirs," said the man holding her. She was both small and large, both a child frightened out of her mind and a woman stunned out of hers, and all she could do was shake as the man's grip tightened. "Did you hear 'em talking?"

Her eyes flickered back towards the table. She wanted her parents, but once her eyes found them, she couldn't bear to look at the glassy eyes and the red spattering the tablecloth. Instead they fell upon the folded newspaper and the bold headline printed at the top: LOCAL FACTORY FIRES MORE WORKERS; FACES CLOSURE.

Her adult mind put the pieces together easily now that she had them. The men had been fired, and they blamed her father, their supervisor, for it. Her child mind simply wailed as the men jeered over her.

"'Ere's an idea," drawled the man who had spotted her. "What if we bloodied 'er up, give 'er the knife—she's mad, people'll think she's the one that did it."

One of the other men snorted. "No one would believe that, look at 'er!"

"It's worth a try," said the man whose grip was leaving bruises on her thin shoulder. Grabbing Alice's arm in his other hand, he thrust it forward against her mother's back, and the blood smeared thick and wet over her hand.

Blood, thick and wet. A much larger hand curling hers around the handle of the knife. She was released, and Alice fell to her knees.

The leader fisted his hand into her long hair and pulled until she cried out. "Don't you tell nobody nothing," he growled. All she could smell was kerosene and blood. "Nobody would believe you, anyhow. Your own parents think you're mad."

"Thought," said one of the other men, and they all laughed.

They were right, weren't they? Mother had said it herself, it wasn't natural. And who would believe the word of a mad little girl ...

"Come on, let's get out of 'ere 'fore the coppers turn up."

There was the heavy tramping of boots as the men rushed past Alice, farther into the kitchen and out the side door. Even when the men left, their shadows remained, dancing against the wallpaper in the firelight. The only sound was the slow *tick—tock—*of her father's bloody watch.

"Cheshire." It was her adult voice coming from a throat far too small for it. "How do I leave this place?"

Soft fur pressed under her empty hand. "You've done it," the cat said with a purr. "You've done it, Alice. All you have to do now is wake up."

"I don't know how."

"Then I'll help. Just don't stab me with that thing." Sharp teeth pierced the skin of her hand, and with a cry, the whole world spun around her into a spiral of wood and fire and shadows and broken china.

Her eyes opened to the canopy of her bed. The room was dark, and she was alone, except for the pair of yellow eyes peering at her through the window.

For a long time she just lay there, panting to the canopy.

She remembered. It wasn't her. She didn't kill her family. She was innocent.

It was far too late to convince anyone else of that, but Alice didn't care. She knew, and that was enough to bring happy tears to her eyes for the first time since that night.

Suddenly the cat poofed into existence in front of her, resting all of his weight on her chest. "Alice," he hissed, bringing his face close enough to hers that she felt the tickle of whiskers.

"Cheshire, I remembered."

"Yes, and I'm very happy for you, but you have another problem." His paw batted at one of her wrists that rested somewhat uncomfortably above her head, and all at once sensation flooded back into her. She was sore, hungry, thirsty, her cheek throbbed, and when she tried to move her hands, she got only the bite of rough fibers as a reward.

A very unladylike curse fell from her lips as she glared up at the ropes holding her wrists to the bedposts. Of course, she had bitten the Doctor, and now that she had disrespected him directly, all pretense of cordiality had evaporated. The Duchess must be throwing a ball in the kitchen right now.

"You must leave here," continued Cheshire. "He will only hurt you, that madman."

Alice couldn't help laughing at the irony. Cheshire glared at her.

"I cannot imagine what you would find funny in this instance."

"Don't be such a dolt, cat. Your claws and teeth are sharp enough, so why don't you—"

The knob on her bedroom door jiggled. The cat vanished in a puff of black smoke.

"Coward!" Alice hissed at the empty air before the door slowly opened, so slowly the hinges didn't even creak.

To her surprise, it wasn't the Doctor who slipped into the room. It was Maryanne.

For a moment the two of them just stared at each other. Even in the dark, Alice could see how tight Maryanne's jaw was and how her body shook.

"What on Earth—" she began, only for Maryanne to dart forward several steps, desperately shushing her.

"Hush, hush, don't make a sound or they'll hear!"

"Why are you here?" Alice whispered back.

Maryanne gulped and stepped to the head of the bed. From her apron pocket she produced a dinner knife.

Stupid, was Alice's first thought. *Killing me would be a lot easier with a proper knife.*

The silver knife glinted in the moonlight as Maryanne shifted her grip. To Alice's surprise, she didn't bring it down towards her; instead she leaned over to the headboard and began to saw through the ropes that kept her bound.

"What are you doing?" she asked again. Maryanne's mouth pressed into a thin white line.

"I heard them talking. They mean to send you back to the asylum."

Alice's heart sank, but: "That doesn't answer the question." Why should Maryanne care what happened to her?

The first rope frayed, making it loose enough for Alice to tug her hand free. Maryanne quickly circled the bed and went at the other one.

"My mother wasn't even mad." Her voice was hard, her eyes glittering with cold determination, her knuckles white around the knife, even as her hands visibly shook. "My father just wanted her out of the way. God would damn my soul to hell if I let the same thing happen to you."

"But I am mad."

Maryanne grimaced and bared her teeth. "I don't care. No one deserves the things they do to people in those places." On that, the two of them could agree.

The second rope came undone. Alice lowered her arms, wincing at the soreness that lanced down them, and gingerly rubbed at her wrists. Maryanne's face was pale as a ghost.

"Where will I go?" Alice ventured to ask.

"There's a halfway house three blocks east of here. They won't ask too many questions."

Lord help her, Alice was almost more afraid of that than the asylum. It was a terrible place, yes, but she knew how it worked. She knew the rules, where she could push and where she couldn't, and what would happen if she pushed too hard. She'd been there more than half her life. What would she even do at a halfway house? She would have to earn her keep, she imagined, but she didn't know how to do anything. The asylum wasn't exactly having trade classes.

What if she failed? What if she was too mad to be of use to anyone? Would they throw her onto the streets? Compared to the idea of endless cold and hunger, the suffocating walls of the asylum and the loneliness of the snow-covered room almost sounded enticing. At the asylum, she didn't have to wonder about her future any further than how painful the next "treatment" would be, if they bothered. Even the concept of a future was baffling.

But Maryanne looked so determined. She was risking her job for this, and if she was fired, the Duchess surely wouldn't give her a good reference. It was her livelihood.

So Alice took a deep breath, and for the hundredth time in the last week, she told herself to be brave.

"Alright."

Maryanne offered Alice a hand to help her up. "Come on, I'll let you out the back."

Together the two of them crept out into the hallway. The floor moved under Alice's feet as the house-beast slumbered, but Maryanne was sure-footed and quick as she led Alice down the stairs, silently pointing out where to step and which places would creak. It was black as pitch without the electric lights humming away. Thankfully Maryanne seemed to know where everything was and didn't let Alice bump into anything.

They went through the kitchen to reach the back door. From her apron pocket, where she had tucked the knife away, Maryanne produced a small key that she must've taken off of the Duchess' key ring. Alice had a half moment to marvel at her bravery before Maryanne pushed the door open. Ahead was a short flight of stone steps leading up into the yard.

"Remember," Maryanne whispered to her. "Three blocks east."

"I'll remember. Thank you."

Then, to Alice's shock, Maryanne grabbed her tight in a hug. Before she could react or even return the gesture, Maryanne shoved her through the door and closed it behind her, the lock clicking shut again.

Alice stood there in her torn stockings and blood-stained dress. She took a deep breath of smoggy London air. She was free. For the first time in so many years, she was *free*.

Now, which way was east?

A weight settled across her shoulders, and a familiar voice spoke in her ear. "That way," said the cat, pointing with his tail. "What would you do without me?"

This one time Alice didn't have a snarky retort. She just reached up to give Cheshire a scratch as she turned in the direction he pointed.

The two of them strode off into the night.

About the Author

Jayde Layne is a graduate of Arizona State University, now residing in Flagstaff, Arizona.

Acknowledgements

Firstly, I would like to thank the extremely talented authors who submitted their stories to this anthology. I am honored to have been able to work with each and every one of you.

Thank you so much to my co-editor, Vanessa Roades, for assisting with the momentous task of editing this book (and for dealing with all the dreaded em-dashes).

Thank you to my sister, Nicole, for designing the awesome cover and illustrations. You're the best!

And thank you to you, dear reader. I hope you enjoyed your journey through the wonderful world of whump.

About the Editor

Kailey Alessi is the founder and editor-in-chief of the Whumpy Printing Press, a publishing company whose mission is to publish the work of the whump community. Kailey has lived in Michigan, Kentucky, Idaho, and Florida (but she's a midwestern girl at heart). She is an archaeologist by day, and by night she writes all sorts of dark fiction. You can find her on tumblr @whumpy-writings

Also By The Whumpy Printing Press

Hurt and Comfort

www.ingramcontent.com/pod-product-compliance
Lightning Source LLC
Chambersburg PA
CBHW022108240626
47153CB00007B/2280